E.R.PUNSHON
DICTATOR'S WAY

Ernest Robertson Punshon was born in London in 1872.

At the age of fourteen he started life in an office. His employers soon informed him that he would never make a really satisfactory clerk, and he, agreeing, spent the next few years wandering about Canada and the United States, endeavouring without great success to earn a living in any occupation that offered. Returning home by way of working a passage on a cattle boat, he began to write. He contributed to many magazines and periodicals, wrote plays, and published nearly fifty novels, among which his detective stories proved the most popular and enduring.

He died in 1956.

Also by E.R. Punshon

E.R. PUNSHON

DICTATOR'S WAY

With an introduction
by Curtis Evans

DEAN STREET PRESS

Published by Dean Street Press 2015

Copyright © 1938 E.R. Punshon

Introduction Copyright © 2015 Curtis Evans

All Rights Reserved

Published by licence, issued under the UK Orphan Works
Licensing Scheme

First published in 1938 by Victor Gollancz

Cover by DSP

ISBN 978 1 911095 40 8

www.deanstreetpress.co.uk

INTRODUCTION

Conventional wisdom about the Golden Age of detective fiction tells us that mystery writers of that era sought to provide readers with escape from the manifold unpleasant realities around them in the 1920s and 1930s. Although Golden Age mysteries "deal with violent death and violent emotions," writes P.D. James in her 2009 genre study, *Talking about Detective Fiction*, "they are novels of escape....Rereading the Golden Age novels with their confident morality, their lack of any empathy with the murderer and the popularity of their rural settings, readers can still enter nostalgically this settled and comfortable world." Similarly, in *Bloody Murder*, Julian Symons' hugely-influential mystery genre study (originally published in 1972), Symons claims that such unpleasant facts as widespread unemployment and the rise of dictatorships "were ignored in almost all the detective stories of the Golden Age." Thus there was in these books, so this argument runs, little talk of--and certainly little empathy for-- strikers and other strife makers at home, and no serious look at human atrocities committed overseas by brutal totalitarian regimes in Germany, the Soviet Union, Italy and Japan.

Whatever its merit in the case of some Golden Age detective fiction authors, this conventional view (challenged of late) certainly does no justice to the detective novels of E.R. Punshon. In 1934, Punshon integrated into the plot of his puzzler *Crossword Mystery* the Nazi ascendance to power in Germany, taking the opportunity to condemn the nascent regime in no uncertain terms. Two years later, in *The Bath Mysteries*, he sympathetically evoked life among the down-and-outs in Thirties Britain, suggesting influence from the politically conscious works of

George Orwell, like Punshon an author in the stable of leftist publisher Victor Gollancz (see particularly Orwell's bracing 1933 book *Down and Out in Paris and London*). In 1937, a year before the publication of *Dictator's Way*, Punshon in *Mystery of Mr. Jessop* was inspired by recent incidents of politically-motivated mob violence in London's East End, such as the so-called "Battle of Cable Street" (4 October 1936) wherein Fascists, Communists and other groups waged a series of violent street clashes involving tens of thousands of fractious combatants. With *Dictator's Way* (1938) E.R. Punshon directly addresses the spread of totalitarian ideologies in Europe, while also finding time at long last to introduce love into the life of his likeable series sleuth, Detective-Sergeant Bobby Owen.

In *Bloody Murder* Julian Symons confidently pronounces that "[i]t is safe to say that almost all the British [detective fiction] writers in the twenties and thirties, and most of the Americans, were unquestionably right-wing." After having spent many years reading Golden Age detective fiction, I am not prepared to concede the safety of Symons' verdict on the political inclinations of "almost all" British mystery writers from this period; yet, in any event, E.R. Punshon surely is one of the clearest exceptions to Symons' rule. Although connected, through his mother's side of the family, to a line of Scottish baronets, the Halkets of Pitfarrane Castle, Punshon's immediate maternal and paternal connections, which sprang from the far northern English counties of Northumberland and Durham, were associated with trade--sometimes successfully, but often not. Both Robert Punshon and David Halket, his father and maternal grandfather, went bankrupt at points in their business careers, and the elder Punshon appears eventually to have separated from his wife and sons. Despite intense imaginative leanings--in later years he recalled "when I was not much older than [seven] my chief pleasure was to escape all alone for long solitary walks during which I told myself...interminable tales with myself for the splendid hero...as I grew older I began to put these dreams down on paper"--Punshon, upon the death of his schoolteacher mother when he was sixteen, most prosaically had to go to work in a railroad company's accounts office. After a few years of what he deemed intolerable drudgery Punshon left office work to pursue a peripatetic life of quixotic career endeavors in the wilds of Canada and the United States, finally returning to England and a fiction writing career around the time of the death of Queen Victoria. Not until late middle age, with the success of his Golden Age mystery fiction, would Punshon achieve in his writing career real "distinction," as Dorothy L. Sayers would so memorably put it in her 1933 *Sunday Times* review of his premier Bobby Owen detective novel (for more on these matters see my introductions to Punshon's *Death Comes to Cambers* and *Information Received*).

All the rest of his life Punshon seems never to have gotten over a feeling that he had been denied material social and educational chances from which, with his own natural intelligence and industry, he could have taken considerable advantage. Over and over in his fiction he condemns class hierarchy and inherited social privilege. His best-known series sleuth, Scotland Yard policeman Bobby Owen, grandson and nephew of earls, feels mostly embarrassment over his high-toned background, hotly resenting whatever allusions to it that are made by police colleagues and private citizens he encounters in the course of his criminal investigations. Yet while Punshon was no conservative, neither was he a socialist; indeed, he seems to have held the Soviet experiment in disdain, especially after Stalin's late Thirties parade of purges and show trials, to which Bobby witheringly alludes in *Mystery of Mr. Jessop*. ("Bump 'em off good and plenty," he says of the "important role" the police have to play in the Communist state.) During the Golden Age of detective fiction and afterward Punshon, a firm believer in moderation, supported Britain's Liberals rather than the Conservative or Labour parties. In 1947 he made his personal political faith quite clear when, in his capacity as a member of the executive committee of the Streatham Liberal Association, he wrote a letter to the Liberal newspaper the *Manchester Guardian*, for which he had reviewed crime fiction between 1935 and 1942, denouncing both the "Tory reactionary" and the "Socialist doctrinaire" as equal menaces to "freedom and general well-being."

Punshon's concern with menaces to "freedom and general well-being" is plainly evident in his tenth Bobby Owen detective novel, *Dictator's Way*, published in 1938, the year that would see the German occupation of Austria and the Sudetenland and the climax of the Great Purge in the Soviet Union. (The Italian invasion of Ethiopia had already taken place a few years earlier.) The title itself has a double meaning, literal and figurative. Literally it refers to a section of London road where wheeled traffic has been debarred at the behest of a "wealthy city man" named Judson, who disliked vehicular traffic near his residence, a mansion known as The Manor. Judson since has decamped to "one of those huge new blocks of flats that of late years have risen in the West End of London like fungi in a field after heavy rain," but he has maintained The Manor as a convenient locale for entertaining special lady friends and hosting parties where cards are played for high stakes and blue films aired to leering appreciation.

After Bobby Owen discovers the man who managed these parties for Judson has been murdered at The Manor, it comes to the attention of both Bobby and Superintendent Ulyett of

Scotland Yard that they have on their hands a murder case with potential political implications, for among those who attended Judson's parties were members of the staff of the Etrurian Embassy, including the Ambassador himself; and most of the suspects seem to have connections to Etruria, a country located between Germany and Italy and ruled over by a despot, the Redeemer, obviously modeled after Hitler and Mussolini. When Punshon describes Bobby's visit to the home of a native Etrurian suspect, fashionable restauranteur Thomas Troya, the author's scorn for Europe's self-aggrandizing totalitarian strongmen is palpable:

> Over the mantelpiece hung a large portrait of the Etrurian dictator, "Redeemer of his country," in his characteristic country-redeeming attitude so strongly reminiscent of Ajax defying the lightning. It was flanked on either side by portraits of his brother dictators of Germany and Italy, though these portraits were of smaller size and had less ornate frames—enough in these days, Bobby thought, to produce an international incident. Between the windows hung another large portrait of the Etrurian Redeemer, in the company of two or three babies, one of whom he was embracing on the well-established Eatandswill precedent. There were various other portraits of the same gentleman scattered about here and there. In all, including those on the side tables and wall brackets, Bobby counted nine….In one corner there was also a picture representing another and different Redeemer, but it hung awry, and was evidently there on sufferance, before final removal.

Through a murder implicating the fictional country of Etruria, E.R. Punshon in *Dictator's Way* decries the rise of aggressive totalitarian states in Europe (here the figurative meaning of the novel's title is suggested). To me there is little about Dictator's Way that seems calculated to offer nostalgia-minded readers of Golden Age detective fiction happy visions of, to again quote P.D. James, a "settled and comfortable world," nor do the characters advance with absolute clarion conviction moral certitudes about murder. When a suspect in the case demands of him, "what is one murder, more or less," compared to the horrific mass slaughter occurring all around the world ("Chinese women and children are blown to bits by the thousands....Sailors are drowned in the Mediterranean, people are shot wholesale in Russia and Spain"), Bobby responds modestly, "It's all over my head"; though he pleas that it is the policeman's job "to see the rules are kept, because if they aren't, there's such an awful mess around."

For those who are less interested in politics than people Dictator's Way also has appeal. Following Dorothy L. Sayers' popular precedent with her characters Lord Peter Wimsey and Harriet Vane, Punshon in this novel has Bobby Owen fall desperately in love with an entrancing suspect, one Olive Farrar, owner of a chic hat shop in Piccadilly. For Cupid 1938 proved a busy period indeed concerning the affairs of handsome gentleman detectives, for that very same year he also aimed his bow with deadly accuracy at Ngaio Marsh's Roderick Alleyn and Margery Allingham's Albert Campion. (John Rhode's charming series police detective, Jimmy Waghorn, would be stricken with amour the next year.) For Bobby the course of true love does not run altogether smooth in Dictator's Way, but I shall leave the readers of this series to peruse the novel and see for themselves just what choppy waters the determined young man encounters.

Curtis Evans

AUTHOR'S NOTE

A pathetic instinct of self-preservation they share with others of the humbler of God's creatures, induces authors to proclaim at the beginning of their books that all characters and incidents therein introduced are entirely imaginary. It is true that this makes not the slightest difference if some far-off, teetotal John Smith the author has never heard of can detect some shadow of resemblance between himself and the John Smith mentioned in the book as having occasionally partaken of the festive cocktail.

For this story, too, one makes the ritual declaration in the hope that at any rate, if a hitherto unheard-of teetotal John Smith does emerge from the darkness of the unknown, the award of damages may be at least a little mitigated. It is declared, therefore, and with emphasis, that all the characters in *Dictator's Way* are entirely imaginary. None of them bears the least resemblance in circumstance or disposition to any living individual. They are, one and all, wholly and solely the creatures of the novelist's imagination. The incidents also are all pure invention.

Nevertheless, it remains to be asserted that everything in the story is drawn from actual occurrences in the life of to-day. Names have been changed. Characters have been invented. The incidents recounted bear no resemblance to any event that has ever taken place. Localities are as different as transfer over land and sea can make them. But the flow and counter-flow of incident, of motive, of idea do present an image, seen through the author's imagination, of certain events, culminating in the deaths by violence of two men of high integrity and character, that took place not so very long ago, upon the continent of Europe. It is true that no hint of such open violence, actual or contemplated, has yet been recorded in this country.

But that may come.

CHAPTER I
THE HON. CHAS. WAVENY

Detective-Sergeant Bobby Owen looked with some surprise at the card his landlady had just brought him. It was one of his rare afternoons off, and he was on the point of starting for Lord's in the hope that Mr. Hammond (90 not out at lunch) would still be batting when he got there. And now this interruption. Yet somehow it seemed to him that the name the card showed – The Hon. Chas. Waveny – was vaguely familiar.

Then recollection flooded back. Of course. It was that match between his own college – St. George's – and Wadham. Bobby had been a member of the St. George's rugby fifteen – he had even been tried for the University team – and in that St. George's-Wadham match there had been a flying tackle that had somehow gone wrong and had ended with one of the other fellow's boots in his face and the other boot pressed firmly home below his belt. How plainly now it came back to him; the mingled taste of mud and leather from the boot heel in his mouth, a tendency to hold himself together in the middle where he seemed to be coming apart, the blood streaming from his nose, his captain's warmly expressed opinion that he was the most hopeless muff that ever threw a goal away and why was he sitting there, looking like a sea-sick rabbit?

It had been, Bobby remembered, the Hon. Charles's boots of which he still seemed to taste the flavour, to feel the impress so firmly planted so exactly in his middle. Nothing like such happy memories of the past for bringing old friends together again; and though that was the only occasion on which Bobby and Mr. Waveny had come into such intimate contact, it was with a beaming face and an outstretched hand that Bobby went out into the hall where a cautious landlady, little impressed by some of Bobby's visitors, had left the Hon. Chas. to wait.

"Hullo," Bobby greeted him. "Haven't seen you since I muffed that tackle and let you get through. Did me out of getting another chance for my blue. Come along in. How's everything?"

Mr. Waveny was a tall, heavily built young man, already showing, as Bobby noticed with regret, a certain tendency to corpulence. He ought to have joined the police, Bobby thought. Eight hours a day directing traffic, or twenty-four hours a day chasing someone who wasn't there, would have lessened the girth of that waistcoat, reduced the fleshiness that showed beneath those pale blue, slightly protuberant eyes. Not but that Waveny was still a fine figure of a man with his light curling hair, his prominent beaked nose above the fair moustache and somewhat small mouth and chin, and that general air of confidence and command which comes so naturally to those born into the British governing classes. But perhaps this was given him by that haughty nose of his that seemed as it were like a flag of triumph, planted there by nature itself. A ruthless, determined nose, Bobby thought, but a little at war with the small mouth and chin and the slightly surprised looking protuberant eyes. He accepted now the cigarette Bobby offered, did not answer the question put him, and coughed in an embarrassed way, a cough indeed quite unworthy of that fierce and domineering nose.

Bobby began to feel slightly uneasy. In the first exuberance of those happy memories of the past that had returned to him so vividly at the sight of Waveny's card, he had been inclined to suppose his visitor had come out of pure friendliness, to chat, perhaps, over the jolly days when they had met upon the football field for a moment brief indeed but of poignant memory. But now he noticed that there was a worried look in Waveny's eyes, a twitching at the corners of his mouth, a nervous movement of his toes inside his smart expensive looking shoes – nervousness often shows itself in movements of the feet people forget to control as they control their hands or their expression. He was fidgeting nervously, too, with the cane he was carrying – one of the variety known as Penang Lawyer. Its handle had been bound round with silver and Bobby noticed that this silver was badly dented as if from a heavy blow.

"You see, Owen," began Mr. Waveny and paused.

Bobby was gloomily certain now of what was coming. There was often a kind of idea that as a member of the C.I.D. he could pull strings, influence the authorities, lend a helping hand to people who felt they both needed and deserved one. Bobby smiled grimly to himself at the idea of a sergeant pulling strings or exercising influence on the authorities to whom sergeants were just there to run errands and do as they were told. People couldn't understand that, though. There had been one young woman, for instance, who had never forgiven him his plea of inability to secure the withdrawal of a summons for exceeding the speed limit.

"There wasn't a creature in sight," she explained, "and I wasn't doing a bit more than fifty and it's so unsporting for the police to be watching when you don't know they are there. If I had seen them I should have slowed down at once," she protested earnestly; and since then, and her forty shilling fine, she had made a point of cutting Bobby dead.

Something of the same sort, Bobby began to suspect, must have caused this unexpected visit. In the hope of heading Waveny off, if that were possible, Bobby said:

"Not often I see any of the old crowd now. Any idea of how old Figgs is doing? Heard he was flying in Spain, but no one seemed to know for which side."

Waveny did not avail himself of the opening. He said:

"There's something I wanted to ask you."

"Oh, my dear chap, don't," interposed Bobby hastily. "I never was good at conundrums. I say, that's a jolly looking stick you've got – Penang Lawyers, they call them, don't they? Handy thing to have when there's a general row going on."

This time Waveny responded. He bestowed a glance of pride upon what was almost as much a weapon as a walking-stick.

"I've got two," he said. "A cousin of mine had a tea garden or something out there and when it went smash and he came home he brought them with him. I gave him a fiver for the two – just backed a winner," he added, apparently in explanation of an evidently somewhat unusual fiver.

But then quite abruptly he remembered what he was there for, since indeed it is not easy to switch a nose like his from the path to which it points.

"I heard you had joined the police. That's why I'm here," he explained.

"My dear chap," protested Bobby, "if it's a police matter, you ought to go to H.Q."

Waveny took no heed. He continued:

"It was a pal of mine in the Home Office told me about you."

"Oh, Lord," said Bobby.

"He told me the Home Secretary –"

"Now look here, Waveny, old man," interrupted Bobby again, even more firmly this time. "The Home Secretary doesn't know me from Adam, and I never set eyes on the blighter in my life. The only thing is when he was a kid he used to leave the milk at uncle's back door, and now he's so thundering cocky about it, he thinks he owns the whole family. I wish," said Bobby bitterly, "he had drowned himself in his own milk can."

Waveny ignored this. Bobby began to perceive that he was a young man of one idea, not easily diverted, a young man indeed of considerable perseverance. That nose, Bobby thought moodily.

"My pal didn't know where you hung out," Waveny went on, "so I looked up Lord Hirlpool – I knew he was your uncle."

"He gave it away, I suppose," Bobby said, meditating removal without letting any of his relatives know.

"It cost me a quid," observed Waveny wistfully, a wistfulness of that small mouth and chin, not of the domineering nose. "He promised to pay it back next week."

"Well, he won't," said Bobby viciously.

Waveny nodded with melancholy resignation.

"So I came along," he said.

Bobby got up from his chair. He felt disturbed. It seemed to him that work threatened. And he had a feeling that now he would arrive at Lord's just in time to see Mr. Hammond bowing his acknowledgements to the cheering crowds as he returned to the pavilion after scoring another double century or so. Waveny remained seated. It was evident his nose was in command now. No shifting a nose like that till it was ready to go.

"Do you know Dictator's Way?" he asked. "It's out by Epping Forest somewhere."

Bobby stared. He knew Dictator's Way very well but he did not wish to say so. Dictator's Way was the name Mr. Judson, a wealthy city man, had given a stretch of roadway he had succeeded in closing to wheeled traffic, though not to pedestrians. There had been a good deal of talk about it at the time. Echoes of the controversy had even reached the London papers in the shape of indignant letters protesting against Mr. Judson's high handed and intolerable action. He had been nicknamed 'Dictator Judson', compared to Hitler, Stalin, and others of those picturesque contemporaries of ours who have done so much to bring back prosperity to the world by inducing us to spend all our money on battleships, bombs, tanks, and other pleasing and instructive toys of modern civilization. In defiance Mr. Judson had retorted, once he had established his legal right to bar wheeled traffic from the piece of road in dispute, by naming it 'Dictator's Way'.

As a matter of fact the whole thing had been very much a storm in a tea-cup, for in the upshot drivers had only to make a brief detour of a few hundred yards that in any case most would have made, both to avoid a sharp bend and for the sake of a better surface. Mr. Judson always protested that all the excitement had been worked up by a local paper anxious to prove its public spirit and to provide its patrons with interesting reading matter. All he really wanted, he said, was the right to prevent people parking their cars, making themselves a nuisance by picnicking there, especially on Bank holidays, and by blocking his own access to the gates admitting to the grounds of a big, rambling old house, known as The Manor, where he was then living.

All this had happened some time previously, it was indeed almost forgotten, even locally. The name, however, 'Dictator's Way', remained, though Mr. Judson had now left The Manor as his usual residence and was established in one of those huge new blocks of flats that of late years have risen in the West End of London like fungi in a field after heavy rain.

But recently Dictator's Way and The Manor had been brought again, as Bobby knew, to the attention of the authorities. There were rumours that Mr. Judson not only used the house, since a block of West End flats must be respectable, as a convenient place where to meet his numerous and successive – even rapidly successive – lady friends, but that he also gave there parties at which cards were played for high stakes and at which sometimes were shown films that had not passed the censor.

But lady friends are no affair of Scotland Yard, the censor's business is his own, and there was no proof that the play was anything but perfectly straightforward, even if occasionally foolish people lost foolish sums. Apparently, too, Mr. Judson was careful to admit none but his own friends, or those for whom his own personal friends vouched. The Yard indeed had taken steps to assure itself that strangers were never admitted, it had also discovered that such high personages as the Etrurian Ambassador were occasional visitors – the Etrurian Military Attaché was a frequent one and was known to have had heavy losses over which he shrugged the shoulders of resignation – and since there is nothing illegal about playing cards in a private house, would have entirely disinterested itself in Dictator's Way and The Manor, but for vague, persistent, quite unsubstantiated rumours that occasionally the evenings did not pass off altogether peaceably. But then Mr. Judson was known to be liberal with his champagne and to possess an excellent brandy – a Denis Mounie of 1830, though not every one got that.

"There's a city chap called Judson –" Waveny went on, but Bobby interrupted him.

"Look here, Waveny," he said, "I don't know what it's all about, but if you think there's anything wrong or have any information to give, it's no good coming to me. You want to go to Scotland Yard. They'll listen to you there. Or the nearest police-station. They'll take it up all right, if there's anything in it. All I could do anyhow would be to go round with you to the one in the High Street, and you can do that just as well by yourself – or better," added Bobby, with a lingering thought of Lord's and the sweet sound of Mr. Hammond's bat meeting the ball full face.

"That's just what I can't do," mumbled Waveny.

But Bobby was not listening. He was watching two newspaper sellers go by, the first with a placard announcing 'Fresh European Crisis', the second proclaiming briefly: 'Hammond Out.'

"I thought as much," said Bobby bitterly, though not making it clear to which placard he referred.

"You see," Waveny went on in his stolid, deliberate way, "there's a girl."

"I thought as much," said Bobby again.

Waveny nodded. His nod seemed to say he was not disappointed in his estimate of Bobby's intelligence and that he had fully expected Bobby to perceive the indicated presence of a girl.

"There's a bounder, too, bothering her," Waveny went on, "I ought to thrash within an inch of his life – or a bit more." He spoke with such a sudden and unexpected vehemence that Bobby gave him a somewhat startled glance. Waveny continued more quietly: "Only, you see, you've got to keep her name out of it, so I thought I would come along to you."

CHAPTER II
MEET CLARENCE

Bobby felt the time had come to make a stand. He went over to the fireplace and planted himself firmly before it, his feet wide apart, his hands in his jacket pockets.

"Now you just listen to me, Waveny," he said. "It's no good talking like that. I can't keep anyone's name out of anything and I wouldn't if I could. If people – girls, anyone – get mixed up in things, well, that's that, and they've got to take the consequences. Another thing," added Bobby, with a somewhat uneasy glance at that formidable stick Waveny seemed to regard with so much affection, "don't you get trying any games like thrashing people within an inch of their lives – or over. It sounds all right but it's apt to have the most unpleasant consequences. I suppose you wouldn't care to do six months' hard, would you?"

Waveny paid no heed to this last remark. Six months' hard and the Hon. Chas. Waveny lived in different streets, so to say, and there was no possible connection. But the first part of Bobby's observations he evidently both understood and approved. To it, he nodded in complete agreement.

"Quite right, too," he approved. "I don't believe in hushing things up myself. Only, of course – well, it's no good making a stink, is it? And then, well, look at the way things are abroad. Look at the Bolshevik rebellion against Franco in Spain. We don't want that sort of thing here, do we? and we shall unless chaps like us stick together."

"I'm not a chap like us," snapped Bobby. "I'm a policeman."

"Jolly good idea, too," declared Waveny, still approving. "One up to Trenchard getting our sort to join. Gives the police a tone, if you see what I mean."

"My God," said Bobby, reaching for his hat.

"All I want," continued Waveny, comfortably certain complete understanding had now been reached, "is for you to come along there to-morrow evening. Not now, because I've something on. To-morrow –"

Bobby interrupted.

"The cigarettes are on the table," he said. "In the left- hand cupboard of the writing-table you'll find whisky and a siphon of soda-water. Make yourself at home and stay as long as you like. When I go on duty to-morrow I'll report what you've said and that I advised you to call at the High Street police-station. So long."

With that he departed and as he went out into the street he saw Waveny staring from the window in open-eyed, open-mouthed bewilderment. Like that, the Hon. Chas.'s protuberant eyes and small round chin and mouth seemed more noticeable, the domineering nose to fade away. In profile, Bobby told himself, that nose, the well-known Waveny nose on which, for generations, judges, generals, admirals of the clan had trumpeted their approval or their disapproval of lesser mortals, would never have allowed him to depart so easily.

He turned into the next street and at the corner waited for a bus to take him to Lord's for what was left of the afternoon. Buses came, of course, for every other conceivable quarter of the globe but none for where he wanted to go. Bobby found himself wondering what had really been the cause of the Hon. Chas.'s visit. Could there be any connection with those vague rumours of which Bobby had some almost equally vague knowledge to the general effect that Mr. Judson's little parties were not so innocent as they seemed. Probably though there was not much foundation for such stories. Bobby knew that discreet inquiry had shown Mr. Judson to be a man of some position in the City, well known and respected. Originally his business had been coal exporting, but the export of coal was less flourishing than once it had been and now for him had become subsidiary to his other interests. He was on the board of one of the smaller discount companies, he did a certain amount of company promoting – his name was worth mentioning when underwriting was being sought – and it was understood that he was a kind of sleeping partner in a successful firm, of stockbrokers. His reputation was that of a cautious speculator who understood that the secret of success was to take a small profit quickly, and then, too, he was careful to bet as a rule only on those certainties the Stock Exchange sometimes knows, when a piece of string can be measured before the public is invited to guess its length.

Altogether, Bobby realized, not at all the kind of man to be mixed up in anything scandalous. After all, nowadays, poker and pretty ladies are rather admired than otherwise, so that he ran no risks of scandal there.

None the less Bobby felt certain that Waveny really knew or suspected something, was really disturbed, and then he woke from his reverie to see the tailboards of two or three of the buses he had been waiting for disappearing in that friendly cluster in which London buses seem to love to run. Another half-hour to wait, he supposed, and somehow now he did not feel quite in the mood for watching cricket. Besides, Mr. Hammond was disappointingly out, though there was always the possibility that to-day might find in form a gentleman Bobby rather liked to refer to as 'Patsy', because once he had been privileged to chat to him for nearly a quarter of an hour (we are all snobs one way or another and the fact may as well be admitted). But then Bobby remembered that Mr. Hendren was not playing in this match and at the same moment a bus bound Epping way drew up.

The coincidence was marked. Just as well perhaps if by any chance anything came of this odd Waveny affair, and if he were questioned about it, to be able to show he knew the locality. In the C.I.D. one was expected to know everything and be able to answer any question off-hand. Bobby could almost hear Superintendent Ulyett asking his snappy questions: 'Dictator's Way, eh? exact position? length? often used? kind of surface? gates to it? lined by a hedge or what? overlooked at all? nearest houses?' And so on. Nice to be able to return equally snappy replies.

A little surprised by the fact, Bobby found himself completing these meditations on the top of the Epping- bound bus. So he lighted a cigarette and devoted himself to surveying with a lazy interest the ever-varying and picturesque panorama of the London streets. It all had its interest for Bobby, often from a professional point of view. There, for instance, stood young Tommy Breeze, eldest son of Sir Thomas Breeze, Bart, (of the first creation), and destined therefore to be Sir Thomas himself some day. Just released from Hendon he was directing traffic at a busy corner and making heavy weather of it, too. And there a little further on was fat old Simmonds, doing the same job with the effortless ease born of twenty years' experience. Bobby waved to Simmonds and as he did so a cultured, drawling, B.B.C. voice hailed him by name. Looking round, Bobby recognized Jimmy Hardwick, expert hotel thief, just released after serving nine months' hard. He seemed quite pleased to see Bobby, passed on a hot tip for to-morrow's three o'clock, and then alighted after further pleasant chat.

"Wonder what he's been up to," Bobby said to himself, and, watching from the top of the bus as it waited for the traffic lights, he saw Mr. Hardwick join Mr. Mullins, a well-known receiver. Probably then Mr. Hardwick had had a good day, and somewhere or another an hotel manager was protesting to an agitated and tearful lady that the hotel was not responsible for jewellery left in an unlocked bedroom.

"Might have been worth while," Bobby thought lazily, "going through his pockets, only most likely someone else had the swag."

Arrived at his destination, Bobby's first thought was for tea. He sought it in an adjacent public-house where a large notice proclaimed 'Teas served in the garden'. It was tea apparently intended to support the trade slogan that 'Beer is Best', but in the C.I.D. a man must be prepared for all, even public-house tea, so Bobby sipped it resignedly and asked for directions how best to get to Dictator's Way. The girl attending to him had never heard of it, so soon does fame pass, for it was only two or three years since the mere name had been enough to let free floods of indignation in all this district. However she undertook to ask one of the barmen and he fortunately was better informed and equally fortunately quite inclined for a gossip in this slack pre-opening hour. He knew, too, about The Manor House, and Mr. Judson, and Mr. Judson's little parties.

"Keep it up all right, they do," said the barman. "I've seen the lights in the windows, and cars waiting, when I was going to work and that wasn't much before six. That's the life," said the barman enviously and then brightened up. "He gets his beer from here and when you deliver and collect the empties, nothing's said about 'em. Not so bad with empties allowed for at fourpence each. It's Mr. Macklin does the ordering and a very nice gent, too."

"Who is Mr. Macklin?" Bobby asked. .

"Sort of a secretary gentleman," the barman explained. "It's him fixes it all up when Mr. Judson's having friends. If there's only a lady coming, Mr. Walker, that's Mr. Judson's chauffeur, sees to things. Handy gentleman, Mr. Walker, cook and manage just like a woman only better than most, and Mr. Judson likes him to do it all when he's just having a lady friend. Mr. Judson ain't no married man, just enjoys himself, he does,*' said the barman still more enviously.

"Aren't there any regular servants?" Bobby asked.

"Not a one," declared the barman. "Hard to get nowadays, them are, especial for a great rambling place like that. Girls won't take it on – miles and miles of passages and rooms and no conveniences like. One reason why Mr. Judson gave it up and why he can't sell."

"For sale, is it?" Bobby said. "But how does he manage if he still uses it sometimes?"

"Contracts, if it's a do," explained the barman, "and if it's only him and a lady, why, then Mr. Walker sees to everything, before and after. Has supper ready at night – champagne, oysters, all the best – and next morning on the spot at eight sharp. Sometimes he has to get their breakfast, sometimes they get it theirselves – and sometimes Mr. Walker says him and the guv'nor is off before the lady wakes up. But always liberal with 'em, always, that's Mr. Judson," added the barman, "a perfect gentleman if ever there was one, and a pity there aren't more like him."

Bobby made no attempt to dispute this verdict. He paid his bill, added a liberal tip, and departed, feeling even more uncomfortable than before. He did not like so much talk of so many successive ladies, or of such lively parties prolonged to hours not so small. Something had certainly disturbed Waveny to a serious extent. He had talked about a girl. So had the barman, though in the plural and using a different word. If Mr. Judson had been extending, or even contemplating extending, his hospitality to any young woman of Waveny's acquaintance, then there was a very clear probability of serious trouble ahead. Bobby began to wonder if it would be as well to suggest to his superiors the advisability of trying to find out a little more about Mr. Judson's evening recreations, and if there was any known rivalry between Waveny and Judson. It might be well, too, to keep an eye on The Manor to-morrow evening. For that a hint to the local people would be enough.

Possibly this Mr. Macklin might know something, or the chauffeur – even more probably the chauffeur. Bobby had acquired a profound respect for the varied and extensive knowledge possessed by chauffeurs. After all, a butler or a footman knows no more than what goes on within. The chauffeur knows in addition all that happens without – 'without' including Road Houses.

Anyhow, it seemed to Bobby that further exploration was indicated, and presently – it was a fairly long walk – he reached the spot where a notice-board announced: 'Dictator's Way. Foot-path only. Wheeled traffic forbidden. Trespassers will be prosecuted.'

In any case, a padlocked gate forbade the way to wheeled traffic. But posts placed at two-feet intervals left it free to walkers, and Bobby strolled on.

On one side lay the expanse of the forest, tamed and trimmed and tidied indeed, its undergrowth kept in check, fallen boughs carefully removed, and yet with its majestic oaks standing as they stood in the days of our Saxon and Norman ancestors, as those from whose acorns these had sprung stood when skin-clad savages hunted in their shade or gathered to watch living victims offered up in fire to the god of the Druids.

On the other side, on Bobby's left as he walked along, lay the neglected and deserted gardens of The Manor. A pity, Bobby thought, to see so much good ground left to lie idle. Not more than a couple of acres, though. A good proportion of it was occupied by an over-grown shrubbery, a damp and gloomy wilderness, it seemed, a shelter for all things that shunned the light of heaven. Dry as the weather had been of late one felt that everything within its shade still rotted in a damp decay. A little further on, nearer the house, was a fair sized pond that a very small degree of attention would have transformed into an excellent swimming-pool of the kind now so popular. But at present its banks were muddy, its waters stagnant and dirty, its presence accentuating the general air of dampness and decay that characterized the whole place and probably explained why Mr. Judson found it difficult to dispose of, as perhaps also why he himself had deserted it for the attractions of a flat in town. Our fathers were less particular, but to-day a damp looking site is small recommendation. No doubt adequate draining would effect much, though at present the whole place looked as though moisture could be squeezed from it as from a sponge.

A large board, drooping dispiritedly to one side, as though it had long abandoned hope, announced that this eligible gentleman's residence was for sale, adding a list of the number of rooms enough in itself to frighten away most prospective purchasers.

The iron entrance gates, rusty and in need of paint, were closed, but near by was an inviting gap in the uncared-for hedge. Bobby pushed through it and went on up the wide and weed grown carriage drive towards the house. He could see that most of the windows were shuttered and that it offered no sign of habitation. On the top floor the windows were curtainless and unshuttered, helping so to produce that blank look of desolation characteristic of uninhabited houses. As he came near the pond Bobby noticed that a grid and drain, evidently intended to draw off surplus water, had become choked with dead leaves and twigs and other rubbish. That probably meant that in rainy weather the pond tended to slop over towards the shrubbery, turning it most likely into a small morass, and then from behind a clump of unkempt bushes rose up a man who had been crouching there and watching ever since Bobby's appearance.

A formidable personage, too, and one well known to Bobby, as to various other members of the police force. His name was Duke, Clarence Duke, often known to his friends as 'Duke Clarence'. He stood well over six feet in height, was broad even out of proportion, weighed sixteen or seventeen stone, and possessed arms like a gorilla's – and a countenance not altogether unlike that of the same animal. Once he had been seriously thought of as an aspirant for the heavy-weight championship. But he was slow on his feet, slower still in his mental processes, and had proved quite incapable of learning boxing. An end had been put to his career by a row in a public-house which had resulted in the death of one of the men concerned from a fractured skull. Clarence had been held responsible, had been lucky to avoid the verdict of murder his dull, sullen air of ferocity in the dock and witness-box had seemed to invite, and had in the end escaped with a sentence of three years for manslaughter.

"Hullo, Clarence," Bobby exclaimed, wondering what on earth this East End bully's presence here might mean.

"All right, all right," the other growled, "you aren't pinching me – I'll do you in first, may as well swing for two as for one."

As he spoke, he charged.

CHAPTER III
BATTLE ROYAL

Bobby had no time for any expression of surprise, protest, remonstrance, no time indeed even for conscious thought as that mountain of a man charged down upon him, with flaming eyes and pounding feet, his arms revolving like those of a windmill.

Instinctively Bobby knew that at close quarters he would stand no chance. As well risk close quarters with a grizzly bear as with oncoming Clarence. His only hope was to keep at a distance and to remember that it had been said of Clarence in his boxing days that to hit him was as easy as to hit a house, even though hitting him seemed to have little more effect than such hitting would have on a house.

Swiftly then, with a speed indeed on which he knew his life depended, for it was murder unmistakable that glared from under those shaggy, overhanging brows, from those small red-rimmed eyes, Bobby sprang to one side, and as Clarence thundered by hit him twice, once on the temple, once just behind the ear.

They were good blows, well timed, well delivered, behind them all the force of Bobby's vigorous young manhood. Either might well, with most opponents, have ended the fight then and there. Clarence gave no sign of having even noticed them.

He swung round and came again, and this time Bobby changed his tactics, leaving that small, bullet-like head alone and aiming instead his blows at the other's heart, leaping in to deliver them, springing away again in time to avoid Clarence's slow enormous fists. This time Clarence paid Bobby's efforts the tribute of a grunt or two, drew back a moment as if to recover breath, and then again came on. But once more Bobby slipped away, getting in as he did so, however, yet another vicious short-arm jab, on the same spot, just above the heart.

Clarence let loose a stream of profanity and again came in pursuit, and still Bobby employed the same tactics, fighting coolly and warily, careful to keep without the range of the other's flail-like arms, taking every chance to let his own fists beat a tattoo on the same spot, just above the heart. Not that this long succession of blows seemed as yet to be having much effect, and the knowledge was clear at the back of Bobby's mind that if even one of those threshing fists of Clarence's got home, that would be the end. So far he had succeeded in either avoiding them altogether, or in taking them on the retreat with diminished force, but the mixture of skill and of good fortune that had hitherto served him so well he knew must in the end break down. But not yet, and once more he ran in under the other's guard and flung all his weight into two more blows on the same spot and was away again, untouched himself.

One hope Bobby had, and that lay in the fact that Clarence was very evidently not in good condition. A steady devotion to the new dogma that 'beer is best' was having its natural and due effect, and then, too, Bobby's fists, thudding home time and again upon that one spot just above the heart, were beginning to produce results. Also Clarence was wasting a great deal of breath in the use of a very great deal of very bad language, as, too, he was expending much of his strength in those bull-like rushes that all the same Bobby was finding it increasingly difficult to avoid.

Once more his fists, with all his weight behind them, got home, and this time Clarence gasped and stood still a moment, slightly dazed, it seemed, so that Bobby had time to leap in and hit, swift right and left, on the same spot and so away again. Not quite unharmed this time, however, for one of Clarence's flail-like swings caught him on the right cheek and sent him reeling back a dozen feet or more.

It was the heaviest blow he had yet received, for another that had cut his lip and set it bleeding, had been comparatively light. For the moment, under the weight of that left-handed swing, it was all Bobby could do to keep his footing, and had Clarence followed it up, the fight might well have ended then and there. But Clarence did not even see his opportunity. He was standing still, trying to get his breath and to get rid of an odd feeling he had, as if his heart was missing a beat occasionally.

The pause gave time for the mists to clear that had gathered before Bobby's eyes. He wiped away the blood trickling from his cut lip into his mouth and he told himself that if only he could get in a few more hits on his opponent's heart, the victory might still be his. A kind of exultation filled him at the thought, a swift energy of combat, so that he knew no longer anything in all the world but this rage of conflict, this urge to conquer.

It was he who was the attacker now. Hitherto he had fought on the defensive, but now he attacked and Clarence was forced to stand and endure his fierce assault. A little bewildered he stood still as Bobby almost danced around, feinting here, threatening there, dodging, leaping in and away again, and yet scarcely ever actually delivering a blow save on that one spot he had made his target.

"Stand still, stand still, can't ye?" Clarence growled, and Bobby laughed aloud, for the sweet joy of battle was alight in him, aflame in every nerve and vein, and once more he feinted and hit and dodged away, unhurt himself.

But now Clarence, a little blue about the lips but still strong upon his feet, and a little tired perhaps of standing to serve as a kind of stationary target, started to follow, slowly, ponderously, determinedly, enduring Bobby's blows, paying almost each one the tribute of a grunt but somehow with the air of knowing that not for long could such a fire and blaze of attack endure and that when it died down, his turn would come.

But Bobby had no feeling that the fierce energy flowing through him would ever slacken, and he had noted that blue tinge come upon the other's lips, and he believed himself assured of victory.

"Now I've got you," Clarence said; and in his turn laughed, if that can be called a laugh which sounded more like a bulldog's growl.

With a start Bobby realized that they had drawn close to the edge of the pond, so that the water behind prevented any further movement in that direction and to one side. And on the other side the ground was damp and sodden from water seeping in from where the choked grid and drain were failing to take it away.

And in front was Clarence, still upon his feet, huge and formidable.

Bobby saw that he had allowed himself to be cornered, that his only chance now was to slip away again into the open. Suddenly he ran straight in at Clarence, hoping to confuse him and then to slip by on one side or the other. But the damp and heavy ground hampered his feet and held them down. For once, too, Clarence guessed right what Bobby intended, received and never heeded another blow, and flung wide his enormous arms so that Bobby found himself caught in the grasp of a man by far his superior in weight and brute strength.

Nor was any referee there to order 'break away', no referee or umpire indeed, nothing between them save the primeval urge to kill and hurt.

With all his force Bobby hit Clarence on the chin. He might as well have hit a brick wall. His own knuckles bled, but that was all. He tried the rabbit punch, for his need was desperate, and the life slowly ebbing from him under the pressure of the grip wherein he was held. But it had no effect, for he could not free his arm enough to deliver it effectively. They fell and rolled together on the ground.

With all the strength despair can give, Bobby tried to wrench himself free, to get his arms free, to make some effective defence against that mountainous grip in which he was held. But he was undermost, and now he saw death glaring at him from the other's red-rimmed, bloodshot eyes, felt now the other's hands groping for his throat, about to squeeze the life from him.

A darkness came before his eyes and a sound of running waters.

Running waters. A splashing, a gurgling. The pressure on his throat relaxed. He perceived that from somewhere a stream of cold water was descending through the bright sunlight, aimed very accurately at Clarence's mouth.

It was wide open. He was trying to shout something, a threat or a curse. The stream of water caught it full. Clarence choked. Bobby wrenched himself free. He perceived he had his own share of the drenching and that he was soaked from head to foot. Clarence, wrathful and wet, was scrambling to his feet, spluttering, gasping, choking. The stream of water continued to play upon his face with extreme accuracy. Probably it was years, not since his childhood's days very likely, since so much pure, unmixed water had found its way into his interior. He disliked it intensely. Nor was he used to cold baths and now he was dripping from head to foot. Thoughts of pneumonia passed through his mind. A girl's voice said:

"Dad taught me that. He always said when two dogs started fighting, there was nothing like a pail of cold water."

"Water," said Clarence, still spluttering. "Water," he repeated as Herr Hitler might say 'Jew' – or a Jew say 'Hitler'.

"Want some more, or is that enough?" asked the girl, deflecting the stream of water.

Bobby perceived now that she had connected up a length of old hose with a stand-pipe some thirty or forty feet away, and from a distance of about ten feet had been directing the stream with considerable accuracy upon the two of them, though with special attention to Clarence's mouth whenever he opened it in an attempt to speak.

She was very tall, very thin, even for these slimming days, with a thin, narrow, dead-white face whereon lips painted a deep crimson made a vivid unnatural patch. Her eyebrows had been plucked to a nearly straight line, her nose was long and straight, her crimsoned lips thin and straight, so that it almost seemed as if there were exemplified in her the modern belief that the straight line and the angle are the lines of beauty. But it was her eyes that were her most noticeable feature, large, dark, fringed with long dark lashes, they gave an odd impression of seeing nothing that was near by, only things that were very far away. Even while she had been aiming that stream of water so accurately at the two struggling men, her gaze had seemed directed not at them but at something she was aware of in the far distance. A strong, unusual personality, Bobby thought, more striking than attractive, neither wholly feminine nor yet in any way masculine, something between the two perhaps, or else something above both, as if sex had been long left behind, forgotten in a greater aim.

"Here, you," Clarence protested fiercely, difficult though it is to be effectively fierce when soaked from head to foot, "you leave us alone, he was going to pinch me, he was, and I'm not standing for it."

"Looked like a good deal more than pinching to me," observed the girl, to whom the technical use of the word 'pinch' was not familiar.

"What for?" Bobby asked Clarence. "Been up to anything lately? I suppose I had better pinch you now," he added. "Evidently you think it's what's wanted."

"No, you don't," said Clarence, glaring.

The girl negligently lifted her hose-pipe.

"If you start again, this starts again," she observed in her cool, detached way.

"Now, look here, lady," began Clarence.

"Wait a moment," Bobby said, beginning to remember the remark with which Clarence had heralded his attack. "What was that you said about 'swinging'? what did that mean? what for?"

"You blokes after me, aren't you? trying to put it on me; always do once a bloke's been sent up, hasn't got a chance then, always after him, you are," Clarence grumbled.

"Well, what are we after you for now?" Bobby asked. "I don't know anything about it, anyhow."

Clarence broke into a long, confused, rambling statement. Bobby listened patiently, asking a question now and then. The girl, apparently convinced that truce had been established, strolled away to turn off the water at the stand-pipe and then came back to listen. Clarence concluded with a fierce declaration that he wasn't going to swing for no woman he had never set eyes on in his life, and never been near where she was found, innocent as the babe unborn he was, but what did the 'busies' care so long as they could pinch someone and get a spot of promotion all round?

"Doubtless, Clarence," Bobby observed meditatively and reminiscently when Clarence was at last silent, "doubtless God could have made a bigger fool than you, but doubtless God never did."

"I should rather like," observed the girl, "to know what it's all about – just as a matter of curiosity, of course. Have you something to do with the police?" she added to Bobby, and, he thought, with less detachment than her voice had shown before.

"Yes," he answered briefly. He went on: "A woman named Wilkinson was found dead on the Hackney marshes last week – drink, exposure, and T.B. Natural death, if you call that natural. But it seems an anonymous letter came along, accusing Clarence here of having murdered her. We get dozens of anonymous letters at Scotland Yard. Generally they're worth nothing – mere spite very often – but once in a way one of them means something, and so they all have to be checked. Probably this letter would be sent on to the Divisional Detective-Inspector and he would send someone round to make inquiries. It does sound as if that hadn't been done quite tactfully, and anyhow Clarence heard inquiries were being made about him in connection with the death of a woman, and promptly got the wind up, and thought he was going to be brought in for it. When he saw me just now he thought I meant to arrest him, and so he decided to make sure of getting hung by doing his best to murder me. He always was the good Lord's prize, champion fool."

"Mean to say you don't want me?" inquired Clarence. "Mean to say you don't think I had nothing to do with it?"

"There's no reason to suppose the woman was murdered at all," Bobby answered, "and no reason to suppose you knew her or that she knew you. Besides, you would be at the Essex greyhound racing track all that evening, I suppose, unless Adams has given you the sack lately."

"Clarence is a bookmaker's bully when he's nothing worse," Bobby added to the girl, somewhat unjustly, but then he was still cross.

"Then you aren't going to arrest him?" the girl asked. "It's all a misunderstanding, is it? I'm glad because he just now threw a horrid little man who was annoying me into the pond."

"Got me orders," said Clarence, and while Bobby was still wondering what these remarks might mean, he added: "It's straight you aren't going to pinch me?"

"I ought to," growled Bobby; "what do you mean by rushing at me the way you did? You ought to get forty shillings or a month at least. Still," he conceded, "it wasn't such a bad little scrap while it lasted."

"For a little 'un," said Clarence magnanimously, "you park a worth-while punch – I've known better but I've known plenty worse, and from bigger nor you."

Bobby was slightly annoyed. He stood six feet and weighed thirteen stone and he was not accustomed to regard himself as a 'little 'un'.

"You weren't fighting fair at the end," he said, "you were trying to throttle me – not in the rules."

"Lor' bless you," said Clarence tolerantly. "I wasn't boxing, I was fighting. So long, Mr. Owen, sir, and much obliged. So long, miss – lummy, she's gone."

She had in fact slipped away, so silently, so quietly, neither of the two men had noticed it. She wasn't visible on the drive, either towards the house or towards the entrance gates. She must have disappeared into the shrubbery, Bobby supposed. He started to follow her and then paused. If she wished to depart, he supposed she had a right to do so. He heard the sound of a car starting up. On an impulse he ran a few yards back towards the entrance and then swung himself into a tree he had noticed from whose branches he guessed he could command a view of the road. He was just in time to see a small 'Bayard Seven' departing. He thought he had better make a note of its number but when he felt for his fountain-pen, he found it was not there. Later he discovered what was left of it on the scene of battle. Evidently it had fallen out during the fight and either he or Clarence had trodden on it with calamitous results. So now the note he wished to make he had to jot down in pencil.

"Rum affair altogether," he decided, and when he returned to the battle-field, though he discovered the remnants there of his fountain-pen, no sign remained of Clarence who had evidently considered the opportunity favourable for departing also.

To Bobby it began to seem that the disappearing act was being
slightly overworked. Still, he did not see what he could do about it.
No doubt in Clarence there was well established by both instinct
and habit a strong inclination to depart from the presence of
anyone in any way connected with the police, and Bobby found
himself wondering if that instinct and inclination were shared,
too, by the unknown young lady of the pale face and strange and
distant eyes.

He felt sure he had not been wrong in thinking that there had
been a slight change in her manner as soon as she understood he
was a policeman. But then she was a motorist, and few indeed are
the motorists whose consciences are clear in the presence of the
police.

It also became borne in upon Bobby that he was extremely
damp, for a proportion of the water played upon Clarence's
resentful countenance had been reflected upon Bobby's prostrate
form.

Trusting that no more young ladies were lurking in the depths
of that damp and joyless shrubbery, Bobby sought the shelter of a
clump of rhododendrons he saw growing on what once had been a
lawn, and there, divesting himself of his clothing, he spread it out
in the rays of a sun fortunately still powerful.

In meditative mood he sat and watched it drying, and now and
again he plucked a rhododendron leaf, dipped it in an old tomato
tin he had found and filled with water, and put it to his cheek and
his cut lip that was still bleeding slightly.

For those of an empty house up for sale, these grounds seemed
to be, he thought, something of a congested area. What, for
instance, was Mr. Clarence Duke doing there so far from his
favourite haunts, the pubs and greyhound racing tracks of the
East End? An odd place, it seemed to Bobby, this neglected
garden, for Clarence to frequent, and what had he meant by saying
he had his orders?

That had been in connection with the girl's remark that he had thrown into the pond a 'horrid little man', who had been molesting her. Bobby wondered who that had been and what the pair of them had been doing here? Apparently the girl must be fairly familiar with the place, too, for she had known where the stand-pipe was situated, known where to find the length of hose she had used so effectively.

Bobby scowled a little as he turned over his clothing to make sure all parts received an equal share of the warm sunshine. Also, risking lurking young ladies in the shrubbery, he moved forward from the shelter of the rhododendrons, grown a trifle chilly, to secure some of the benefit for his own bare body of that same sunshine. It was comforting but he still scowled, for he remembered the tone in which she had remarked that her father had recommended cold water for fighting dogs. It was a tone very wounding to the feelings. Hang it all, what was a fellow to do if another fellow went for him, hammer and tongs?

At any rate, he hoped that her presence here did not mean that she was one of those who at times enjoyed Mr. Judson's doubtful hospitality. Somehow, he did not much think so, even though certainly this was not the first time she had visited the place.

Then there was the 'horrid little man' mentioned so casually as having been thrown into the pond, as if throwing people into ponds were a part of the ordinary routine of life. At any rate it was to be hoped that having been thrown into the pond, he had come out of it again. A somewhat uneasy glance it was that Bobby now directed towards those placid and anything but clear waters, nor was it only the after effects of the chilly rhododendron shade that made him shiver as he sat, in spite of the hot sun upon his back.

And was any one of the three of them – Clarence, the girl, the unknown 'horrid little man' – in any way connected with whatever it was interested the Hon. Chas. Waveny in The Manor? Had he had any knowledge of the likely presence here this afternoon of any or all of these three people? And, if so, had such knowledge been his reason for naming to-morrow, and not to-day, for the visit suggested?

Puzzling; and Bobby began to wish he had allowed Waveny to tell his tale in full, even though it had not seemed then, it did not seem now for that matter, any direct concern of his. Waveny had made no direct allegation of any conduct calling for police action. The girl was a trespasser, no doubt, but no more so than was Bobby himself, and anyhow trespassing in itself is not a criminal action. Most likely, too, there was some perfectly simple explanation for her presence and her knowledge of where to find stand-pipe and hose. As for the 'horrid little man', his very existence was only a matter of hearsay evidence. Clarence – odd about Clarence certainly. He could no doubt be brought in for a breach of the peace, but somehow Bobby felt that would be an unworthy termination to what had been quite a jolly little scrap.

Thoughtfully Bobby plucked another rhododendron leaf, wet it, laid it against his cheek.

Yes, a jolly little scrap, and a shame to expose it to the cold, unsympathetic eye of the law. After all, one could understand how it had happened. Anonymous letters had to be investigated. Once in donkey's years they were important. Clarence had heard that inquiries were being made about him in connection with the death of a woman. Very likely he had been teased by his pals, told that now the 'busies' had made up their minds that this time he was to swing 'and no error'. He had fallen into a panic, felt the rope as good as round his neck, come here to hide – why here? – and on seeing Bobby arrive he had, like the muddle-headed fool he was, jumped to the conclusion that Bobby's errand was to arrest him. To him, with his record, no doubt arrest and conviction meant the same.

It began to come slowly into Bobby's mind that perhaps the oddest incident in the whole business might turn out to be that anonymous letter of accusation. Mere silly spite though, most likely, well calculated, too, to give a really bad scare to a man like Clarence.

But then who should want to frighten Clarence, and why?

Supposing Waveny for instance – but here Bobby felt that now he was no longer trying to think things out but merely indulging in wild guesses. He got firmly to his feet, resolute to spend no more time in speculation; unless and until further developments occurred. The sun had done its work now and his clothes were dry enough to put on. He dressed accordingly, and as he did so watched with curiosity the empty house behind him, and how from those uncurtained, unshuttered windows on the top floor the rays of the nearly setting sun winked back at him, as though to remind him how much more they knew than did he.

He decided that now he was here he might as well have a look round the building. Of course, he was a trespasser, but if he were challenged, since in spite of its deserted air the place seemed so populated, what with large, angry men, small, horrid men, tall, pale young women, he could always plead the notice-board offering the house and grounds for sale. Easy to pass for the interested, or even merely curious, possible purchaser.

But first of all he strolled down to the edge of the pond and was not long in finding on the muddy bank a medley of footprints and other signs of a struggle that seemed to confirm the tale of the 'horrid little man' flung into its water. An expert might, Bobby supposed, be able to read the whole story from those various marks and signs, and at any rate he, though he was no expert, was able to pick out two or three footmarks, a man's and yet too small to be those of Clarence, that were still damp and that pointed from the pond as if someone, very wet, had been going away from it.

Well, that at any rate suggested the 'horrid little man' had not remained under its calm and unclean surface. Reassured on this point, Bobby turned his steps towards the house. The facade seemed to offer nothing of interest. Bobby tried the front door, found it secure, knocked, rang, waited a little, tried knocking and ringing again, got no answer. The bell was of the electric type and he could hear its shrill summons sound within the house. So that had been kept in order, and Bobby noticed, too, that there was a telephone wire running to the house, though of course it did not follow the instrument itself was still in position.

He walked on round by the side of the building without noticing anything unusual. On the south side there was a verandah and a side door opening on it. He tried this door and found it securely fastened, nor did it show any sign of recent use. Mr.

Judson's visitors were probably of the nocturnal type and not much interested in verandahs or garden doors. There was a large conservatory here, too, quite empty and looking very desolate. Passing round it, Bobby came to the back of the house. Here was a large paved courtyard, two or three outbuildings, and a certain amount of debris, including two or three empty, rusting and overturned dustbins. There was a large garden roller, too, standing in one corner, and Bobby supposed he might as well try the back door and make sure that was fast. Approaching, he saw lying quite near three one-pound notes.

Curious, he thought. What could they be doing there? They couldn't have been there long, anyhow. Very odd, he thought, and odder still he thought it when he stooped to examine them more closely, and saw upon the corner of one a red stain that looked to him very much as though it had been caused by blood freshly spilt.

He knelt down to examine them more closely, and then to his extreme annoyance, and by a piece of unforeseen bad luck, a tiny drop of blood from his own cut lip that had now started bleeding afresh fell on another of the notes. Just the sort of thing cross-examining counsel would make play with, if it ever came into court. ['You were I believe, Sergeant, yourself bleeding freely at the time from a wound received in honourable combat?' (loud and prolonged laughter.)] If this affair had any sequence, that was the sort of thing he would have to expect, not to mention all the pointed remarks his superiors would address to him on the necessity of at least keeping irrelevant bloodstains (bloodstains!) off exhibits in criminal cases.

He could only hope the whole wretched business would prove to be without significance and that nothing much would need to be done about it.

One had to make sure, though. He produced his pocket book, copied in it the numbers of the notes, made an accurate sketch of their position with exact measurements and intersecting lines to show precisely where they lay, and reflected that it was all a lot of red tape, but then the Yard was like that. There was no wind and the spot was sheltered, but to make sure they did not blow away he found and placed a small stone on each. Then he made a closer search of the vicinity. The paving of the courtyard held no footprints, he found no trace of any recent visitor, no sign of any unusual happening till inside one of the overturned dustbins he discovered a few ashes as if paper had been burnt there, very thoroughly burnt, too, for the ashes had been crushed together and crumbled so as to make any reconstruction evidently impossible. Yet close by lay other charred fragments that seemed to show it was only a copy of the morning's *Daily Announcer* that had been destroyed.

"I wonder," said Bobby, looking at them thoughtfully, and that red stain upon the pound note by the back door of the house began to seem to him more ominous still.

He made a note, too, of the position of the dustbin – one has to be ready to answer all the questions – and then went across to the back door. Gingerly, there might be finger-prints on it, he tried the handle. To his surprise, the door opened at once. He crossed the threshold and listened. It was all perfectly still within, still and silent with such stillness and such silence as are only in places whence has departed the noise and bustle of healthy normal human activity.

He was standing in the entrance to a wide passage, where now lay heavily the shadows of the coming night. The windows that once had admitted the day were now barred and shuttered so that no light entered. Bobby bent down and examined the floor. It was of boarding, covered with linoleum, and the dust on it did not appear to be sufficiently thick to show footprints. Keeping as close as he could to the wall, walking carefully so that his own should not interfere with any marks that might in fact be there, Bobby moved forward. On his right was an open door, by which some light entered, though already his eyes were growing accustomed to the gloom. He saw a spacious apartment that evidently had formerly been the kitchen but now was empty of any furnishing. At the further end were two closed doors, admitting probably to pantry or scullery, and there was an enormous, built-in cooking range, now red with rust. Further on were other doors, but all closed and Bobby did not open them. To search thoroughly a house of this size would take time and indeed could not be done effectively by one person. Besides, his first care must be to find out if there was anyone within. If so, some simple explanation might at once be offered. If there was no one to be found, then Bobby felt that the sooner he got on the telephone, reported, and asked for instructions, the better. In front, too, he could now see a door covered with green baize, probably the service door separating the part of the house occupied by the owner from that used by the domestic staff.

Walking as carefully as before, for who could tell what footmarks or other signs might not be visible to expert examination, Bobby reached the baize door. It was not fastened. He pushed it open and listened. All seemed perfectly still and quiet. Not even the scuffling of a mouse, the movement of a spider, disturbed the utter immobility that was here, as though here time was not and motion had for ever ceased.

At the top of his voice, Bobby shouted:

"Is there anybody here?"

CHAPTER V
STRANGE CORPSE

Once again Bobby cried aloud his question. Again there was no answer, only the heavy silence that filled the house from floor to roof, as though there no one ever came.

He let the baize-covered door close behind him and walked on. It was difficult to see much at first, for little light penetrated through the closed and shuttered windows, but gradually his eyes were growing still more accustomed to the gloom and then he found the switches that controlled the electric lighting. He tried them, and at once a huge chandelier shone out overhead.

He was standing in a great hall. It was entirely empty. The only sign of recent use was that the parquet flooring showed traces of having been swept and polished at not too distant a date. Bobby saw also that the stairway rising at the back of the hall was carpeted. On either hand doors opened into various rooms. They were not locked and he looked into them all, in each case trying the switches but without result as all bulbs here had been removed from the fittings. The light entering from the hall was enough, however, to show him all the rooms were empty, except for one at the back where he found a few chairs and, piled against the wall, trestles and boards evidently intended for use as tables. In this room the bulbs were still in place in the lamp sockets and at one side was an elaborate electrical hot plate arrangement. Bobby guessed that when Mr. Judson gave one of his parties, this apartment was used by the contractors as the service room.

All that was without interest for him. He thought he might as well look through the rest of the house. If there was still a telephone here and he could find it, he had better, he supposed, ring up the nearest police station, report finding the back door open and ask them to let Mr. Judson know. Mr. Judson ought to be told, too, about those three one-pound notes lying near the back door. He might know to whom they probably belonged.

Bobby went back to the great lighted hall, his tread echoing heavily through the deserted spaces of the house. He found himself endeavouring to walk more lightly so as to make less noise. The silence, the brooding, patient stillness of the house, must be getting on his nerves, he thought, or why was it that there kept returning to his memory that red stain he had noticed on one of the pound notes. A cut finger, a slip of the razor when shaving, might easily account for it. Why then did it keep returning to his memory as if in some way it made an evil harmony with the silence of an empty house, with the heavy gloom these shuttered windows caused?

He made his way slowly up the wide, carpeted stairway, though not till once again he had sent a shout echoing before him:

"Is there anyone there, anyone up there?"

He expected no answer and none came. The carpet was in good condition and of fine quality, and he noticed that the stair rods were bright and polished. There was dust on the banister rail, and in the corners, and at the sides of the treads, but evidently some cleaning and sweeping was done from time to time.

At the top of the stairs was a wide landing, so wide that the American use of 'hall' for 'landing' would here have been fully justified. Opposite were double doors admitting to a fine, large, well-proportioned room, very comfortably and even luxuriously furnished. In the middle stood a long, mahogany table. At one end was a small round table. There were various armchairs, large and small, settees, a big sideboard, a carpet into whose soft pile the foot seemed to sink. A ribbon of light ran all round the walls behind the picture rail, and at intervals panels of frosted glass of different colours helped the general illumination, which, with all the lights on, was as bright and clear as that of direct sunshine. Nor was there any shadow anywhere. Warmth was evidently provided at need by electrically heated panels, and Bobby mused for a moment on this modern luxury by which light and heat lay dormant as it were, ready to be called into being by the pressing of a button, the touching of a switch. This room was, he told himself, the one where Mr. Judson received his guests when he gave parties here, and Bobby noticed that in one corner stood an elaborate radio gramophone. The room was big enough for dancing, since it ran nearly the whole length of that side of the house. The long table in the middle of the room would serve equally well for supper or for baccarat or *trente-et-quarante*, and the smaller round table for poker or any similar game.

But in all this there was nothing to interest Bobby, nor could he see any sign of a telephone.

He began to search the other rooms, going into them all in turn. In all, the electric bulbs were still in position so that he could light up as he entered. One apartment was a bedroom, luxuriously furnished with every imaginable modern fitting. Opening from it was a large dressing-room and a bathroom fitted up in the latest style, with all the complications modern civilization has added to the simple act of washing. Another room was apparently a store-room holding brooms, brushes, crockery, a vacuum cleaner, and so on. Two smaller rooms were more simply furnished with armchairs and small tables, as if for sitting in, and then Bobby entered one, at the end of the passage, with its windows facing east, that was evidently meant for a small dining or breakfast-room. Presumably it was where Mr. Judson took supper and breakfast when he came to spend the night here. There was a small sideboard, a small round table in the middle of the room, comfortable chairs, and in one corner, the telephone for which Bobby had been looking. He moved towards it, and as he did so he saw where there lay behind the table, between it and the electric stove, the body of a man.

It needed only a glance to tell the man was dead, had been dead some time. There is that about a body whence life has fled that once seen is not easily mistaken. No need for the testimony of the blood that had come from a wound in the head and that had formed a little pool near by.

For a minute or two Bobby stood very still under the shock of this discovery and yet he knew that ever since he had crossed the threshold of the house, it was something of this kind that he had in part anticipated. Very still he stood, and intently he gazed at the dead body, as intently as the staring, protruding eyes gazed back at him.

A thousand thoughts raced through Bobby's mind. Who was it, he wondered? Mr. Judson himself perhaps. Was this why Waveny had wished him, Bobby, to come here, but not now, not to-day?

Why not now, why not to-day?

Stepping carefully he went to the telephone and there when he put out his hand to pick up the receiver he drew it back again quickly. On the receiver were stains of blood marks; he thought, of a blood-stained hand.

Of murderer or of victim, Bobby wondered?

Using every precaution to avoid touching these stains, he rang up the Yard and reported briefly, asking them too, to let the local people know, since he wished to use the 'phone as little as possible.

There was nothing more he could do till help arrived. He locked the door of the room behind him and then went down to the back entrance to wait there.

The three one-pound notes were still where he had left them, to his relief for he had been afraid they might have vanished.

Help would come quickly, he knew, but all the same it seemed long to wait. His thoughts were busy with many speculations, many questions. Useless, though, to wonder, till more facts were known on which to build some theory of what had happened.

Names buzzed in his mind. Waveny. Waveny would have to be asked a good many questions. Was Waveny a murderer? That nose of his might contemplate murder perhaps, but would the small round mouth and chin ever carry it out? One never knew, though. Perhaps, in emergency, the nose might win. Or Clarence? Had that shout of his that you might as well swing for two as for one, now taken on a new significance? The pale, thin faced girl, too. What had she been doing here? Good thing he had taken a note of the number of her car. There had been something said, too, about a 'horrid little man'. Who was he?

But it was no good asking questions at this stage of the investigation. He did not even know the identity of the dead man. Mr. Judson presumably, since the house was his and he was often there, but it might easily turn out to be someone else.

He wondered, too, if those ashes he had found in one of the disused dustbins had any significance. After burning, they had plainly been very carefully crushed and destroyed, as if for some reason it was important no possible effort at reconstruction should succeed. And then those three one-pound notes lying by the back door almost as if they had been placed there on purpose. Had they been left for collection by some person expected to come for them? If they had been dropped accidentally, one would hardly expect them to be lying so neatly together. Yet why should a murderer leave three one-pound notes behind? why indeed should anyone leave them lying about like that? Even a millionaire has a certain respect for pound notes. In modern life, pound notes have an extreme significance. But a general significance is one thing; the particular meaning of their presence here in this strange affair of death and violence was more difficult to guess.

Bobby was still deep in thought when he heard the sound of motor-cars approaching. He had suggested arrival by the back so that the front entrance might remain undisturbed, and now quite a procession swept into view.

Superintendent Ulyett himself was the first to alight. He had chanced to be still in his office when Bobby's message came through, and the case had seemed of sufficient importance and interest to require his personal attention. Then there was

Inspector Ferris, one or two other of Bobby's colleagues, a photographer, a fingerprint expert, the Divisional Detective-Inspector, named Rose, and one or two of his assistants, and a couple of uniform men. From a smaller car alighted the police surgeon, Dr. Andrews, and from a large and imposing car that had brought up the rear of the procession emerged a tall, powerfully built man, smartly dressed, with an air of well being and authority. He came thrusting forward as if he meant to assert himself at once.

"My name's Judson," he announced. "I got a message. What's it all about?"

Superintendent Ulyett turned to him.

"Mr. Judson?" he repeated. "Owner of these premises?"

"Yes. Well?"

"From information received," said Ulyett with professional caution, "we have reason to believe that a dead man has been found here."

"A dead man?" repeated Judson with every appearance of astonishment and incredulity. "Nonsense. There couldn't be. Why should there? Who is it, anyhow?" Bobby moved forward.

"I made no attempt to examine the body," he said. "The back door was open and I thought it well to investigate in case of robbery or unauthorized entrance. I found a dead man in one of the rooms upstairs."

Mr. Judson stared at him, but Bobby thought there was now a certain uneasiness in his eyes, as though he had not much liked that reference to the rooms upstairs.

"Well, I don't understand," he muttered. "Why was the back door open? it's never used."

"You live here, Mr. Judson?" Ulyett asked.

"I've a flat in town. Park House, Park Lane. Convenient, but a bit cramped. I have a few friends to spend the evening here sometimes. I sleep here too occasionally. It's hardly living here."

"Is there a caretaker?" Ulyett asked.

Mr. Judson shook his head.

"I don't understand about the back door," he repeated. "It was locked and bolted, no one ever used it."

"There are three one-pound notes lying near the entrance," Bobby said, pointing to them, though he knew they had been already noticed by his colleagues. Mr. Judson went across to stare at them. Bobby said quickly to Ulyett: "Papers have been burnt in that dustbin, the one to the right, lying on its side. I don't know if that means anything."

One of the police chauffeurs was told to keep an eye on the pound notes and the burnt ashes in the dustbin, and the rest of the party entered the house and ascended the stairs. Bobby unlocked the door of the room and then waited outside with the rest of the party while Ulyett, the doctor and Mr. Judson went in. The doctor said at once:

"Nothing I can do. Rigor's set in already, look at the neck."

"Do you know him, sir?" Ulyett asked Judson.

Judson had become very pale. He was trembling slightly. He stammered:

"It's Macklin. Macklin. One of my staff, manager of the coal export branch. I don't understand."

CHAPTER VI
INQUIRY BEGINS

The activity in the house became intense as there began the usual busy routine of an investigation. With it, of course, now that it had passed into the hands of the specialists, Bobby had for the moment little to do.

The next hour or two in fact he spent patiently doing nothing, in which indeed consists a large share of the work of the C.I.D. Meanwhile the experts and specialists bustled about, arrived, consulted, departed. The photographer photographed; the finger-print expert used up enormous quantities of his grey powder; a famous pathologist strolled in; an eager journalist, forerunner of a host of others, made an excited appearance, though how he had come to hear so soon of what had happened, not even he himself seemed to know. Instinct, perhaps, or the mysterious workings of the unconscious, since that nowadays can be used to explain anything. Or more probably the mere sight of three or four cars in procession with uniformed policemen in one of them. The burnt ash in the overturned dustbin was carefully collected – something for Hendon to try its teeth on, as one man with little faith in science remarked scornfully to Bobby. Of the three one-pound notes the one with the stain upon it was marked for the analyst, in the hope that he might be able to say whether the stain was really blood, and, if so, if it belonged to the same group as that of the victim. The famous medical expert and the police surgeon ended at last their long discussion by arriving at the same conclusions – or rather by arriving at the famous medical expert's conclusions, since the police surgeon was a prudent man and knew who carried the heavier guns. And in one of the smaller rooms sat Superintendent Ulyett, interviewing everybody in turn, taking reports and statements, issuing instructions.

It was getting on for the small hours before at last he sent for Bobby who had already written out a full report of the evening's events as they concerned him. Ulyett asked a few questions on various details and informed Bobby that the doctors seemed fairly certain that death had taken place about, or soon after, five o'clock that evening.

"They seem more certain about the time than doctors are as a rule," Ulyett remarked, not quite sure whether to be pleased by, or suspicious of, such unusual dogmatism. "Say there are two or three different pointers they can go by. What's odd, though, is that they say suffocation was the cause of death."

"Suffocation," repeated Bobby, very surprised. "Not the head injury?"

"No. They say that was a nasty crack all right and probably knocked the chap out. Fractured the skull, but not necessarily fatal. The way they figure it is that somebody clubbed him and he passed out. But he recovered sufficiently to try to 'phone. He may have been too weak and collapsed or he may even have forgotten what he wanted to do – he must have been in a dazed state – or he may have put his call through. No telling. Anyhow, he must have touched both the receiver and the dial after being knocked out because of blood stains on them that agree with his fingerprints. But when you found the body it was lying some distance away and the doctors are clear death resulted from suffocation. They've found a cushion on one of the chairs with marks of blood and sputum on it."

Bobby listened gravely. He seemed to see the picture so clearly. A quarrel or dispute of some kind. A blow given with something blunt and heavy – something in the shape of a life-preserver perhaps, or even a heavy walking-stick. There flashed back into Bobby's memory a recollection of Waveny's cane – the 'Penang Lawyer' with the heavy silver fitting to the handle. Afterwards the injured man recovering to some degree and trying to get to the 'phone to summon help. And his assailant, panic-stricken, dragging him away, completing the dreadful task.

There seemed thus introduced into the affair an element of fiendish cold-bloodedness. Bobby's mouth set in grim, hard lines. A blow, even a fatal blow, might be given in sudden passion, without malice or premeditation, but this slow and deliberate completion of the deed was different altogether. To Bobby, too, it seemed that about the method used, suffocation, there was something especially repulsive. Who was guilty of such a deed must not be let go free, must answer for it to the full.

"No money, no watch, no valuables, no papers, on the body," Ulyett said abruptly. "Looks like a robbery and murder. Where did the three pound notes come from and what were they doing outside there?"

Bobby had no answer to make. Ulyett went on:

"You heard Mr. Judson identify him as one of his staff. Mark Macklin's the name. Had a good job apparently. Manager of the coal export department. Judson says he was at the office this morning as usual, up to lunch time, anyhow. He's not sure after that. Says Macklin was often out, hunting business. Doesn't seem to know much about him out of office hours. We've got his address though, a flat in St. John's Wood. When we go through it, we may get a pointer or two. Judson can't account for Macklin's presence here."

"I believe Macklin used to see to things when Mr. Judson was asking friends here," Bobby said.

"Judson mentioned that," agreed Ulyett, "but he says nothing of the kind was in prospect at present. Judson gave Macklin the key if there was anything on like that, but Macklin always returned it. I suppose he could easily have had another made."

"It seems a little unusual," Bobby remarked, "for the manager of a department to arrange his employer's private parties. More like a secretary's job."

"Judson mentioned that. Said it was Macklin's own idea. It was worth an invite to him and then Judson says his secretary at the office is a girl, quite efficient and all that, but he didn't want to risk shocking her, as he admits the affairs were a bit unconventional. But he won't have it there is anything in the stories of the films shown being a trifle hot. Says they were generally 'Mickey Mouse', only sometimes they were war pictures from Spain or that sort of thing – one of a lynching scene in America, for instance. All right in a way, but not quite the thing for public showing. I put it to him the play was pretty high, and he hummed and ha'd a bit, and said his friends were mostly people used to risking big sums on the Stock Exchange and it wasn't high for them. He let out Macklin was rather a plunger, but says he generally won. Judson claims there was always a limit to the play but admits it varied."

"Did he give the names of any of the people he used to ask?" Bobby inquired.

"Refused point blank," Ulyett answered. "Says they are all important people and in good positions and he's not going to mix them up in a thing like this if he can help it. We'll have a try to find out on our own, or he may change his mind."

"It looks to me as if there must be some connection between Judson's parties and Macklin coming here to-day," Bobby mused.

"I pressed Judson two or three times, but he stuck to it, he can't account for it at all. I suppose it is just possible Macklin remembered something that needed attention, came along, disturbed a tramp or someone who thought an empty house made a nice, rent-free shelter. Macklin may have threatened to give him in charge and the tramp knocked him out and then when Macklin tried to 'phone for help, finished him off. Only there's no sign of the presence of any tramp and no sign of forcible entry."

"If it was like that, it's difficult, too, to explain the pound notes left by the back door," Bobby remarked. "They hardly looked as if they had been dropped accidentally. Then there's the paper someone burnt out there."

"May have nothing to do with it," Ulyett said. "May have been something the murderer wanted to get rid of. Envelope with an address or paper he had cleaned his hands on or anything. Don't see much help there. Now, about this Mr. Waveny who called on you. What's his address? You don't give it."

But Bobby didn't know it nor had he much information to offer about Mr. Waveny. Until to-day, he had not seen him since the occasion when they had played against each other in an inter-college football match. But it would not be difficult, Bobby thought, to find him.

"Swell, is he? An 'hon.' and all that," grumbled Ulyett, who disliked very much having anything to do with 'swells'. One never knew what they might be up to, behind the scenes. You pinched someone for misbehaving and then found half the peerage, and all the bench of bishops, ready to swear to his respectability. As if other peers, and the bench of bishops, ever saw the nonrespectable side. Well, it was all in the day's work. "Have to be asked a few questions," decided Ulyett. "Pick him up and bring him along to the Yard as soon as you can. Make that your first job."

"Very good, sir," said Bobby.

"I suppose," Ulyett continued, "Waveny could have reached here before you and got away again without your seeing him?"

"Yes, sir," agreed Bobby uncomfortably. "I didn't hurry, I don't think I came the nearest way, and I stopped to have some tea. And anyone could have left by the back without my having any chance of seeing them."

"Made a point of your not coming along here before tomorrow, didn't he?" Ulyett went on. "Must know something all right. If we dig up any connection between him and Macklin –"

He left the sentence unfinished and Bobby said nothing but felt more uncomfortable still.

Rather awful to think of Waveny like that. Well, he wouldn't, not just yet, anyhow. Ten to one Waveny would have a perfectly plain, simple, straightforward explanation to give.

"Have to pick up Duke Clarence, too," Ulyett went on. "What was he doing here? Got a record, hasn't he?"

"Yes, sir," agreed Bobby, "but if he had anything to do with it, would he still have been hanging around? He strikes me as the type whose first instinct would be to run." Bobby added slowly: "To my mind, almost the oddest thing in the whole case is the anonymous letter accusing Clarence of being guilty of the murder of that woman who was found dead in Hackney somewhere. It wasn't murder at all, it's quite clear Clarence never knew her and had nothing to do with it, so what can have been the idea?"

"Spite," suggested Ulyett. "It generally is. Someone had it in for him. May have really thought he had something to do with it, or else just wanted to put him in bad with us. Anyhow, he ought to be able to say something and perhaps give us a description of the chap he talked about who annoyed the lady. We want both of them. Good thing you got her car number – if it was hers. If you can't find Waveny at once, you had better get in touch with her as soon as we trace her. She may be more willing to talk to you as she's seen you before, and as this affair won't be in the morning papers you can tell her about it and see what she has to say and if she seems to know anything."

"Very good, sir," said Bobby.

"If she can give any information about the man said to have been annoying her, it may be very important. Bring her along to the Yard but have a talk to her first. More informal, she may be willing to say more. Hang it all, Owen, with all these people buzzing round the place just at the time a murder was being committed, they must know something."

"Yes, sir," agreed Bobby. "Did Mr. Judson say where he happened to be about five?"

Ulyett stared and then pulled thoughtfully at his chin. "He did. Said he was in the City till late. That's why we got him at once when we 'phoned his office. He was still there. No reason to suspect him, I suppose?"

"Oh, no, sir," said Bobby.

Ulyett sighed and looked at his watch.

"I'm going home to bed," he said. "Even a couple of hours is better than nothing and we can't do much more till morning. Mr. Judson has given us a free hand here and Rose is arranging for two of his men to stay. As soon as it's light there'll have to be a thorough search of the grounds – of the house, too, in case anything's been overlooked. I've told Ferris to arrange for a squad."

"Shall I stay too, sir?" Bobby asked. "I should like another look round myself when it's light, and I could explain where it was Clarence and I scrapped, and so on."

"All right," said Ulyett. "Get a bit of sleep while you can."

"Lots of comfortable chairs here, sir," Bobby remarked, and in fact managed to get an hour or two of good sound sleep on one of the settees. Then, soon after daybreak, he was out in the grounds, ready for the search-party when presently it arrived.

The weather had been dry recently so that the ground was generally hard and in no condition to take impressions easily. But one of the searchers found a spot near the house, in the shelter of a tree, where somebody had apparently been resting for a considerable time, to judge from various marks and signs, and from the stumps of two cigars lying near. A band also found near identified the cigars as a cheap and not very popular Swiss make. Two cigar stumps did not seem a very promising clue to the identity of the smoker but they and the band, with the name of the make on it, were carefully preserved.

The other discovery was one that Bobby made. By the short piece of private road known as 'Dictator's Way' was a patch of ground kept almost permanently damp by water draining from the shrubbery. Here were plainly visible tyre marks showing a large car had been standing for some time. Footprints were also visible where presumably the occupants of the car had descended and left their traces on the damp ground before reaching the hard dry road surface. There were two sets of these impressions, one set larger than the other. Bobby called attention to them, they were carefully examined and measured, plaster casts were made, photographs taken, and presently, on trials being carried out, it was found that the shoes worn by Macklin fitted the smaller prints exactly. The larger prints were less distinct and clear, all that could be said for certain was that they had been made by a much taller man.

The tyre marks were closely scrutinized as well, but they had less to tell for there seemed little about them to serve for any possible identification. At Bobby's suggestion, however, he and Inspector Rose, who was early on the scene, compared them carefully with those made by Mr. Judson's car. But these last were faint and all that could be said was that there existed a general similarity.

"Du Guesclin Twenty with Dunlop tyres," Rose remarked, "that was Judson's car, and those marks by Dictator's Way were made by the same size and make, most probably. But then there are hundreds of Du Guesclin's Twenties on the roads."

Bobby agreed, and, no other discovery of any importance having been made, he went back to his rooms to get a wash, a shave, and breakfast before beginning the tasks to which his superintendent had assigned him.

CHAPTER VII
THE HAT SHOP

A look in the telephone directory gave Waveny's address, but when Bobby dialled his number there was no reply. The address was that of a block of service flats not far distant and Bobby thought the best thing to do was to go there at once. But before he did so he rang up a large tobacco firm and made some inquiries about that inexpensive and not very well-known brand of Swiss cigars of which stumps had been found in The Manor garden. In reply Bobby received an offer to supply him at a cut rate two and a half per cent below that he would be charged anywhere else, and the information that the cigar was one popular with members of the catering trades, especially those of foreign birth.

Bobby expressed his thanks both for the offer and for the information, and continued on his way to the block of service flats. There he was informed by the maid he found in possession, busy tidying up the rooms, that Mr. Waveny had gone out an hour or so previously – unusually early for him, she admitted – and that he had not said anything about either where he was going or when he would be returning. The maid indicated with some dignity that had he done so she would have considered that he was taking a liberty. All tenants knew that at whatever hour of the day or night they either went or returned their rooms would always be in a state of perfect readiness for them and the restaurant on the premises equally ready at any hour of the day or night to provide them with meals.

A little abashed by such efficiency Bobby retreated and from the nearest call-box rang up headquarters to report. In return he was informed that the owner of the car of which he had noted the number was a Miss Olive Farrar and that her address was in a street just behind Piccadilly. He was accordingly to proceed thither, enter into tactful conversation with Miss Farrar, see if she appeared to have anything interesting to say, and try to make an appointment for her to call at Scotland Yard, since any information she had to give would be of considerable importance.

Bobby had supposed that the address given would be that of another block of flats. He found instead an exceedingly smart little hat shop, the whole of its window given up to the display in splendid isolation of what Bobby's masculine intuition told him must be a hat. Otherwise he might have thought it was a bundle of bits of ribbon, lace, three straws, and an artificial flower or two tied up together ready for the dustbin. Two girls were gazing at it in a state of almost religious ecstasy, and as Bobby paused he heard one of them say in a tone of timid defiance:

"I could make it up all right myself if I could remember how."

And the other answered:

"It wouldn't have the chick if you did."

Bobby thought this remark mysterious, since he could see no sign of any chicken, or any egg or hen either, for that matter. He supposed you did something like pulling a hidden string and then a chicken appeared on a kind of jack-in-the-box principle. Only afterwards did it occur to him that 'chic' had been intended.

The name above the shop – if indeed so common a designation may be given to an establishment so rare and precious – was 'Olive' in gold script with olive branches twining in and out and round the lettering, and Bobby, hoping there was no mistake, but a trifle nervous about it, penetrated within.

The interior was very wonderful, a discreet and most successful mingling of the temple and the cocktail bar. The temple atmosphere resulted from the prevailing hush, a kind of reverential calm indeed, from the soft, subdued lighting, from the rich embroidered hangings that hinted of the mysteries they concealed. The cocktail suggestion came from the presence of an obvious cocktail cabinet with a sofa table like a bar before it, from two chromium stools drawn up to this table, from a mildly 'daring' figure that stood near and served as a cigarette lighter. From somewhere in the distance a deep, husky voice chanted:

"Travellers are only seen between the hours of two and four in the afternoon on Tuesdays and Thursdays."

"But," said Bobby timidly, "I'm not a traveller."

There emerged then from the background a stately vision of imperial dignity, tall, slender, magnificently languid, attired in flowing robes that rustled and trailed as their wearer advanced. She paused. She surveyed Bobby. Bobby's impression was that she controlled with difficulty a shudder of repugnance. She conquered herself, and, but not hopefully, for somehow Bobby did not look to her like one of those rare and valued males who occasionally dropped in and ordered half a dozen hats to be sent round at once to Miss So-and-so, for her to choose as many as were wanted, she said:

"Can I help you?"

"Is Miss Olive Farrar here?" Bobby asked.

"Madam is out at present," the vision answered, accompanying the words by a slightly surprised lifting of mathematically curved eyebrows.

"Could you tell me where I can find her?"

"If you care to leave your name and a message," came the cold reply, "I will communicate them to Madam on her return."

Bobby produced his official card. The vision thereupon became almost human. She shook with indignation. A kind of cold fury came upon her. She pointed at Bobby a long white finger, ending in a nail pointed like an arrow and stained as with the gore the arrow had drunk. She said intensely:

"If ever there's a revolution in this country, if ever there's Bolshevism – bombs and things," she explained to make it clear, "it'll be because of the way you chase motorists."

Bobby retreated nervously, scared of where that stabbing finger might stab next, for he did not wish his blood to add to its crimson hue. Useless, the finger followed him still.

"Only last week," said the vibrant, quivering voice, "a client hadn't left her car outside more than an hour or two and she had almost nearly made up her mind when a policeman called her out to tell her she would be summonsed. She came back and she flung the hat she had almost nearly chosen right in my face and we haven't seen her since – and she owes us nearly fifty pounds."

"Dear, dear," said Bobby.

"If you ask me," declared the girl, "in this country, we want Hitler."

"Too bad," said Bobby. "Er – Miss Farrar's private address?"

"Is it speeding or obstruction?" she inquired, quite human now. "It isn't dangerous driving, is it? If you've got the summons with you, you might as well leave it."

Bobby explained that it wasn't a summons, that it wasn't even motoring, but that it was important. The girl explained that this was Miss Farrar's private as well as her business address. She occupied two rooms above for living purposes. She was out at the moment and would not be back for some time. She had mentioned that she was lunching with a friend. It was someone she was to meet at the Twin Wolves and as that was some distance away it would probably be well on in the afternoon before she returned. Bobby might try again about half-past three or four.

The reference to the 'Twin Wolves' had been dropped casually but Bobby was evidently expected to be impressed. The 'Twin Wolves' was indeed a recent discovery of the people who like to consider themselves 'smart'. Anyone can discover a little restaurant in Soho, and as for the Ritz and the Savoy the difficulty is to avoid discovering them. But to find in an entirely out of the way quarter of the town a restaurant of such quality was quite a thrill, and there's not a gossip writer on any London paper but would sell his immortal soul for something new to talk about. So they had fallen with avidity on the 'Twin Wolves' and its almost romantic suburban isolation. Now it was the rage.

To tell your friends you were dining at the Savoy was merely snobbish, to say you knew a wonderful little place in Soho entirely commonplace, since so did everyone else, but to remark that you were motoring out to the suburbs for dinner and that nothing would induce you to say whether you were bound for Brixton, Islington, or Kilburn, that did indeed make your friends stare and talk and wonder. Then you chatted a little about the 'Twin Wolves' – you didn't mind giving the name of the restaurant, but not its address, you didn't want it overrun and ruined in a week or two – and you expatiated on the absolutely marvellous food. The wines you agreed could be matched in the West End, for rare wines are a matter of money and the expert knowledge that money can buy. But cooking's an individual thing, a thing of taste, of instinct, of innate genius. Think of the great Boulestin, had he ever had a lesson? Was not his pre-eminence due to such a direct gift from Heaven as that which enabled Pascal to re-write Euclid for himself at the age of ten? The same sort of thing at the 'Twin Wolves', only there even *in excelsis*. One awe-stricken patron had been heard to murmur that there they could turn cold boiled mutton into ambrosia and make nectar out of stewed tea.

You had to know the ropes, too. If you were one of the common herd you sat downstairs and might even order such things as – excuse their mention – steak and kidney pie, fish and chips, or even suet pudding, yes, suet pudding itself as often as not with raisins in it. But, being instructed, you found the almost hidden stairs at the back, and in the long, plain room upstairs, you could be served with Etrurian delicacies as 'Oie farcie à l'imperial' or 'poulet pourri caesarian'. The restaurant was in fact kept by a fat little Etrurian, long resident in England. His name was Troya – Thomas Troya – and his recent leap to fame was said to be accounted for very largely by the culinary genius of his second wife. During the lifetime of Mr. Troya's first wife and during his brief widowhood, the 'Twin Wolves' had been a restaurant good among others of its class but in no way remarkable. But after his second marriage Mr. Troya had begun to serve to his more favoured customers national Etrurian dishes – and even in Paris itself Etrurian dishes and Etrurian cooking are famous. Gradually the news had spread. The Etrurian Ambassador himself had paid a visit there – incognito, of course – and was reported to have sworn that he would recommend the proprietor for the 'Insignia of the Tearing Vulture', the highest Etrurian order. The smart young Etrurian attaches, too, would sometimes whisper its praises to those of their English friends they thought worthy of the knowledge, and indeed at the Embassy it was a common joke that as a result of his visits there the Military Attaché, Major Cathay, had so much increased his girth he had had to order an entirely new set of uniforms. It was said, too, that in an effort to bring his figure back to its former more graceful outline he was beginning to make a point of walking to and from the remote district of London where the 'Twin Wolves' still so modestly existed. For very wisely Mr. Troya turned a deaf ear to all suggestions that he should migrate to the West End, to all offers of capital from friendly financiers ready to advance him any cash needed for the change.

"No, no," he would say, "here I am freehold. Up there, it is for the landlord one works and for the mortgage holder. One becomes simply a cow to be milked. Is it too much," he would demand with the Etrurian's dramatic gestures, "to ask of those who understand how to dine, that they should take just one little car drive?"

Of all this Bobby was well aware. He had in fact dined at the 'Twin Wolves' himself, though modestly and on the ground floor, not in the privileged upper chamber. As it happened, the 'Twin Wolves', though situated in a suburb respectable even among suburbs, was within a short distance of a district to which, as by some natural instinct, half the less dangerous but more violent of London's criminals seemed to gravitate, so that duty had called Bobby to the neighbourhood more than once. He had entered the 'Twin Wolves' by chance, and had been amused afterwards to find that his modest cutlet had been eaten in so renowned a temple of gastronomy.

He had heard, too, though he had not been personally concerned, the tale of how a gang of roughs from the adjoining district already mentioned had thought it would be a good idea to invade the premises and demand food without payment, and of how the fierce little proprietor, a carving knife in one hand and a soup ladle in the other, had headed a charge of his staff that had driven the invaders pell-mell into the street so that on the arrival of the police there had been nothing for them to do but pick up one of the gang knocked senseless by a swinging blow from the aforesaid soup ladle. Subsequent dark threats of vengeance had induced Mr. Troya to apply for permission to keep a pistol in his office, a pistol which had been the chief booty of a burglary carried out later on, apparently in pursuit of the threatened vengeance. Now Mr. Troya carried both the new pistol he had obtained and the evening's receipts back to his home each night, and had let it be known that if he were interfered with, he meant to shoot.

However Bobby made no mention of all this to the presiding priestess of Miss Farrar's establishment. He thanked her, said how sorry he was to have troubled her and to have missed Miss Farrar and how he hoped that if he came again he would have better luck. Therewith he departed and in due time arrived at the 'Twin Wolves'. He passed through what might be called the steak and kidney pie section, found the half hidden stairs at the back and ascended them, conscious that two or three of the waiters were watching. He wondered why, for he could never bring himself to believe that his tall form, well-disciplined bearing more alert and lively than that of most soldiers, something even in his way of looking around as if all he saw might be of interest to him, were all a little apt to suggest police to those who had any reason to suppose that police might be interested in them.

"Has there been any serving drinks after hours?" a comparatively new waiter whispered, and was told sharply by a senior colleague that that sort of thing was not done at the 'Twin Wolves'.

"Here Madame sees that all is correct," added another, and, as an afterthought: "So does the patron. It may be there is a client who is wanted."

In the room above Bobby chose a corner whence he thought he could see without being seen, ordered a glass of sherry, and devoted himself to a study of the menu to see what was the cheapest dish available – cheapest being purely a matter of comparison, for up here the prices were a little devastating considered in relation to a detective-sergeant's pocket. However, before he could decide he saw enter the room the tall, pale, thin faced girl, with the eager features and the vivid eyes, who the evening before had known how to use a hose so effectively. With her was a young man of middle height, but well and sturdily built, with strongly marked features, a bronzed complexion that told he was no city dweller, and the clear, far looking eyes of the sailor, eyes used to search far horizons.

Almost immediately Olive caught sight of Bobby, though in his sheltered corner he had thought himself fairly safe from observation. Evidently she recognized him and he saw that she was saying something to her companion. Bobby rose to his feet. They were coming towards him. She said aloud:

"I told you so, Peter, they are after me already." To Bobby she said: "Is it about the murder? Well, I can prove I didn't get there in time to murder anyone or even to go inside the house."

Her companion put his hand quickly on her arm. It was a warning gesture. Of that Bobby was certain. He said:

"Madam, how did you know there had been a murder?"

CHAPTER VIII
AT THE "TWIN WOLVES"

Olive did not answer. She might not even have heard, so impassive, so unmoved did she seem. It was her companion who replied. He said swiftly:

"Miss Farrar knew because I told her."

Bobby turned his attention to him, wondering whether this was the truth or just an effort to save the girl from awkward questioning.

"Is that so?" he asked her sharply.

"You heard what Mr. Albert said," she answered, and Bobby supposed it was not possible for her face to be more pale, her eyes more bright and glittering and feverish.

She was not looking directly at him and yet he was aware of an impression that never had two people been more vividly aware of each other's presence.

"My good chap, of course it's so," interposed the young man she had referred to as Mr. Albert. He was smiling a little, but his eyes were alert and watchful and in them showed no mirth at all. "I told Miss Farrar a minute or two ago and she said at once she was at the Manor and so she would probably be suspected, and then she said she had only just got there when you saw her, so she wouldn't have had time."

"How was it you knew?" Bobby asked.

"Oh, that's simple," Albert answered. "Let's sit down and I'll tell you. Sitting's as cheap as standing. Have a Grey Lady, Olive?" To Bobby he explained: "One of their specials here – it's a White Lady, only different. Their secret. What about you?"

Bobby shook his head.

"Ah, you've a sherry," Albert said. "O.K. Two Grey Ladies," he said to the waiter. "Bring them to the table in the corner over there, by the window. Come along, or someone else will bag it first."

He hustled his companion off to the table indicated and Bobby followed, telling himself grimly that all this simply meant that young Mr. Albert was playing for time while he tried to think up some plausible story. He saw that Bobby was following and called to another waiter:

"Bring this gentleman's sherry over here, will you?" They seated themselves. Bobby waited. Albert said: "You can see a lot here, everyone else in the room and all down the street. By the way, you are police, aren't you?"

Bobby put his official card on the table.

"I am waiting to hear," he said, "how you knew about the murder?"

"Chap rang me up and told me."

"Who was it?"

"Now, there you've got me," said Albert, bestowing on Bobby his most ingenuous smile. "Ah, here come the Grey Ladies. Next time you're here, try one. Their sherry – well, it's just sherry. Sherry always is, isn't it? But their Grey Lady is all their own."

"Are you asking me to believe," Bobby said, "that someone rang you up and told you a murder had taken place but you don't know who or why?"

"I daresay I could find out," said Albert brightly. Bobby looked at him, feeling a little baffled. He looked at Olive, too, and felt more baffled still. She might not have heard a word they said, so impassive was her attitude, so unmoved her thin, pale features, so aloof the distant gaze of her bright and eager eyes. Bobby did not know what to make of her. He had the impression that she was hiding behind a mask. There was something in her rapt, intent expression that seemed familiar in a way and yet he could not think why. He perceived that she was aware of his scrutiny, but he could not tell whether she resented it, or feared it, or was merely indifferent. He transferred his attention to her companion. A more ordinary type, Bobby thought. Young, frank, pleasant, clean living, athletic, so Bobby would have summed him up. One of the finer products of the public school system, with all the readiness to take responsibility the public school teaches, but with perhaps a clearer sense of what responsibility implies. Like the heroes of Homer he would feel he was entitled to the warmer seat by the fire, to the richer food and the stronger wine, but would know as clearly as they what he must give in return.

Bobby sighed. Neither of them criminal types, he felt. Nor yet of that unbalanced hysterical type which is ready to be swayed by any gust of passion and then find for it some high-sounding name. Yet both of them apparently in some way implicated in this dread business of murder and neither being frank with him.

"I think I ought to warn you," he said presently, "that in police work we find it advisable to accept nothing that is told us until it is confirmed."

Olive spoke for the first time, though still without looking at either of them, her gaze still directed down the long, straight London street that led at last to the open country far beyond.

"Lies everywhere," she said, "it's all lies – even Nature never tells you what she is."

"That's right," Albert agreed. "All a put-up job, appearance one thing, reality another. Well, I suppose I had better start at the beginning. May as well feed at the same time, though. Miss Farrar has to get back to business and I've an engagement myself."

"I may have to ask you to come to Scotland Yard with me," Bobby said gravely.

"Bad as that," said Albert and glanced at Olive who, however, Bobby saw, now seemed to have lapsed again into indifference, as though nothing of all this was of any interest to her. Yet Bobby was well convinced that nothing that they said, no least change even in the inflection of their voices, was lost upon her, so aloof and so indifferent as she seemed. He had the feeling that he was watching an intense activity held fiercely in restraint, but a restraint that might at any moment give way, the activity as it were of flood waters held by a dam on the point of yielding.

Bobby said to her sharply and suddenly:

"Do you care to say anything? or do you prefer to wait till we get to the Yard?"

"I will wait," she answered and somehow made the words sound as if they meant for ever.

"Well, you'll let us lunch first, won't you?" said her companion cheerfully. "Hang it all, murders may come and murders may go but man must lunch. Especially at the 'Twin Wolves'." He beckoned the hovering waiter and gave a careful order, asking for counsel now and then as from one expert to another, choosing with knowledge and discretion. Bobby listened gloomily. For all Mr. Albert's frank, ingenuous, almost boyish appearance, he was showing very great skill in postponing his answers to Bobby's questions. All the time, probably, behind that open smiling exterior, he was busy concocting a plausible story. Grapefruit, truite de la maison, grouse a la reine Marguerite, peche Melba, with a chateau wine to follow, that was the final decision. Plainly the young man was not short of ready cash. A meal like that was going to put him down three or four pounds, and Bobby was perfectly sure that Olive would have appreciated equally a soft boiled egg and two cream buns. This may be woman's century of triumph but she has not yet conquered all her natural weaknesses.

Bobby declined an invitation to join in the meal. He would wait, he said, and tried, but failed, to give 'wait' as he uttered it something of the significance with which Olive had managed to invest the word.

"Right-ho," said Albert cheerfully. "Bit delicate to feed with a fellow and be feeling for the handcuffs all the time. Why not have your own eats here, though? Bit trying for us, you know, feeding with someone else looking on. Embarrassing, but have your own way." The waiter appeared with the grape-fruit and Albert said to him: "Where's Mr. Troya? I don't see him about."

"He is not well," the waiter explained. "He has a cold and madame is afraid it may turn to pneumonia."

"Cold? in this weather? how did he manage that?" Albert asked.

There was something in his tone that caught Bobby's attention and an idea struck him suddenly.

"Did Mr. Troya get wet yesterday?" he asked.

"I don't know, sir, I don't think so," the waiter answered, plainly surprised. "It didn't rain yesterday."

But Bobby saw that Olive's attitude of frozen indifference had grown more tense still, that her companion's hold on the grapefruit glass had tightened suddenly. Bobby once more produced his official card:

"There is a photograph of Mr. Troya in his private office," he said. "Bring it here."

The startled waiter retreated hurriedly and Bobby saw him consulting a colleague by the service trap. He sent them a warning frown to show them he meant it, and thereon they vanished precipitately into the back regions. Albert said to Bobby:

"How on earth did you know Troya had his photo there?"

Bobby did not answer. It was never wise, he knew, for a detective to explain his methods. In this case he had not even known that Mr. Troya did in fact possess a private office. But it seemed a fair guess; and a fair guess, too, that it would be decorated with a photograph of the occupant. And if he were wrong, no great harm would be done. Instead of replying to the other's question, he said:

"You are a very long time starting your story, Mr. Albert. Of course, if you prefer to wait till we get to headquarters rather than say anything to me now, that will be quite all right."

"Oh, no," Albert answered. "Not at all, only, well, you see, I'm rather like the celebrated knife grinder, no story to tell. By the way, oughtn't you to be warning us that anything we say may be used in evidence against us?" Bobby shook his head.

"No question of evidence against you yet, is there?" he said, "and anyhow, that warning business is only a rather stupid convention. You know you are talking to a police-officer and you know why. Nothing else is necessary."

"Well, then here goes," said the young man. "Name, Peter Albert. Address, Imperial Building, Mayfair Square. Occupation, one of the unemployed but unemployment mitigated by the possession of a certain amount of coin. Shan't tell you how much, because I try to keep the Income Tax from knowing and you might go and tell. Not that it would matter much if you did because the Income Tax people represent Omniscience here below, only some of mine comes from Etruria and that's less their business than they seem to think. Age twenty-seven. Hobbies, Bach – the only musician God ever sent into the world; yachting – the only real fun in the world; and bridge – the only game that is a game and not a bore. Yacht for cruising, not racing, sails and motor auxiliary. Crew, three men, me, and a boy. Name, *Charlie Chaplin* after the only truly great man alive, I did think of calling her the *Oswald Mosley*, only that did seem so like asking for shipwreck and total loss. Wanted to join the British Navy, but they turned me down hard as not being hundred per cent British."

"Not British?" repeated Bobby, surprised, for the young man spoke with no trace of accent and seemed indeed typically British.

"Oh, I am now."

"You are naturalized?"

"No. Opted. You can, you know. My father was English. He was an artist and went on a painting tour in Etruria and to study Etrurian art. Dad liked Etruria in general and one Etrurian in particular. So he married her and settled down there on land that had been in her family for centuries and that she had some interest in. It was all rather complicated and the complications were made worse by her marriage with an Englishman, and becoming English in consequence, so the obvious thing seemed for Dad to get naturalized there, and then Mother would be an Etrurian again. In those days we weren't all so nationality mad as we are now and I don't suppose Dad thought it mattered much one way or another. Good for business, too, because as soon as he was understood to be a foreigner the English began to buy his pictures, especially when they realized that his wife belonged to the landed classes and owned a castle. So they used to come to London every year to see the dealers and during one of their visits I was born, so I'm British born. Then both Dad and Mother died, and there was a bit of a tug of war over me between my Etrurian relatives and my British. Rather wearing for me, because I was keen on getting into the British Navy, and yet I hated my British relatives and liked my Etrurian ones. Even as a kid I felt they wanted me for myself, as one of the family, and Dad's people only wanted me because they thought all foreigners disreputable, and there was a bit of money foreigners shouldn't be allowed to get hold of. Anyhow I was brought up between the two lots – shuttlecock and battledore sort of business. The British Navy turned me down as of doubtful nationality. My Etrurian aunts and uncles spoiled me, my English ones bullied me for my own good. All the same when I came of age I opted for England on the ground of being British born."

"But all that, very interesting of course," Bobby said, "doesn't explain how it was some unknown person rang you up to tell you a murder had taken place."

"Persistent, aren't you?" sighed Peter Albert. "Well, it's this way. Miss Farrar has been once or twice to Mr. Judson's parties at that Manor place of his. Olive and I are old pals – Dad did a portrait of her when she was two, sucking her thumb."

"I wasn't," said Olive dispassionately.

"It's in the Tate now," Peter Albert explained, "but they don't show it. Because you can tell first guess what it is. Kid in blue with doll, sucking –"

"No," said Olive.

"Not sucking her thumb," agreed Peter Albert amiably. "Old fashioned, Dad was, and when he painted a frying-pan, it was a frying-pan he painted, not a symbolical pattern in green and gamboge of the frying-pan's ultimate reality. Good idea, though, because when it's a frying-pan, well, anyone can check up on a frying-pan, but when it's the frying-pan's ultimate reality, you have to open your mouth and shut your eyes and take what's given you. I daresay you know Judson's shows at the Manor have the name of being a bit hot? No business of mine –"

"None," interposed Olive, though without resentment. "– but all the same I made a few inquiries on my own, meaning to head old Olive off if the shows were really what I heard. I asked quite a lot of blokes off and on, newspaper johnnies because they generally know all the worst, and at the club, and so on, and it must have been some bird like that who rang me this morning because he said: 'That you, Albert?' – sounds like a waiter, doesn't it? Some day I shall put a 'd' and an apostrophe before it and make the 't' mute – D'Al-berrr – sounds a lot better that way. 'That you, Albert?' the bloke said. 'You were wanting to know about Judson's shows? Well, last night he was done in there – at his place near Epping Forest. Found murdered.' Well, I was a bit bowled over. When I started to speak again, the line had gone dead. The other fellow had rung off. And that was that."

"You have no idea who was speaking?"

"No, but I'll try to find out."

"I hope you will succeed," Bobby said, not without irony.

He had little faith in Peter Albert's story and he suspected the error in the identity of the victim had been made on purpose so as to avoid showing too much knowledge. He added slowly: "Any confirmation of what you have just told me, Mr. Albert, would be exceedingly welcome."

"Do what I can," Peter Albert declared. "Can't make any promises, but you may be sure I'll do my best." Bobby nearly said: 'Yes, but best which way?' Instead he asked abruptly:

"Do you know Mr. Macklin?"

Peter Albert shook his head.

"Never heard of him," he said.

"Yes, you have," Olive interposed. "I told you. I met him at Mr. Judson's – at least, if it's the same man. He's a partner or manager or something in Mr. Judson's business."

"Oh, him," said Peter Albert.

A waiter came up to their table. He had a photographic frame holding three cabinet photographs. Frail looking old people, man and woman, at the right and left, and in the centre a fat little man, though broad-shouldered, who was smirking into the camera, exactly as if he were asking it for its order.

"Mr. Troya's photograph, sir, you asked for," the waiter said.

"The one in the middle, I suppose?" Bobby said. "Who are the old people?"

"Mr. Troya's father and mother, sir," the man answered with a faint snigger as if all the staff found something amusing in their employer's devotion to his parents.

In fact, as Bobby knew, there is an exceedingly strong family sense among the Etrurians, stronger as it often is among the Latin races than in the Anglo-Saxon peoples.

Bobby showed the centre photograph to Olive.

"Is it anyone you know?" he asked, "anyone you have ever seen?"

CHAPTER IX
DICTATORS' PORTRAITS

Olive gave the photographs only one glance and then looked away, her gaze travelling down the long, crowded London street as though an urge were on her to take that way of escape. She drew a deep breath, but still did not speak, and Bobby gave the photographs back to the waiter.

"Thank you," he said, and then asked if they had in stock any of those inexpensive Swiss cigars he had learnt were often smoked by hotel and restaurant workers of foreign nationality.

"I don't think so, sir," the waiter answered, evidently again surprised by the question, "we aren't often asked for them. I could inquire."

"Mr. Troya smokes them himself, doesn't he?" Bobby persisted.

"I believe he does sometimes," the waiter agreed. "I could ask if there are any in the office," he offered.

"Never mind," Bobby said. "It's all right. Don't bother. You can take away the photo., too."

The waiter retired, bewildered and uneasy. He did not know what all this meant, but he wondered whether it would not be better to look out for another place. With the police, one never knew. Both Olive and Peter Albert were looking surprised, too. Olive had even withdrawn her abstracted gaze from the street to bestow it upon Bobby, and Peter Albert was smiling more broadly than ever, though still there was no mirth in those watchful eyes of his.

"Quite in the best tradition of Hawkseye the detective," he said chaffingly, "but I do wonder what Troya's cigars have to do with it, and why you lost interest in them all at once?"

"Hawkseye never explains," retorted Bobby and turned to Olive: "I think," he said, "Mr. Albert brought you here to-day to see if you could identify Mr. Troya as the man who annoyed you yesterday?"

"You seem to know it all," Peter Albert grumbled.

Bobby continued:

"You recognized the photograph?" Olive agreed with a slight affirmative gesture of the head. Bobby went on: "Would you like to say how it is you happened to be there?"

"It was quite by chance," she answered. "I like to get away for a drive sometimes – I don't often get a chance, there's the shop and there's going out, cocktail parties and all that. I have to go to them whenever I can. Advertisement. If there's a smart, new model I can wear, people may notice it, and if they do, it may mean sales."

"I see," said Bobby, and yet was not quite satisfied, for this aloof, silent girl with the pale face and the burning eyes did not seem to him exactly the born saleswoman type.

Indeed he found the idea of her frequenting cocktail parties in order to sell hats somehow vaguely displeasing. Wrong somehow, he felt. Nor could he rid himself of the impression that her mind was occupied with quite other things than the selling of hats, that into the framework of modern commercial publicity her eager and passionate personality seemed to fit but badly.

"Sometimes I feel I must get away from it all," she continued, "and then I get out the car and drive fast – fast," she repeated with a little catch in her breath, the first sign of any yielding to emotion he had seen in her. "One gets – away," she said. "It was like that yesterday and then I remembered I had never been to Mr. Judson's place except at night and I thought I would like to see what it looked like in the daytime. That's all."

"Ah, yes," Bobby said and looked at her moodily. "I thought perhaps," he said, "you knew the place pretty well as you seemed to spot that stand-pipe and the hose at once."

"Oh, I just noticed them," she mumbled. "That's all."

It was possible, Bobby supposed. Possible, too, that her visit to The Manor had resulted merely from a sudden impulse of curiosity, but an odd coincidence that that impulse of curiosity should have occurred on the day and about the hour of a murder. And Bobby had a great dislike for coincidences. If they really happened, it was confusion. If they hadn't happened, then that was worse still.

"Bit of a novel idea," Peter Albert interposed, "those parties in an empty house. Makes people talk no end. I've been asked myself what sort of a place The Manor is and so I asked Miss Farrar. I expect that's what made her think of having a squint at it in daylight."

"Ah, yes," said Bobby, thinking that once again Peter Albert had come to the girl's assistance.

He found himself wondering what connection there was between them. They were not married apparently, nor close relatives, and yet there was an air of intimacy between them as if they were very close to each other. Yet they exchanged no lover-like glances. Perhaps, however, that phase was over. Peter was talking again, a little as if he did not wish Bobby to spend too much time in thought.

"Any bit of novelty," he was saying, "sets people talking like one o'clock nowadays when everything is exactly like everything else. I'm told the main street in Kamchatka is entirely occupied by Boot's, Woolworth's, and picture theatres showing Mr. Robert Taylor's last film."

Bobby ignored this and said to Olive:

"Did you mention to anyone before you started where you were going?"

"I only thought of it afterwards," she said.

Bobby got to his feet.

"You won't be leaving just yet, will you?" he asked. "I'll ring up, if you don't mind, and ask if they would like you to call at the Yard, if you can spare the time."

He asked the waiter for the 'phone and was shown an extension in a small room on the same floor. There was no telephone directory visible so he asked for one, and Peter Albert, watching, saw it being taken to him.

"If he's ringing the Yard," Peter Albert said slowly, "doesn't he know the number?"

Olive did not answer but after a time she said:

"He seems so ordinary and then he asks just the very questions you don't want him to."

As a matter of fact Bobby had inquired for the directory in order to ascertain from it the private address of Mr. Troya. It was not far from the restaurant and Bobby, having made a note of it, rang up Headquarters, reported, and asked for instructions. They were given him to the effect that Mr. Albert and Miss Farrar were to be asked to come on to the Yard at once. His own proposal that he should proceed immediately to interview Mr. Troya was approved.

Accordingly Bobby went back, paid for his sherry, explained that he wouldn't have time to stop for his lunch, fortunately not yet ordered, and informed Mr. Albert and Miss Farrar of the official desire to interview them as soon as possible, if they would be so kind.

"Suppose we prefer to be unkind?" asked Peter Albert.

"We are hoping you won't," Bobby answered blandly. "Any time round about three would suit. A little later if you like. Ask for

Superintendent Ulyett and explain you are expected. Then you won't be kept waiting."

"Aren't you coming, too?" Peter Albert asked. "Gyves upon our wrists, and all that?"

"We've hardly got that far yet, have we?" Bobby retorted.

"I suppose," Peter Albert mused, "the idea is, you make your report afterwards, and then you check up and see if we've told the same story and if we haven't, then you've got us by the short hairs. Deep, eh?"

"But easily countered by the simple method of keeping to the same story," Bobby pointed out. "If you do want to change it, please say so at once. And I would very strongly ask you both to be entirely frank and open. Oh, and we do like things confirmed. Red tape, I suppose. I expect if you told us two and two made four, we should send round to the appropriate expert to get it confirmed before we accepted it."

"You don't think of getting signed and sealed certificates for everything you do," Peter Albert grumbled. "I was busy all yesterday afternoon working out a cruise I have in mind, totting up the supplies I shall want, and so on. But I never thought of calling in a porter every half hour or so to testify that I was really there. Why on earth should I?"

"I know, it's often like that," Bobby agreed.

"Look here, about this murder," Peter Albert went on, "of course, Miss Farrar happened to be there and frightful bad luck, too, but you can't seriously think she did it – or Troya either. Hang it, why on earth should either of them want to do in poor old Judson?"

"I haven't the least idea," said Bobby, and took his departure, more than a little troubled in his mind.

Miss Farrar could hardly be the actual murderer, he supposed, and yet there was that identity of time and place it is always so important to establish. The method, the blow on the head, suggested a man, certainly, but a woman can hit out, too, on occasion, and this girl gave an odd impression of the strongest passions in reserve. As for her own statement that she had only arrived a minute or two before Bobby got there and so had not had time even to enter the house – well, it does not take long to commit a murder. A margin of ten minutes would be enough; less, for that matter. It would be odd if times could be established with sufficient accuracy to prove an alibi for her, seeing she was admittedly so near when the crime was committed.

Bobby had the impression, too, that Peter Albert had been exceedingly nervous – more than nervous, afraid. That ready flow of talk of his, chatter almost, it had been, Bobby put down confidently as not natural to his character but a cloak assumed for the occasion. But then had that been for his own protection, or for Olive's, or perhaps for that of some third person unknown? A question with no answer as yet. Bobby frowned reflectively as he remembered that Peter Albert had claimed to have been at home all that afternoon, busy with his affairs, and yet emphasized that he had no witnesses to the fact.

Arrived at his destination, Bobby found Mr. Troya's residence to be situated in a quiet, old-fashioned street, once occupied by the prosperous business-man class but now showing signs of decadence as its former inhabitants died off and their successors preferred the modern flat or the country – with garage. There was already one 'Private Hotel' in the street, and several of the houses showed by a diversity of window curtains that they were in the occupation of different families. Mr. Troya's was one of the more prosperous-looking establishments, and the maid who answered Bobby's knock explained that Mr. Troya was not well enough to see anyone, and that Madame had gone to town on business, and would not be home till late, but might possibly be found earlier at the restaurant.

Bobby explained that his business was urgent. He produced his official card and the maid looked suitably impressed and showed him into a comfortable, though slightly ornate drawing-room. Over the mantelpiece hung a large portrait of the Etrurian dictator, 'Redeemer of his country', in his characteristic country-redeeming attitude so strongly reminiscent of Ajax defying the lightning. It was flanked on each side by portraits of his brother dictators of Germany and Italy, though these portraits were of smaller size and had less ornate frames – enough in these days,

Bobby thought, to produce an international incident. Between the windows hung another large portrait of the Etrurian Redeemer, in the company of two or three babies, one of whom he was embracing on the well-established Eatandswill precedent. There were various other portraits of the same gentleman scattered about here and there. In all, including those on the side tables and wall brackets, Bobby counted nine, and decided that Mr. Troya must be indeed a loyal and devoted adherent of the existing regime. But then perhaps that was only natural on the part of a restaurant keeper largely dependent on the patronage of that regime's Ambassador. In one corner there was also a picture representing another and a different Redeemer, but it hung awry, and was evidently there on sufferance, before final removal.

The door opened and Mr. Troya came in, heralding his arrival with a sneeze or two. He was a short, sturdily built little man, a trifle run to fat now, but with broad shoulders and a deep chest that explained how effectively that soup ladle of his had been wielded on a certain occasion. His eyes were small, bright, and shrewd, set in a wide fat face, above a bristling little black moustache with waxed ends. He was wearing a dressing-gown and Bobby noticed that there were fresh ink stains on the forefinger of his right hand, as though he had been busy writing with a fountain-pen that leaked a little.

"Is. there any complaint, anything not satisfactory?" he asked, glancing nervously from Bobby's card he held in one hand to Bobby himself and then back to the card again. "I assure you I am most careful – always. Never, never do I permit in my restaurant –"

"Nothing to do with your restaurant, Mr. Troya," Bobby assured him.

"It is about the murder, then?" Troya asked, and grew more pale even than before. "I know nothing about it, nothing at all. It is true I knew poor Mr. Macklin. It was a shock to me, naturally. But only in business did I know him, purely business. He was not a friend, you understand, a client, a valued, a most valued client."

"How did you know there had been a murder, Mr. Troya?" Bobby asked.

Troya jumped – literally jumped.

"But – but –" he stammered. "But –"

Bobby waited.

"I heard – it was a message," Troya stammered. "On the 'phone. I was rung up."

"Who by?"

Troya gulped and looked round wildly, a little as if seeking help and counsel from his country's redeemer.

Bobby waited.

Waiting was always effective. If you stood and waited silently, then those who had reason to be nervous became generally very nervous indeed and soon felt it incumbent on them to do or say something. Troya wiped his forehead. It was wet with perspiration, but Bobby had in justice to admit that Mr. Troya looked as if he perspired frequently and on small provocation. At last he stammered out:

"I assure you, I do not know, it was someone, but who I do not know."

"You don't – know?" repeated Bobby with some emphasis on the last word.

Troya let loose a stream of language, half English, half Etrurian, with an appeal at almost every word to every saint he could remember, each in turn, in the hope apparently that if one could not help another would, or perhaps on the simple theory that there is safety in numbers. He repeated that no name had been given and he had not recognized the voice. The news had so startled him he had not even wondered who his informant might be. He had been too 'bowled over' 'as you say here in England,' to think about that. Then, too, the speaker had rung off almost immediately and attempts to obtain further information had been useless.

It was a possible story, Bobby supposed.

But a little odd that Peter Albert had told one so similar.

Noticeable, though, that Troya's informant had given the right name.

"Mr. Macklin was a client of yours?" Bobby asked.

"Of the most valued," Mr. Troya asserted, and then paused, but seemed to decide he might as well tell the truth since it would infallibly come to be known sooner or later.

"It was for the suppers," he explained, "the suppers Mr. Judson gave at this house where the tragedy has happened. I supplied the food, the wines, the service – all of the highest, the most superb quality."

"I see," said Bobby. "Do you do much of that kind of work?"

"As much as I can get – but only of the best, for those who understand and who can pay. I am not a universal provider," said Mr. Troya with a touch of professional pride.

"You know Mr. Macklin was murdered and you realize I am a police-officer engaged on the investigation," Bobby said formally. "You understand also that it is your duty to give all the information you can and that it may be of great value?"

Mr. Troya protested that there was nothing he could say. The news was terrible. To him it had been a shock of the utmost. Horrible. One did not expect such things to happen to people one knew oneself – even though purely in business. Above all, not in England, so calm, so peaceful, above all with a police so admirable, so courteous, so obliging. The mere sight of an English policeman filled Mr. Troya with a sense of peace and complete security, and the odd thing was that he seemed quite sincere in saying this even though the presence of Detective-Sergeant Bobby Owen was very plainly inspiring in him sensations altogether different.

In answer to further questions he considered Mr. Macklin to have been one of the most friendly and kindly of men. He could not conceive the possibility of Mr. Macklin's having an enemy in the world. Admittedly he knew nothing of Mr. Macklin's private life, but one could tell, could one not? A little hard in driving a bargain, no doubt, but that one had to expect, and the bargain once made, everything that was most desirable.

All this came out in a torrent, a spate of words, every fresh question Bobby asked releasing a fresh outpouring, accompanied always by much gesticulation and appeals to different saints of whom Mr. Troya seemed to know as many as the mate of an

American tramp knows swear words. Then Bobby fired a final question.

"You haven't explained what it was took you there yesterday afternoon?"

"I wasn't," fairly screamed Mr. Troya. "Mother of God, why should I have been there? There was no reason, nothing to arrange, no supper, it was only for that I ever went, for the arrangements when Mr. Judson was expecting friends. It was for that alone I ever saw Mr. Macklin – may his soul rest in peace," added Mr. Troya, and Bobby wondered if it was only a fancy that made him think this aspiration was one for which Mr. Troya did not consider there existed much solid ground.

"Mr. Troya," he said, "I remind you again – a man has been murdered and I am a police-officer trying to discover what happened. From information we have received, we believe you were on or near the spot when the murder took place."

"No, no," said Mr. Troya faintly. "Oh, no."

"Our information is," Bobby continued, "that you sat there for some time under a tree, that you smoked two cigars – the stumps are in our possession."

Mr. Troya flung up his hands with a groan of despair, evidently thinking, as Bobby had rather hoped he would, that the two cigar stumps were conclusive evidence. He moaned:

"You were watching me then all the time?"

"We are also informed," Bobby continued, prudently ignoring this, "that you saw a lady in the grounds, that you spoke to her, that she resented your conduct –"

"Mother of God, St. Luke, St. Joy, St. Christopher," screamed Mr. Troya and now his forehead not so much perspired as overflowed, "you will not tell my wife?"

"That entirely depends," Bobby answered coldly, "on the course of the investigation. The more we know, the fewer questions we shall have to ask, the fewer people we shall have to see. Would you not prefer to tell us the whole truth?"

"Very well," sighed Mr. Troya, "I will try."

There was a silence, a long silence. Bobby waited. He had an air of being prepared to go on waiting, as if indeed he had no thought in all the world but to sit and wait. Mr. Troya began to feel a trifle easier in his mind. Just another stolid English policeman, he told himself. Well, was it for nothing that Etrurian subtlety was famous the world over?

Mr. Troya spread out his hands.

"I will tell you the whole truth," he announced firmly.

Bobby looked depressed. He knew that gambit. It was an almost infallible warning that a pack of lies was coming. But he said nothing, only looked more stolid than ever, and Mr. Troya continued fluently:

"No one has any idea of the competition in the catering trades. It is terrific, unheard of, unparalleled. Our association will shortly approach the Government with a demand – it is not too strong a word – that no more restaurants shall be permitted –"

"Mr. Troya," interrupted Bobby, "I don't want to hear about your business difficulties. I want to know why you were in the garden of The Manor at the time of the murder, and what happened while you were there."

"But I explain," protested Mr. Troya, hurt and indignant, for what is the good of subtlety against an ox-like stolidity that will not even listen? "I heard that Mr. Judson had been complaining – oh, not at the quality of the food, the wine, the service, that would have been impossible – but at my, in fact, incredibly small charges. Perhaps it was only a story. But I thought it would be best to see Mr. Macklin. I heard he was visiting The Manor yesterday and that he was to meet there some representative or another of one of the coffee-stall establishments."

"Coffee-stalls?" repeated Bobby, surprised.

"I call them coffee-stalls," explained Mr. Troya severely. "What else are they, these wholesalers of the art of dining, so delicate, so individual, with their establishments at every street corner?"

"Oh," said Bobby enlightened. "Well, did you see Mr. Macklin?"

Mr. Troya shook his head.

"It was warm, it was sunny. I sat there in the shade. I smoked a cigar, another. I dozed. I was happy. There was no heat from the kitchen, no complaint from the clients, no quarrelling between the chefs and the waiters. In my mind I composed two new dishes. How was I to know that hidden agents of the police were watching my every movement, waiting to seize even the stumps of my cigars when I flung them away so heedlessly, poor innocent that I am?"

He nearly wept here at the thought of how Etrurian simple faith had been so meanly taken advantage of.

"Curious," remarked Bobby, "that you did not see anything of Mr. Macklin."

Mr. Troya rose to his feet and made fresh appeals to numerous saints to witness he was telling the truth. Indeed he would probably have gone through the whole calendar and then started afresh had not Bobby stopped him.

"It may be that I slept a little," Mr. Troya admitted, "it may be that Mr. Macklin arrived while I reposed, it may be that he was already there. I repeat, I saw nothing of him. I saw nothing of anyone till I had given up hope and had decided to return home. Then I saw arrive a girl. Not pretty, plain, pale, thin – it breaks the heart how women now are thin. Why is it do they think that there exists a restaurant of the first order, such as the 'Twin Wolves'? – ah, pardon," for Bobby had made an impatient movement. "Nevertheless, it was a woman, and it was only natural, was it not? to suppose that she was one of the pretty ladies Mr. Judson entertains and that she had returned for some reason, perhaps in the hope of seeing again Mr. Judson, perhaps merely to meet Mr. Macklin, and that therefore since Mr. Judson was not there, and Mr. Macklin not visible, the opportunity was favourable for a friendly salute from one who is not yet perhaps – ah, pardon, yes, I keep to my story. She misunderstood. They often have that air. Well, as a rule, with a little persistence, one can remove that misunderstanding. But before there was time for that, there arrived literally from nowhere – literally, I repeat," emphasized

Mr. Troya who had chiefly learnt his English from a study of the popular Press – "a ruffian, a giant, an ogre, an animal of unbelievable size and stature. And then – by misfortune, in stepping backwards to defend myself, I slipped by the very edge of the lake."

"You mean he picked you up and chucked you in, head over heels?" interposed Bobby.

"Sir," said Mr. Troya with dignity, "you express it with a crudity and a vulgarity that I resent, but that I overlook."

"What happened next?" asked Bobby.

"Nothing. It was enough," answered Mr. Troya with still greater dignity.

Bobby asked a few more questions. Mr. Troya protested that he had never even seen Mr. Judson. Of the nature of Mr. Judson's parties, he knew nothing. There was talk, of course, among the staff, chatter about card playing, about the fabulous sums that changed hands, about the nature of the films shown, about this, that, and the other. But all of it only gossip, hearsay, inference. No member of the staff was allowed to be present when the films were being shown. The doors were locked, the windows were curtained and on the first floor, no one was permitted to go in or out. It was the same when cards were being played. Perhaps there was roulette also. No waiter was allowed in the room. One of the smaller adjoining rooms was fitted up as a bar, and any of Mr. Judson's friends wanting a drink had to come there for it, and, if he wished, carry it himself into the room where the gambling was going on. All that of course made plenty of talk, but talk it remained. There was always a bully in attendance in case of trouble, but his services had never been required, except once or twice when smart young gentlemen had tried to gatecrash, under the impression perhaps that The Manor was some kind of night-club.

"What happens then?" Bobby asked.

"The bully, he is a boxing champion, a giant, he picks them up and throws them in the lake," explained Mr. Troya, chuckling. "It is very funny that, my staff laugh and laugh when they tell me. Oh, very funny indeed."

Mr. Troya admitted that naturally the staff came in contact with the guests, but they did not know their names, though occasionally they recognized some well-known and outstanding personality, Major Cathay, for example, the Etrurian military attaché. As a rule the guests tended to be rather elderly than otherwise, middle-aged, anyhow. The younger element was very much in the minority. That is, as regarded the men. The lady guests were generally younger, even much younger.

But that, Mr. Troya supposed, was nothing to do with the police?

Bobby agreed that the police had nothing to do with questions of morality as such. Their duty was the preservation of public order – the keeping of the King's peace as the old phrase runs.

For the rest Mr. Troy a stuck to his story. He had seen, heard, known nothing except for the incident already recounted of the pale young woman and the brutal Goliath who in what did not concern him had interfered with what was – Mr. Troya must be permitted to say – a typical British lack of *savoir faire*. After that he returned home, explaining to his wife that he had got wet in helping to rescue a child fallen into the Thames from the steps opposite the Temple station.

"All that I have told you," he added anxiously, "it is all in complete confidence?"

"Mr. Troya," said Bobby, "everything that is told the police is in complete confidence but always in complete subordination to the interests of justice."

"The interests of humanity, of a husband, of the sanctity of the family, that is all nothing, I suppose?" said Mr. Troya with a kind of bitter resignation. "There is in the English official no sign, no trace, no scrap of human sympathy?"

"None at all," agreed Bobby cheerfully. "Well, Mr. Troya, I shall report of course your explanation of how you came to be present in the vicinity at the time of the murder."

"Mother of God," protested Mr. Troya indignantly, "what a way to put it – is it my fault then if a murderer commits his crime while I am innocently near?"

"It seems," Bobby continued, "that you have nothing to tell us," and was only just in time to check another torrent of appeals to all known saints. "If you do remember anything else or want to add anything to your statement or change it in any way, please don't hesitate. You have only to ring us up any time, day or night."

"Why should you think I am likely to have forgotten anything?" Mr. Troya asked sulkily.

"Oh," Bobby explained, "we often find people's memories improve wonderfully after they have had time to think things over. That is why a preliminary informal chat like this is so useful. I don't know, of course, it doesn't depend on me, but I think headquarters will probably want you to make a formal statement in writing. But they'll let you know if they do."

Mr. Troya made no comment, but looked thoroughly uncomfortable and very frightened, which is what Bobby wanted, for he felt fairly certain that while the little man was probably telling the truth as far as it went, there was certainly very much more he could have told if he had wished.

His story of having gone there on the mere chance of meeting Mr. Macklin sounded very thin, for instance. It might be true or it might be that his real object was to discover the identity of the rival caterer Mr. Macklin was supposed to be negotiating with. But there was no proof that any such person had been present, though inquiries could be made from likely firms, and by advertisement in the trade papers, to see if any confirmation could be obtained.

Not that Bobby was much inclined to suspect Troya of being the actual murderer. He did not look much like a murderer somehow, though of course murderers seldom do, so individual, indeed unique, in cause and circumstance, is the crime of murder. But it was hard to imagine any motive, and hard, too, to imagine a murderer emphasizing his presence on the spot by making unwelcome advances to a strange girl. Only then of course that again might be an example of extreme subtlety.

How often has not counsel for the defence declaimed:

"Gentlemen of the jury, is it reasonable, is it even possible, to suppose that the accused or any man could have behaved –" as there was abundant proof the accused had in fact behaved.

Bobby told himself that Troya must at present remain on the list of suspects, though not in a very prominent position.

He was on his feet now, ready to depart, much to Mr. Troya's very evident relief. But that is the moment it is often wise to choose for asking a final question, and Bobby said:

"Oh, by the way, would you give me the name and address of the person who told you Macklin would be at The Manor yesterday?"

"His name, yes, Jules, but I don't know his address," Troya answered with a readiness that might mean he was simply telling the truth or equally well that he had had his story already thought out. "He came to the 'Twin Wolves' to ask me for a job. I had no vacancy. He tried to persuade me. He said he had important connections in the trade – they all have. Certainly he had experience, he knew our ways. To prove he could be useful he told me about Mr. Macklin. I gave him a ten-shilling note and told him to come back in a week. I thought if his information was true, then it might be worth while to take him on. But if he was only bluffing, then I did not want him."

Bobby pressed for further particulars but got none. The description, a middle-aged man of average height, clean shaven, dark hair, dark complexion; colour of eyes, shape of nose, ears, not noticed; mouth like anyone else's; was far too vague to be of any help, and yet Mr. Troya managed to give an impression of trying his best to remember.

"I see so many people," he sighed, "so many of them so much alike."

Nor could he say exactly when or where he had heard that Mr. Judson had been grumbling at the size of his bill. It was just an impression, a word here, a look there, most likely he would never have given it another thought but for the story Jules told of Macklin's appointment.

"It is unlucky," said Bobby grimly, "that you can't tell us more about this Jules, that you don't know who rang you up to tell you of the murder, that you can't say exactly when you heard Mr. Judson was not quite satisfied – it is all very unlucky indeed."

Mr. Troya agreed that it was, very unlucky indeed, no one felt that more than he did himself. But there it was.

No good, Bobby decided, pressing him further. If he were telling the truth, there was nothing more to be learnt. If he were lying, then further questioning would only produce more lies, and make it more difficult for him to retract if presently he did decide to give the further information Bobby felt sure he was holding back. So Bobby thought it might be as well to drop a few genial remarks about the results of withholding information and the penalties attaching to those found guilty of having been 'accessory after the fact*. They were remarks that, as Bobby observed with interest, threw Mr. Troya into a state of quivering terror, and such streaming perspiration it was a wonder anything soluble was left in his body. Nevertheless, for all that he seemed none the more inclined to add anything to his previous statements.

Bobby thought it would be as well also to make a note of the description, vague as it was, Troya had given of the illusive 'Jules Some of the trade employment agencies might know him. But then Bobby discovered he had not yet replaced the fountain-pen that had been the chief casualty of his encounter with Clarence. Mr. Troya offered to lend him his he produced from an inner pocket, and when Bobby got his own fingers stained with ink from it, offered profuse apologies.

"It is in fact time," he said, "that I got another, even though economy is certainly so necessary. The one I did buy for myself when this one began to leak, my wife uses now," he added sadly.

Bobby deduced from this, as well as from one or two remarks previously heard, that Madam Troya was very definitely the senior partner. A small point, and not of much interest, though hard lines on poor little Mr. Troya that he was not allowed another pen when his old one leaked and his new one had been apparently commandeered by his wife. Much more interesting, Bobby thought, to know why Troya, evidently very badly frightened, yet remained so obstinately silent? Was it perhaps that he was controlled by a greater, more immediate fear?

There was no more to be said for the present, however, so Bobby took his leave, and almost as the front door closed behind him a big motor-car drew up in front of the house. From it there descended Mr. Judson. The recognition was mutual, and, on Mr. Judson's part, unwelcome, or so Bobby thought.

CHAPTER XI
CLARENCE PAYS A VISIT

For a moment or two they stood there like that, watching each other, Mr. Judson startled and scowling, Bobby wondering what to do.

He had no instructions to question Mr. Judson and he knew enough of Mr. Judson's standing in the city and his many influential business friends to be very well aware that he must be handled with extreme care – unless there was soon to be an erstwhile detective-sergeant returned to the uniform branch as a constable on a beat. All the same, Judson's appearance here seemed odd to Bobby, and he thought, too, that the city magnate's deepening scowl testified not only to annoyance but to fear as well. Mr. Judson was the first to speak, for Bobby, as usual, preferred to wait.

"You've been to see Troya?" Judson asked, and without waiting for an answer went on to explain somewhat lengthily, too lengthily, Bobby thought, that he himself wanted to talk to Troya on one or two small matters of business. Apparently there was an account outstanding. Poor Macklin had dealt with Troya on behalf of Mr. Judson. There were one or two small matters to be cleared up, Mr. Judson explained, and if Bobby wondered why for that a personal interview was necessary, he did not say so. Mr. Judson's probable retort would have been that it was no concern of the police whether he chose to do his business by word of mouth or by letter. Bobby said thoughtfully:

"Mr. Troya told me he did business with Mr. Macklin. He doesn't seem able to tell us anything useful, though. We are very anxious to know what took Mr. Macklin to The Manor. I believe you yourself hadn't seen him since he left the office at lunch-time?"

"I should very much like to know myself what he was doing there," Judson said gloomily. "I can't understand it."

Bobby noticed that his question had had no direct answer. He decided that for the present it would be more prudent not to press for a reply. He remarked casually:

"Mr. Troya was there, too, about the time of the murder, but he denies entering the house."

Mr. Judson made no comment. Nor did he seem surprised. He might almost have known before of Troya's presence. He said moodily:

"I wish to hell –"

"Yes?"

"Nothing," said Mr. Judson.

But in Bobby's experience 'nothing' generally meant 'something', and very often something of importance. He was looking at the car. There could be no way of proving that this was the car that had made those tyre marks near The Manor he had noticed and examined so carefully. But certainly it could have made them, certainly the marks had been made by a car resembling this. He took a chance. It was risking a reprimand for going beyond his instructions, but one was often faced with that necessity. The High-Ups were the lucky ones. On clover. If you did take a chance and it came off, they got the kudos for their successful handling of the case. If it didn't come off, then the discipline board for you. And if you prudently turned your back upon the offered chance, then you were lacking in initiative and good-bye to your chance of promotion.

Bobby paid the sharp horns of his dilemma the tribute of a sigh, as so many juniors have and will, and then, making his choice, he said:

"There were tyre marks showing Mr. Macklin arrived in a car" – Bobby paused – "in a car the size and make of yours, Mr. Judson."

Mr. Judson said nothing. His flushed, florid face went suddenly pale. He turned away and got back into the car. It moved off with increasing speed, and for a long time Bobby stood looking after it.

"Well, that's that," he said to himself profoundly.

Returning to Headquarters, he set himself to writing out his report, and while he was busy with it, one of the other men engaged on the case came in and told him it had been ascertained that after leaving his office at lunch time, Mr. Macklin had called in at the bank. There, on Mr. Judson's behalf, he had arranged some financial business about the payments due for a recent consignment of coal sent abroad, and, on his own behalf, had drawn the sum of one hundred pounds in one-pound notes.

"The bank's being sticky about giving details of his account, as per usual," said the other man, "but they'll come through in time all right. Got to do their stuff first, I suppose. They did admit Macklin had rather big dealings with them – big, that is, for a man not in business on his own."

"If Macklin drew a hundred that morning, what's become of it?" Bobby asked. "There was no money on him."

"There's a bit more," said his colleague. "It was brand new notes the bank gave Macklin, and the numbers were all in series they have a note of. The three one-pound notes outside the back door at The Manor were from the same lot."

"Ninety-seven missing then," said Bobby thoughtfully.

"Gives the motive," said the other man. "Theft. Makes it simpler – someone did Macklin in to pinch the cash. Clarence, if you ask me. What was he doing there, anyway? You know he's done a fade out? Not a sign of him round about where he hangs out, or in the pubs he uses. None of his pals seen him. Won't take long to pick him up, of course, but he's keeping out of the way all right. What for?"

"If theft was the motive for the murder," Bobby asked, "what about the three notes left at The Manor back door? what was that for?"

"Whoever it was, was in a hurry to get away and dropped them without noticing," answered the other. "That's all."

"If he was in such a hurry as all that," Bobby mused, "why did he stop to burn some papers in a dustbin? and what were they?"

"Oh, you want to know too much," retorted his colleague. "Immaterial, anyhow."

With that he went off, and Bobby handed in his report in which he touched only lightly on the Judson episode. He felt that too much emphasis laid on it at present might easily earn him an official rap on the knuckles. But he decided thoughtfully that it might be worth while to keep an eye on Mr. Judson and perhaps in the future draw further attention to the incident when sufficient time had elapsed for it to have been accepted, forgotten, and therefore in a way condoned.

It was late by now and Bobby was permitted to sign off duty and go home. He wondered what progress was being made with the other lines of investigation that were being followed up and he was worried by a feeling that this missing money somehow did not quite fit in.

Nevertheless, it was a fact, and the thing about a fact is that of necessity it does fit – somewhere.

After supper, with an hour or two to spare and no inclination for bed, he went to a near-by cinema and there, following the fortunes of the flickering shadows on the screen, tried to forget the puzzle and the worries of the day. Wonderful how the cinema could empty your mind of all thought, all conscious activity. You just sat there, only semi-conscious, lulled, your mind as blank as a new-born babe's. A kind of mental bath. Afterwards, you started again, fresh and invigorated by the rest from all thought, all emotion. To-night, though, odd and annoying how a thin, white face with distant, enigmatic eyes kept coming between you and the screen.

Bobby set himself grimly and resolutely to regard Olive Farrar as a possible murderess.

"She could do it," he thought as he remembered those intent and passionate eyes. "She could do anything," he repeated, half aloud, and was astonished, looking at the screen, to find another picture had begun. "Oh, well," he said moodily.

He found himself wondering in what relationship she stood towards the bronzed young yachtsman, Peter Albert.

Of course, a fellow like Peter Albert had simply everything to attract a girl. Money – or why the yacht? – position, good looks, a friendship dating from childhood, an attractive manner.

Bobby felt depressed.

He wondered why he had ever been born.

He wondered, too, why Peter Albert had chattered quite so freely. Just good spirits, perhaps a kind of bubbling over, an effervescence, a joy in life natural to one with nothing else to think about but how to plan out jolly cruises. Very likely, Bobby supposed, he and Olive were engaged. That seemed probable. Why not? So probable indeed as to be almost certain. Well, he wished them luck.

Also he wished very much that Olive had not been so near the scene of the murder at the time of its commission, and he wished also that Peter Albert had not been quite so chatty. Nervous people, people with something to conceal, often took refuge in a flow of inconsequential chatter, a kind of screen of words, but then, too, it was natural for a man just engaged – Bobby felt quite certain now that Peter Albert and Olive were engaged – to be cheerful and chatty. As for himself, Bobby wondered afresh why he had ever been born.

So unnecessary, he felt.

He got up abruptly and left the cinema, thus earning the undying hate of several young ladies whose view he entirely spoilt of the perhaps most ecstatic kiss the films have ever given to the world.

He went straight back to his rooms and in the passage met his landlady. She knew where he had been and she said to him eagerly:

"Oh, Mr. Owen, isn't she wonderful?"

Bobby considered the point.

"Much too thin, too pale," he decided. "Wants feeding up, too. Wants some colour in her cheeks. Might be a ghost with a mission. Personally I don't care for ghosts."

"Well," said the landlady, bewildered and a little hurt, "I must say that's not most people's idea of Greta Garbo."

"Greta Garbo?" repeated Bobby, bewildered in his turn, "Oh, yes, of course, I forgot it was her. Good night."

The landlady shook her head as she watched him ascend the stairs. She did hope he hadn't been drinking? Imagine forgetting

Greta Garbo! The landlady was really hurt. To her Greta Garbo symbolized woman's eternal triumph, the proof that in the end the victory was hers. For what are votes for women and equal pay for equal work and the rest of it compared with the triumphs that are truly feminine? The landlady herself might not be able by a word or a glance to reduce men to abject slavery, but it was as thrilling to watch Greta doing it as it is to the schoolboy to watch the dauntless hero with fist and gun triumphing over a host of gangster enemies. Dreams of power, both.

In his room Bobby slowly undressed, resolutely turning his mind from Olive and her fiancé – not much doubt of that – to other aspects of the case.

Troya, for instance, and that extremely thin, not to say tenuous tale of his? What was the truth that lay behind it?

Mr. Judson too. Why his visit to Troya, why his panic flight at the mention of the tyre marks his own car might have made?

Clarence as well. What was Clarence Duke doing in The Manor grounds? Was it only chivalry had made him interfere? What was the real cause of the panic into which Bobby's appearance had thrown him? What had become of him? And did the disappearance of the missing ninety- seven pound notes explain both it and him? Well, if Clarence could be traced and was found in any unusual condition of affluence, he would have a good deal to explain. But then if he had been guilty of murder and theft, would he have remained one minute longer than necessary in the neighbourhood, girls in distress or none?

Certainly it seemed likely that Clarence was the 'bully' employed on the nights of Mr. Judson's parties to keep intruders away, and in any case he ought to be able to give a good deal of useful information.

There was Waveny, too? why had Waveny been interested in The Manor parties and why so insistent on postponing their proposed visit? and what had become of him?

With such thoughts buzzing in his head, Bobby prepared for bed. Then, when he was ready, by a strong effort of his will, he dismissed them all, made his mind a blank, put his head upon the pillow and at once was sound asleep – according to plan.

Dreaming was a rare experience with him but to-night he dreamed that he was waiting outside a church. He did not know what for, only he wished very much he was elsewhere, especially as it was snowing hard, only was it snow that was falling so thickly or was it just confetti? Someone inside the church was trying to open the door now, only not the door, a window, his window. He did not move, he gave no sign he had wakened, he lay still and made his breathing as soft and regular and deep as he could, only very slowly, very cautiously, his right hand stole out and grasped the hanging control by which he could switch on the light above the bed.

The window was wide open now. Someone was climbing in, very slowly and cautiously. He was in the room. A person of experience, evidently, for Bobby noticed that every movement was timed to coincide with his own exhaled breaths. The intruder was nearer now, but not quite near enough, and, wishing to please and to encourage, Bobby contributed quite a good snore.

"Guv'nor," said a hoarse voice, "guv'nor, Mr. Owen, sir, are you awake?"

Slightly vexed, Bobby sat up in bed and switched on the light.

"Clarence," he said, "Clarence, what in thunder do you think you are playing at?"

"Wanted to tell you something, guv'nor," Clarence explained apologetically.

"Why on earth," demanded Bobby, "in the middle of the night?"

"'Cause," said Clarence, "there's them as I don't want to know I've been talking."

"Why not?"

"Along," explained Clarence, "of not wanting to be a found deader in the Thames."

"Oh, rot," said Bobby.

"That there Macklin bloke, was that rot?"

"You know something about that?" Bobby asked, preparing to get out of bed.

"You stop where you are, guv'nor," Clarence warned him, retreating towards the window. "You put a foot on the floor and

I'm off – I've got my car what I pinched just round the corner and I can be miles away before you've had time to blow your whistle."

"Don't be a fool," said Bobby, but staying in bed all the same, for he felt Clarence meant it.

"Want me to talk or not?" demanded Clarence.

"Do you know who killed Macklin?"

"No, and it wasn't me, neither," Clarence retorted. "Why do you think anyone should suppose it was?"

"You blokes after me, ain't you? Making inquiries you call it. I know," said Clarence bitterly. "Pinch a bloke and ask him and ask him till he don't know where he is and then you've got him where you want him. I'm not having any, not me. And all about a bit of skirt as I never even heard of."

"No one is going to worry you about that," Bobby told him. "We know you had nothing to do with it."

"No more I hadn't," declared Clarence, "but I ain't taking no risks. How do I know them as tried to do the dirty on me with their ruddy an-on-mous letters won't have another go? So I thinks as I'll go along and talk it over with Mr. Owen, what I knows is a gent after you and me had that bit of a turn-up together."

"It wasn't such a bad little do," admitted Bobby reminiscently.

"It's your feet what does it," declared Clarence as a connoisseur, "all the tip-toppers fight with their feet – here and there and gone again. You've a punch, too. I wouldn't say but that if you took the profession up serious like and worked hard, you mightn't get well up among the second raters."

"Awfully good of you to say so," Bobby said, though with a touch of reserve in his voice. "Did you break in here in the middle of the night to tell me that?"

"No," answered Clarence seriously, "it's about that there nonmous letter saying I done in a lady what I hadn't never seen. I've been – thinking."

Bobby looked at him incredulously, but said nothing.

"Having thought it all out," continued Clarence, not without pride, "which it took some doing and made me go all funny in the head like copping a near K.O., I arrives at the conclusion as it was to do with me having been asked to corpse a cove, all a part of the same game."

"Do you mean," Bobby asked, not quite sure whether to take this seriously or not, "you've been asked to murder somebody?"

"That's right."

"Who?"

"We didn't get that far," Clarence explained, "me not liking the job and saying so. No, thank you, I says, polite like, not for me, and I aimed to land him one to make him remember same, but he outs with a gun so we parted, cursing mutual. So then what I says is he wrote that nonmous letter to put me in wrong with you blokes and get me fixed so as I'd do anything wanted."

"Who was it?" Bobby asked sharply.

"It was dark, at night, out Epping way. I never saw his face and he was wearing something over it as well. He drove up in a car and talked standing on the footboard."

"What sort of car was it?"

"Du Guesclin Twenty same as Mr. Judson drives. Mr. Macklin used it, too, sometimes."

"Ah, yes," said Bobby slowly. "Was it Macklin, do you think?"

"I couldn't tell, guv'nor," Clarence answered earnestly, "I wisht I could. But it was dark and he was wearing a long loose coat. I couldn't even tell whether he was a big 'un or just a light weight. He wasn't no bantam, anyways. Stood all humped up on the footboard, if you know what I mean, and when I took a swipe at him out with his gun, he did. I never did hold with guns," Clarence said meditatively. "What was we given fists for if it wasn't to bash each other with?"

"It's a queer story," Bobby said. "You have no idea who it was?"

"There's times I think it was Macklin," Clarence observed, "wanting me to do in his guv'nor, but now he's been and gone and got done in hisself."

"Not conclusive one way or the other," Bobby said.

"And times I thought it was Mr. Judson wanting to get Macklin done in," Clarence continued, "and now he has."

"Judson murdered Macklin? Why?"

"Macklin had the screws on him, if you arst me," explained Clarence. "That's why."

Bobby, sitting up in bed, his hands clasped round his knees, considered this. If it were true, it provided motive, and motive is always of the first importance.

"What makes you say so?" he asked. "Look here, Clarence, you start at the beginning, will you? and I'll take a note of what you say. Just chuck me over that pad from the table. There's a pencil there, too, somewhere. Or I'll get 'em myself."

He made a movement to throw off the bedclothes but from his place of vantage near the open window Clarence motioned to him to remain where he was.

"Guv'nor," he said simply, "you move and I hops it."

"Don't be an ass," snapped Bobby, but none the less staying where he was, for he had no wish to see this odd, nocturnal interview degenerate into a tip and run match.

"Nor no more," continued Clarence, "I'm not going to make no statements, not me, having had some already, what was read out in court, and not never again, not if I knows it."

Rather a hail of negatives, Bobby thought, but though two may make an affirmative, all these certainly added up to a refusal. Nor from that position would Clarence budge, one hand always on the sill ready to vault out and down the drain pipe whereby he had obtained access.

"I'll talk," he said, "as one gentleman to another. But no writing nothing down. Take it or leave it."

Bobby decided to take it. If necessary, Clarence could always be brought in later for more severe interrogation. For the present, it would be best to listen to what he wanted to say.

"Oh, have your own way," he said, settling down comfortably in bed. "Any objection to a cigarette? They are somewhere about. Help yourself and throw me one. There's a lighter on the dressing-table. Thanks. Now, how about starting at the beginning. How did you first come to know Mr. Judson?"

It appeared that Mr. Judson, something of an athlete in his youth, and still, even in middle age, of fine physique, was interested in boxing. He had been himself an amateur boxer of some standing. Also he had been one of Clarence's backers in the last heavy-weight contest Clarence had taken part in.

"I'd have won all right," Clarence interposed, "had it all my own way till I sort of slipped, and my head went whack against one of the ring posts, and them calling it a K.O. Yah."

He paused to spit out of the window as a sign of disgust and then continued. It seemed that Mr. Judson, being in need of a real tip-topper, thoroughly trustworthy, honest as the day, straight as they're made, had inevitably, in Clarence's opinion, thought of Clarence. For one of the disadvantages of the generous hospitality Mr. Judson liked to extend to ladies of his acquaintance at The Manor – as being more private than hotels or the flat – was that occasionally friends and relations of the said ladies desired further pecuniary rewards, under threat of a publicity from which it was hoped Mr. Judson would shrink.

"Blackmail," said Clarence who, never having been in the Foreign Office in his life, was able to give things their own names. "When they tried it on, Mr. Judson told 'em to come along to The Manor and talk it over and they'd get what was right. Only when they come, there was me waiting, with instructions to dump 'em in the lake. Which being done according, they never came back no more."

"If Macklin was trying blackmail, too," Bobby said, "why didn't Judson treat him in the same way?"

"What I says," Clarence answered slowly, "is as how Macklin, he knew something. Them others, they was just small change. Their lay was, here's a swell city gent., what won't want nothing known, or why don't he take 'em to Brighton for a week-end, like anyone else? Something behind that, they thought, wife and family he don't want to know – ought to be good enough to cop a tenner on, says they, the poor suckers. But that's where they backed a wrong 'un, Mr. Judson not being respectable and his wife knowing it all and not caring, being on the same lay herself, if all stories are true."

"Nice couple," observed Bobby.

"It takes all sorts to make a world," Clarence pointed out, "and then he's a gentleman, he is, and she's class, too. Plenty of money as well."

"Money covers a multitude of sins," agreed Bobby.

"So it wasn't no tenners, only the lake for them, the poor dubs," explained Clarence, "and two quid for me, let alone the fun. The young lady t'other afternoon only came through with a nice new pound note, but ladies ain't never free like with the ready – always mean like, is ladies." So it had been no impulse of chivalry surging up in his rough, untutored, but manly bosom that had urged Clarence to Olive's rescue, but merely a keen eye for a business opportunity!

"Got that note still? Bobby asked, and seldom had more difficulty in getting words pronounced, for suppose Clarence had, and suppose the number proved to be one of the series originally paid out by the bank to Macklin?

He hated having to ask the question, he hated still more the doubts that made him hate it so, but Clarence looked at him with a certain pity and said:

"What do you think? Reckon with a thirst like I had I was going to hang on to it for a keepsake? 'The Manor Arms' may have got it still, if you ask 'em."

"Never mind. Go ahead," said Bobby, refusing to admit to himself that it was a relief to know there could be no hope of tracing a pound note paid in the usual way over the counter of a busy public-house. Nor did the fact that Clarence had noticed it was a brand new one count for much, since all banks frequently pay out notes fresh from the printing press.

Clarence continued his story. He had also been employed, as Bobby already knew, as a kind of guardian of the door when Mr. Judson entertained his friends at The Manor. If, as sometimes happened, uninvited guests appeared, then it was his duty to deal with them – to see them outside the grounds if they went willingly, and inside the lake if they showed any reluctance to depart.

"Your blokes tried it on once," said Clarence, closing his eyes with a beatific smile at the thought of that happy memory. "You did ought to have heard the telling off I gave 'em – one of your inspectors it was, Ferris his name is, I told him things about himself all the way to the entrance gates. Never said a word back neither," Clarence added with a little sigh of disappointment.

"Discipline," explained Bobby, though secretly wishing he had been there to hear Clarence taking advantage of such a heaven-sent opportunity to tell a dignitary of Scotland Yard exactly what he thought of him. Bobby remembered having seen Ferris's report, which had somehow forgotten to mention Clarence and had merely stated briefly that no foundation appeared to exist for the rumours that strangers were admitted to The Manor entertainments.

"Top dog – that was me," said Clarence happily.

"We all have our turn," agreed Bobby.

It seemed further that Mr. Judson's guests were often aware of the fact that Clarence had been tried for murder, had narrowly escaped conviction, and had served a term of penal servitude on the lesser charge of manslaughter. In consequence, some of them sometimes questioned Clarence on his experiences, which, as he now admitted, lost little in the telling and were often worth a liberal tip.

"When they was good and screwed and ready to put it up," Clarence explained, "I used to throw in another murder what no one had never found out but kept me awake at night, dreaming of the blood flowing free from the cove's throat what I cut from ear to ear. Copped a fiver, that did, one time, and a quid as often as not. Got me a repitition, too."

"A repitition? repeated Bobby, puzzled for the moment, "Oh, a reputation. I see. Go on."

"It got so as some of 'em," explained Clarence, "would give me half a crown soon as I looked at 'em, for fear of being handed out the same – especial if I showed 'em the knife I done it with, sharpening it all the while on my boot. But I had to drop that."

"Why?" asked Bobby.

"Same gent, but not the same knife," explained Clarence. 'Slipped up I did when one time I showed him the carving knife what I done it with, and next time it was a razor I showed with the spots on it what was the blood before wiping off. So he called me a liar," said Clarence sadly, "and didn't turn up not even a copper."

"Hard luck," agreed Bobby sympathetically. "That means all Judson's guests knew about you?" he added reflectively, thinking to himself that this meant that any one of them, believing Clarence guilty once of murder, might have had the idea of hiring him to commit another.

"All of 'em," admitted Clarence proudly. "You could see 'em looking," he added, pushing out his chest. Then he added, for though he loved the reputation thus gained, he had his scruples about it, too: "But I never done no murder all the same. All I done that time I was pinched was to out a bloke with a straight one to the chin when he come at me with a knife. It was another bloke he copped the kick on the head from what did him in."

Bobby nodded. The doubts existing on the identity of the person actually responsible for the fatal kick had, he knew, been enough to save Clarence from the gallows in spite of some hard swearing on the part of others implicated and chiefly anxious to save their own skins. In the end the verdict had been manslaughter and a lenient judge had passed a sentence comparatively light and certainly no more than Clarence had thoroughly deserved for his part in the affair, even if that had stopped far short of murder.

Clarence continued. In the course of his employment by Mr. Judson he had been obliged now and again to present himself at Mr. Judson's offices. Sometimes, too, he had been there on errands connected with Mr. Judson's boxing interests, as an occasional backer of likely youngsters. In this way he had picked up an acquaintance with some of the staff, and had heard that it was the general opinion in the office that Macklin had some, kind of hold over Mr. Judson. Macklin had made his appearance suddenly about three years previously, he had been taken into the office at once, within three weeks he had been appointed manager of the coal export department over the heads of exceedingly disgruntled employees of long service who felt one of them ought to have been given the post. Moreover he had shown himself utterly inexperienced, though he had picked up the routine quickly enough. He had in fact proved to be quick and intelligent, though very apt to leave all the work to be done by the very men over

whose head he had been appointed. He had always been amiable
and friendly in the office, and so was not unpopular personally,
and then Mr. Judson had, since Macklin's arrival, been generous
in the matter of rises, as if in compensation for missed promotion.
As a result, what with the unnecessary Mr. Macklin's own salary
and the extra rises given, Mr. Judson was paying out in overhead
office costs some six or seven hundred a year more than before,
and that amount made so big a hole in the already exiguous profits
of the coal export department some of the staff expected it would
soon be closed down altogether.

"They say," Clarence explained, "as there's a deal of money
owing along of them foreigners not paying up and no business
could stand it, not carrying on just on all debt and no pay, only
Mr. Judson has to, along of not never getting none, if he don't."

Bobby nodded. He knew, of course, that to-day, with the whole
world in a 'state of chassis', to quote a celebrated saying, it is often
the creditor who has to dance to the debtor's tune.

After that had come the mysterious attempt to hire Clarence in
the role of first murderer. He had received a message instructing
him to go to a call-box and ring up, at the hour given him, a
specified number. He had done so and had been told to proceed to
a described spot, not very far from The Manor, where the road ran
by the edge of Epping Forest, and there wait. Presently a big car
had drawn up. Without much preliminary, for it had apparently
been assumed he would be ready to undertake the job, he had
been offered five hundred pounds to carry out a killing, one
hundred down, and four hundred on completion of the task,
complete safety guaranteed. Arrangements, he was told, would be
made to provide an absolutely sure alibi on testimony that would
have to be accepted.

Clarence's story was that he had not at first understood that
the offer was made in sober earnest, and when he did understand
it was seriously meant, he had responded by a flat refusal and an
effort, as he put it, to 'swipe the bloke one as would learn him
better'. The 'bloke', however, had dodged the blow and produced a
gun. Clarence, scared, for the gun had a nasty look, dodged away
into the trees, and the 'bloke' drove off with a final shouted

warning to Clarence to hold his tongue about the events of the
night, if, that is, he wanted to go on living.

"Which I do, guv'nor," said Clarence earnestly, "which is why
I've come the way I have to-night, so as no one wouldn't know, for
there's been them tailing me, which I thought was your busies at
first, only it wasn't, and a note come through the post, too, telling
me as I was to watch out if I didn't want to cop it some night. So I
don't and I ain't making no signed statements neither, and from
now on I'm lying low, the way you can count me out, till this here
game's cleared up."

Nor from that determination could Bobby move him, either by
threats or promises. Nor could he give any clear description either
of man or car. Nor had he kept either of the notes sent him. The
first note he had flung away at once, thinking it of no importance.
The second note he had destroyed, because, as he said, he hadn't
half liked the looks of it. He remembered, however, that the
writing had been in block capitals so that every precaution had
probably been taken to prevent the sender being traced. Nor did
Clarence remember the 'phone number he had been instructed to
ring up, but then almost certainly that would have been some
restaurant or public-house – possibly even another call-box.

"One thing more," Bobby said as Clarence began to show signs
of wishing to depart, "how was it you happened to be at The
Manor that day? You are sure you saw no one?"

"No one," repeated Clarence earnestly, "except the young lady,
and the cove I dumped in the lake, and you, guv'nor, what I
scrapped with."

"You didn't see Macklin? or go into the house?" Clarence
asserted with various oaths that he had neither seen Macklin nor
entered the house. He had only got there a few minutes before
Bobby. Further questioned, he admitted he had come on foot
through the forest and had no evidence to prove what time he had
actually arrived. His reason for going there was that he had been
hanging about in the neighbourhood of Mr. Judson's city offices
with some vague idea in his mind of trying to find out who had
wanted to hire him to commit a murder and for what reason.

"I thought as I might get to know something," he explained, "and then I saw Mr. Judson and Mr. Macklin go by in Mr. Judson's car and they was heading Epping way so I thought I would follow and see if I could twig what was up. Five hundred pounds is worth copping, and more than you most ever get a smell of all your life, though I ain't no murderer. Only there you are."

"That's right," agreed Bobby, wondering a little if Clarence had on second thoughts been inclined to regret a too precipitate refusal.

Was it even possible that on those second thoughts he had accepted the offer – and was the death of Macklin the proof that he had carried out his instructions?

"What time was it when you saw Judson and Macklin in the car together?" Bobby asked.

Clarence wasn't very sure. Time was a thing he was always somewhat vague about. But he was clear that it was after lunch – and Judson had told Bobby in so many words that he had not seen Macklin after Macklin had left the office before lunch.

Then either Clarence was lying or Judson. But why should Clarence lie?

And if Judson were the liar, then again – why? It was a question to which the answer seemed full of dark and sinister suggestions.

Only at present the fact, if it were one, depended on Clarence's testimony, and Clarence was not the sort of witness one could afford to put in the box. How blandly would defending counsel ask: 'I think, Mr. Duke, you have had the misfortune to stand your trial on a capital charge?' and how entirely after that would his evidence be held by any jury as utterly unreliable, indeed probably to be interpreted by the rule of opposites.

Someone else might be dug up, though, who also had seen Judson and Macklin together, and then there would be something to build on.

"Time I hopped it," the voice of Clarence broke in on these meditations. "I thought it was only right to come and tell you, Mr. Owen, sir, and I hope it'll help you, me not standing for putting no bloke's light out."

"What you've said may be a very great help," agreed Bobby.

"Worth a quid, guv'nor?" suggested Clarence, always the keen business man.

"In the middle of the night?" Bobby retorted. "Think I'm a millionaire? Think my pocket's stuffed with quids? I'm about broke till next pay day. Tell you what. There's my wrist-watch – on the table there. You can take that if you like and pawn it – you ought to get near a quid, it's only a gun metal case, but it's a good make, only mind you send me the ticket so I can get it back. Mind, no tricks. I'll have it in for you if you don't send on the ticket."

"Guv'nor," said Clarence earnestly, "you're a gent, and I know I can trust you, though there's some as might do the dirty and make out as how I had pinched it."

"That's all right, I won't do that," Bobby promised. "I don't think any of our chaps would, for that matter. Mind, I'm trusting you to send me the ticket after you've popped it. I don't want to lose it."

"Between gentlemen, it's a do," said Clarence, and departed by the way he had come, shinning down the drain pipe into the street and leaving Bobby with a barb in his conscience, for though his offer to Clarence had been genuine enough, undoubtedly he was hoping that the receipt of the pawn ticket would give some hint of the locality where Clarence might best be sought, should it become necessary to find him – as it almost certainly would.

The rest of the night was tranquil, and Bobby, up early, was still shaving, when there came a tap at the bathroom door.

"Gentleman to see you, sir," said his landlady's voice. "Mr. Charles Waveny."

Only the invention of the safety razor saved Bobby from cutting his throat, as he would inevitably have done had he been using the old-style razor, so violent was the start he gave at this unexpected announcement.

"Oh, all right," he said then; "tell him I'll be down in a minute. Ask him if he'll have some breakfast. You might do another couple of kippers if you don't mind."

"They're big ones, Mr. Owen, two to the pound pretty near," the landlady remonstrated.

"That's fine," said Bobby, and with a note of passion in his voice, he added: "I do so hate a starveling kipper."

Nevertheless the kippers, in spite of their size and succulence, were not a success. For one thing, the Hon. Chas. Waveny had a kind of sub-conscious impression that kippers for breakfast were slightly vulgar, proletarian indeed, if not almost Bolshevik in tendency. For him kippers were associated with three o'clock in the morning refreshment after fashionable dances, at £5 5s. a ticket, in aid of some charity no one had ever heard of, and a general belief that '*La Vie de Bohème*' had been plumbed to its depths. Even more important was the fact that he had no appetite at all, and indeed his breakfast consisted entirely of coffee and cigarettes.

"It's this murder," he explained, "what have I got to do with it? I tell you I don't like it, if you know what I mean. Police chaps calling at the flats and asking questions – at the garage, too. I don't want to make a fuss... I thought I'd come along and see you first. But I want it stopped."

"That's all right," said Bobby easily. "We'll stop it fast enough as soon as we've got to know anything you can tell us – why you talked to me the way you did, and why you were interested in Judson's parties, and all that. My boss was trying to get in touch with you all yesterday. Where were you, by the way? No one seemed to know."

"Had to go and see Aunt Tilly," Waveny explained, "up Bedford way. She's dying."

"Dear me," said Bobby sympathetically.

"Been dying for the last ten years," said Waveny with some bitterness, "and will be for the next twenty most likely. But she comes through with a cheque now and then, and every so often I have to rush off to hear her last wishes. Or there would be a new will jolly quick."

"I see," said Bobby. "How about trotting along to the Yard with me?"

"I don't see what for," Waveny grumbled. "It's nothing to do with me."

Bobby wondered. There was a kind of unease, a restlessness in Waveny's manner that might be caused by the not unnatural disinclination many people would feel at the prospect of being in any way concerned in a sensational murder case or that might have some other cause altogether.

"Well, old man," Bobby said slowly, "you know you did seem interested in the place, and then a murder happens there the same afternoon, so you can't wonder if our people are a bit curious, especially when they know you had been talking about giving the murdered man a good thrashing. Yes, I know," he added, as Waveny tried to interrupt, "a thrashing's one thing and murder's another."

"It's a girl," Waveny explained, "he was getting fresh about her." He paused, blushed slightly, looked embarrassed. "She's a girl... well, if you know what I mean –"

"I don't," said Bobby.

"Well, she's... well, she's a girl."

"So you said before," observed Bobby, devoting himself to his kipper. "Lots of 'em."

"Not like her," said Waveny with unexpected decision. "Her people lost all their coin and now she's running a hat shop in the West End, just behind Piccadilly. Sort of thing lots of the best people do, you know."

Bobby made no answer but the kipper suffered badly. An Honourable now, he thought bitterly, and not only an Honourable, but one who had as well a wealthy aunt on her death-bed. It was, Bobby considered, hardly fair. Peter Albert was bad enough with his yacht, his ready smile, his frank, engaging manner, and now here was Waveny with a title in the background and his periodically dying aunt. Of course, Aunt Tilly – otherwise as Bobby knew, the Dowager Duchess of Blegborough – might go on living for years, but anyhow she 'came through' with cheques at apparently not infrequent intervals. Bobby found himself wondering if a detective-sergeant of the C.I.D. had any chance of wangling a job in the police- force of, say, the Fiji Isles.

Waveny continued:

"You see, a chap like me, family name, all that – well, he's got to be careful, hasn't he?"

"He has," said Bobby grimly, "especially if there's a discipline board hanging around."

"Oh, that's different," declared Waveny, "I mean – well, all this Bolshevism about, chaps like us have got to look out. That's not all. There's aunt."

"The dying one?"

"Yes. She's always on at me about getting married and if I did and she thought it all O.K. – well, very likely there would be a sort of settlement, if you see what I mean."

"I do," said Bobby.

"Only she's a bit starchy, old-fashioned, all that sort of thing. If there was any hint of a scandal or any gossip about her – if you see what I mean?"

"About your aunt?"

"Good lord, no. About any girl I got engaged to. Put the hat on any chance of any coin or any settlement either."

"Well, that seems your private look-out," remarked Bobby. "Our people won't be interested. All they'll want to know is why you came to see me, and why you seemed interested in The Manor the day before a man got murdered there."

"That's what I'm saying," Waveny protested. "I told Olive she ought to cut 'em. I told her they weren't fit for any decent girl to go to. I asked her to stop it. I put it to her as plainly as I could. After all, chaps like me, we can't think only of ourselves. There's a tradition."

"So there is," agreed Bobby, suspending his operations on the kipper to regard his companion with a certain awe. "A tradition. As you say. What did Miss Olive say?"

"There's no need to go into that," said Waveny with some dignity.

"Well, what happened next?"

"I determined to take a firm line," declared Waveny, as it were suddenly thrusting that nose of his into prominence. "I told her she might laugh but she would see."

"She laughed, then?" murmured Bobby.

"Girls are always giggling," Waveny pointed out. "At nothing. She didn't understand how serious it was. I decided to arrange for the police to raid the next party Judson gave."

"Oh, did you?" said Bobby. "Really?"

"That's why I came to see you," continued Waveny. "I was in a position to tell you exactly what went on, as I had been there."

"As Mr. Judson's guest?" murmured Bobby.

Waveny nodded, apparently without noticing the slight stress Bobby laid on the last word.

"Roulette," he said. "High play, too. Poker. *Chemin de Fer.* Films, too. Hot, very hot." He paused, smiled, even giggled. "Of course," he explained, "if there had only been men there –"

"We must protect our women," Bobby agreed.

"That's right," said Waveny, brightening up a little, for hitherto even he had been aware of a certain lack of sympathy in Bobby's manner. "So what I thought was I would take you round, show you the place, tell you all about what went on so you could make your arrangements, and let you know next time. Then you could raid 'em. I would take care Miss Farrar wasn't there, and when she knew what I had saved her from – you see what I mean?"

"I think I get the idea," Bobby said. "Did you think that all out by yourself?"

Waveny nodded, not without complacence.

"Didn't strike you, I suppose," Bobby asked, "that it was a private party in a private house? Anyhow, we needn't go into that. You can tell 'em all about it at Headquarters. They mightn't believe me but they'll have to when it's you telling them. You made rather a point of not taking me to The Manor that afternoon. Any special reason? "

"I had an idea Judson might be there."

"Why did you think that?" Bobby asked sharply. "Oh, it was something he said at the club the night before. We were playing bridge and someone wanted to make an appointment with him and he said, sorry, he couldn't, he was engaged, had to see a man out Epping way."

"Where did you go after leaving me that afternoon?"

"I thought I would run down and see how Aunt Tilly was – she appreciates it if you pop in and say you've been feeling anxious."

"Rather sudden, wasn't it?"

"Well, when I got back to my place –"

"Yes?"

"Well, there had been some bounder writing, some lawyer fellow. Wanted a hundred in twenty-four hours. Talked about one of those beastly writ things. I thought Aunt Tilly –"

"Did she?"

"Well, as it happened, I didn't need. She don't like it if you touch her openly, she likes to think it's a surprise. A chap I hadn't seen for months – Monty Evans – dropped in. He's owed me a hundred since the Derby last year and he just walked in and clapped it down on the table – notes, too, not a cheque. He said he was cleaning up before he went abroad."

"Bit of luck," said Bobby. "You went on to Aunt Tilly all the same?"

"Well, I had rung up to say I was coming, so I couldn't very well cry off. Besides, I knew she would be pleased if I went to see her and never even dropped a hint about being hard up."

Bobby questioned him somewhat closely about times, but Waveny was very vague. According to his story he was on the way to his aunt's from about half-past three till he arrived at his destination in time for dinner. He hadn't hurried. He hadn't met anyone he knew. He had stopped once for a drink at a pub he passed, but he wasn't sure which pub or where; it was quite plain that no alibi could be established by his story. He could quite well have spent half an hour or so at The Manor about the time the murder had taken place. There was no evidence to prove that was so, but the possibility was one that had to be considered. The story of the demand for the immediate payment of a hundred pounds under threat of legal proceedings and of the opportune appearance of a debtor to repay exactly that amount, seemed a little odd, too. Suppose that necessary hundred pounds – the necessity for repayment more urgent than Waveny had allowed to appear – suppose it had come from no convenient debtor appearing in the very nick of time, but from some quite other source?

Suppose Waveny's knowledge of Judson's errand at The Manor had included knowledge that Judson intended to pay over to Macklin that exact sum of a hundred pounds, and suppose it had seemed to Waveny a good opportunity to secure the amount he needed – that possibly again he needed very badly? He might have known his aunt would give him nothing. He was a young man, powerfully built. Macklin was an older and a smaller man.

Then again there was the admitted fact that Waveny had used threats against Macklin. Jealousy, theft, murder, did they all run together?

Well, if the thoughts of his superiors at the Yard ran on the same lines, it would be for them to decide what steps to take. Thankful was Bobby indeed that the responsibility did not lie with him. In this drama he felt that all the personalities touched him too closely. Even for Waveny, though Bobby considered him a kind of museum piece, he felt a friendliness born of the football field and the taste of a muddy boot in the mouth, and between Clarence and himself, too, was the blood bond of bleeding noses and of blackened eyes.

Breakfast was over now, and Waveny, though with obvious reluctance, agreed to accompany Bobby to the Yard.

"Don't see what for," he grumbled. "I've told you the whole thing. Hang it all, if you mean to marry a girl, it's up to you to see she doesn't get mixed up with that sort of thing. Aunt Tilly –"

He paused. He evidently felt that to mention Aunt Tilly was enough.

"You intend to marry Miss Farrar, then?" Bobby asked.

Waveny nodded, and somehow once again his nose came into prominence so that that small round mouth and chin of his were utterly eclipsed.

"Does Miss Farrar know?" Bobby inquired.

"If you ask me," said Waveny profoundly, "a girl always knows."

Bobby agreed, and during most of the journey to Scotland Yard was very silent. Arrived at Headquarters, he handed over Waveny to the tender mercies of Superintendent Ulyett, while Bobby himself was instructed to write out a full report of his nocturnal interview with Clarence.

When he had handed it in he was told to stand by for a time, and was then informed that Superintendent Ulyett, having finished with Waveny, had gone in person to conduct a further examination of Macklin's flat, and that Bobby was to report to him there.

"I expect he wants you to see if you can get on the trail of this Clarence bird," explained Inspector Ferris who gave Bobby these orders. "Looks to me as if it was him all right. He's offered five hundred to do a bloke in and a bloke gets done in – cause and effect, I say."

Bobby never disagreed with what inspectors said and made his way to the address given him. Ulyett, busy in the flat itself, one on the ground floor of a fairly large building, sent out word that Sergeant Owen was to stand by, and Bobby accordingly stood by, a duty in which like all other C.I.D. men, he was much experienced. The porter of the flats was, naturally enough, very excited and interested, since it is not every day a murder case impinges on the somewhat dull routine of a porter's life. So he was very ready to talk, and Bobby equally ready to listen, since he knew truth is as often to be found in casual chatter, as at the bottom of a well. He knew also that the humble and the lowly, sergeants, for instance, are often told more than large, imposing, and somewhat terrifying dignitaries like Superintendent Ulyett, so he was quite willing to encourage the porter to talk as much as he liked.

Reward soon came.

"One of our tenants won't be putting on mourning," the porter told him presently. "Mr. Yates, I mean. I've seen Mr. Yates looking at Mr. Macklin as if he wouldn't have minded putting a bullet in him himself. He's said as much to me once or twice when he was a bit lit up."

"Oh," said Bobby, though without showing too much interest. "Bad feeling between them, was there? What was the trouble? Wireless?"

"Oh, no, nothing like that. Mr. Macklin's flat's this one, on the ground floor. Mr. Yates lodges with tenants on the third – of course, rightly speaking, tenants aren't allowed to take lodgers, but you can't stop 'em having friends on a visit, and it's no affair of the office how long the visit lasts or if any coin passes. Nothing we can say, even though we knows. Funny thing is, it was through Mr. Yates as Mr. Macklin come here."

"That was before they quarrelled perhaps?"

"It wasn't exactly a quarrel. Mr. Macklin was always friendly, and so was Mr. Yates to his face, had to be. They was in the same office, and Mr. Macklin got the job Mr. Yates thought ought to have been his. Seems Mr. Macklin turned up sudden from foreign parts and got took on. Mr. Macklin was looking for a place to live, so Mr. Yates told him about there being to-lets here, and Mr. Macklin came along to have a look and took one. Quite changed Mr. Yates was though when Mr. Macklin got the post he thought he ought to have had by rights – Mr. Yates, I mean. Seemed as if all the life went out of him. Used to go about muttering to himself and I've seen him look at Mr. Macklin very queer like."

Bobby decided it would be best to report all this to the Superintendent for him to deal with as he thought best. Ulyett might not like it if Bobby went on with questioning that looked as if it would turn out to be of first-class importance.

"Anyone else here on bad terms with Mr. Macklin or specially friendly with him?" he asked.

"No, very quiet gentleman, Mr. Macklin – but the biggest 'phone bill I ever saw. I noticed it lying on his table once when I was in there and the bell ringing constant, like a bookie's almost."

"I suppose he wasn't anything in that line?"

"Lor', no," answered the porter, laughing at the idea. He added that he didn't suppose many of the other tenants knew Mr. Macklin even by sight. There was one gentleman who had seemed interested in him and had thought at first he must have met him somewhere. But that was eighteen months ago and the gentleman wasn't often there. He was a sailor, a mate on a coasting steamer, and only came when his boat happened to be calling at London. He lent his flat to friends though, sometimes. Foreign gentlemen he met abroad very often.

Bobby said nothing but he wondered how it was a mate on a coasting steamer met people abroad, and, still more, he wondered that a mate on a coasting steamer should be able to afford to keep for occasional use even a small London flat.

CHAPTER XIV
SUSPECTS A TO G

As a result of his report of the information imparted to him by the chatty porter at the flats, Bobby was relieved of the task to which he had been previously assigned, of searching for the vanished Clarence, and was instructed instead to continue to perform his familiar duty of 'standing by'.

It is a restful occupation but Bobby was very tired of it when at last the tedium was relieved first by an order to draw as best he could from memory a sketch of Peter Albert and then, this completed and delivered to the waiting messenger, a summons, after yet another long wait, to Superintendent Ulyett's room.

He found that high official somewhat shamefacedly slipping his boots off.

"Haven't sat down since I got up," he explained, "breakfast on the hop and no lunch unless you call a glass of beer lunch, standing up, too. I suppose you've been knocking the billiard balls about all day, lucky young devil."

"Yes, sir," said Bobby meekly, though in point of fact he had not been near the billiard room, but a wise sergeant always begins conversation with a Superintendent by saying: 'Yes, sir.'

From among the pile of papers on his desk, Ulyett produced Bobby's sketch, scowled at it, examined it closely, held it upside down, shook his head, might indeed have been an art critic inspecting the work of a not yet established artist.

"Give me a photo, every time," he said finally.

"Yes, sir," agreed Bobby. "Best I could manage, sir. I've only seen Mr. Albert once."

"What about the ears?" demanded Ulyett.

"I've tried to be very careful about them, sir," answered Bobby, for indeed there is some reason for considering that the ears are always the most distinctive human feature. "Of course I noticed them specially."

Ulyett grumbled a little longer over Bobby's sketch and then explained that the porter from the flats was waiting below.

"Want to see," Ulyett explained, "if he recognizes his mate of a coasting steamer. Says the chap's name is Phillip Adams – same initials as Mr. Peter Albert. If it is the same man, looks as though we're on to something, and there won't be any difficulty in identifying him without the porter's help, so it'll be all right showing him your sketch. If the porter says it's someone else, we shall be saved a bit of time. Albert himself has gone out for the day apparently and no one seems to know where." Ulyett paused to grunt his disapproval. "People in this case seem fond of going out for the day and no one knows where – don't like it."

"Yes, sir," said Bobby.

The sketch was duly dispatched by an attendant constable for the consideration and opinion of the waiting porter, and then Ulyett began again rummaging in the piles of papers on his desk.

"How and When and Where are simple enough," he remarked, "but not much help to the Who. It's the Why and the Who that's the puzzle. Take 'em all in turn. Mr. Judson for the first. Call him 'Suspect A.'"

"Yes, sir," said Bobby.

"The yarn," Ulyett continued, "that Clarence told you about Macklin having a hold on him seems confirmed. It's the general office gossip. Macklin drops in out of the blue. In less than a month he's head of an important branch of the business. Must be some explanation. Then those wheel tracks near the house of the car Macklin apparently came in could have been made by Judson's car, and again there's Clarence's story of his having seen Macklin and Judson driving together shortly before the murder in the direction of The Manor.

"I've had a talk with Judson. He's jumpy. Natural enough. Swears black and blue Macklin had no hold on him. Very indignant at the suggestion. Says if anyone tried to blackmail him, he would know how to handle it. Thinking of Clarence and The Manor pond most likely. That's as may be. Says he knows there was office jealousy, but insists Macklin got the job simply because he gave the impression of being a first-class man and first-class men are rare. Sticks to his denial that he saw Macklin after lunch, but didn't like it when he knew someone swore to having seen him and Macklin in the car together. Wanted to know who it was said that and got quite raggy when I wouldn't tell him. No alibi. Says he drove out after lunch to visit a business associate in the country and then when he was nearly there remembered the business associate was abroad so he drove back to the office. Not too good. Left the office again about half-past three or a quarter to four and drove out to dine with another business friend in Essex. Confirmed as far as it goes, but evidently gives ample time by a bit of speeding to stop off for half an hour on the way at The Manor and do the job there. What do you think of all that?"

"No case as it stands, sir," answered Bobby promptly. "No evidence Macklin blackmailed Judson, no evidence Judson wanted to get rid of him, no proof Judson was near The Manor, no evidence he was with Macklin that afternoon except what Clarence says, and Clarence isn't the kind of witness you can rely on. If we can dig up any confirmation of Clarence's story, any witness who can prove Judson was near The Manor that afternoon, anything to show Macklin was actually blackmailing him – then there might be something to show Treasury Counsel."

"Have to work on those lines," agreed Ulyett. "Have to tell off someone to take that on – let me see, who had it better be?"

He began to jot down names on a piece of paper and then asked abruptly:

"How did Judson strike you? Sort of man to pull off a murder?"

"Might," agreed Bobby cautiously. "I think so, if he was cornered. Hard, pushing type of business man, I think. His interest in boxing suggests a bit of violence wouldn't scare him. These affairs at The Manor show he's a bit of a gambler, ready to take risks. He's in touch with shady types, too – like Clarence, and probably the people he gets his films from are a doubtful lot. And the way he reacts to the petty attempts to blackmail him do suggest that he might react more seriously to a more serious attempt."

Ulyett nodded.

"That's logic," he said approvingly. "Gambler, reacts to threats by violence – dumping people in ponds – and in touch with bad characters. Quite suggestive. Not a conventional, respectable type, anyhow, or he wouldn't have a name for showing hot films to his pals. Yes, Mr. Judson stays on the list all right. Now what about this Yates bird you turned in a report about?"

"Well, sir," Bobby pointed out, "I only know what the porter at the flats told me. Apparently there were threats. But they may not have meant much. I haven't seen Yates."

"I have," Ulyett said. "In hysterics pretty near. Tall thin chap, long thin face, looks as if he hadn't had a square meal for a month, and eyes so far back in his head you can't hardly see them. Lost a finger in the war. Defiant about it, might have been an S.I.W. Sort of bird you feel might have got the V.C. or never stopped running, just as it happened to take him. Couldn't get much out of him except that he didn't do it. Admits to having used threats but says he never meant them. No alibi. Felt unwell after lunch and went home. No one saw him there. No one at home till the people he lives with get back about half past six. Plenty of time between leaving office and half past six to do the job. Looks as if he drinks a bit, too."

"No direct evidence against him?" Bobby said thoughtfully.

"No, but he'll have to stay on the list for the present. There's a motive and threats all right, but if everyone in an office murdered the fellow who got the job the other chap thought he ought to have – well, do they?"

"It might be this way, sir," Bobby suggested. "Suppose Yates thought Macklin had some sort of hold on Judson. That was the office gossip apparently. Suppose Yates thought he would try to find out what it was and shammed unwell for an excuse to leave the office and follow Macklin. Suppose Macklin spotted him, there was a row – and Macklin got the worst of it. The method of the murder doesn't suggest premeditation, more like a sudden quarrel, Macklin knocked out, and then the murderer making sure with a handy cushion."

"We'll have to follow that line up," agreed Ulyett. "Who can I spare for the job?" He scowled and frowned over his list of names. "We are so short handed," he complained. "Well, anyway, Yates is Suspect B. What about Suspect C, Clarence. That yarn of his – pretty thin, eh?"

"Well, sir, I thought it a bit thick myself," agreed Bobby, and both were too engrossed to think of pausing to admire the resources of the English language. "Of course, he is quite unreliable. But there is some confirmation. An anonymous letter making accusations against him was actually received."

"He's a natural born liar," observed Ulyett. "May have written the letter himself."

"I don't think he has brains enough for that, sir," Bobby said, "or enough to invent the yarn he told me, for that matter."

"There's an offer of money to kill and someone was killed," Ulyett pointed out. "Cause and effect, Ferris says. Clarence has sense enough to see he must be suspected, so he comes along with half the truth, half the truth being always the best lie. If that's giving him more brains than he's got, how about someone in the background putting him up to it?"

"It's possible," agreed Bobby. "It might be, too, that his story is true as far as it goes, only he knew Macklin would be at The Manor – perhaps had a message to meet him there – knew that Macklin had a hundred pounds on him and what began as an attempt at robbery ended in murder. Only again – no direct evidence."

"He'll have to stay Suspect C, he'll have to be brought in and questioned," declared Ulyett. "Who on earth can I put on the job?" He contemplated his list of those who could in theory be spared and shook a despairing head. "Suppose I'll have to invent someone special for the job," he said finally. "Clarence seems to have disappeared and no one knows where he's gone – as per usual. I wonder if that pawn ticket stunt of yours will come off to give us a hint where to look for him."

"It hasn't, sir," said Bobby sadly. "I rang up my rooms to ask if there had been any message, and they say a street urchin left a pawn ticket about noon. It's from a shop close by. Clarence must have pawned the thing there first thing this morning and then given a boy twopence or so to leave the ticket for me."

"Well, it was worth trying, long shots like that do come off sometimes. What about this Waveny bird? Friend of yours, is he?"

"I've only met him once or twice, it's years since I saw him," Bobby answered. He added in rather a worried tone: "I don't know what to think of him."

"In love with the Farrar girl?"

"He says he wants to marry her," agreed Bobby, wincing.

"Threatened to go for Macklin, hadn't he?" mused Ulyett. "Says Macklin was getting fresh with Miss Farrar, doesn't he? Jealousy. How about his watching for a chance to have it out with Macklin – and it ends in murder?"

"It might be like that, I suppose," admitted Bobby gloomily.

"Have to see what she has to say herself," decided Ulyett. "Or – how about this? Waveny admits he was threatened with a writ and then he tells this yarn about a debtor turning up unexpectedly with the exact amount required. Not the sort of thing debtors do as a rule. Debtor vanished abroad, too, so there's no chance of checking up, and Waveny has no alibi. He could easily have got to The Manor and done the job on his way to this aunt he talks about. Another motive there. He may have known she had strict ideas about debt and would cut him out of her will if she heard about the writ. Old ladies are like that sometimes. All the rest of his yarn may have been just to make you think it couldn't be him when he was actually offering to take you to the place – next day. Looks as if it was his idea to be the one to discover the corpse with you as witness – to provide proof he had nothing to do with it."

"Yes, sir," agreed Bobby, "only not much direct evidence again." -

"He'll have to stop Suspect D," declared Ulyett. "It'll be another line to follow up," and this time he did not even look at his list of names, so little hope now had he in it. "Oh, well, what about Suspect E?"

"Who's that, sir?" asked Bobby uneasily.

"The Farrar girl. She was on the spot. Clarence says she gave him a new one-pound note and we know the money stolen from Macklin was in new notes."

"Not very much in that, sir, is there?" Bobby asked. "Plenty of new notes issued by the banks. She has a shop as well."

"Yes, there's that," agreed Ulyett, "but she went to Judson's parties. Macklin is suspected of blackmail. Suppose he tried the same game on her. She was in a hole – desperate. She was to meet him and brought a life preserver or something like that with her – flat-iron in the end of a stocking perhaps. I've known a woman try that on. She may have brought it just for protection. Perhaps Macklin did get fresh with her and she let him have it. A woman can hit hard enough all right once she gets worked up. Then she makes sure with a cushion – that might be a woman's idea. A man wanting to make sure would go on hitting. What do you think?"

Bobby, incapable of thinking, was equally incapable of speech, and therefore said nothing. Ulyett did not seem to notice and continued:

"Another line to follow up. You'll have to take her, I think. It's promising, you've met her already, a girl might be more likely to come through to a young chap like you."

Bobby thought wildly of resigning on the spot. But one did not resign simply because one did not like the job offered. Besides, though he hated the idea with a great hatred, yet he knew also that it was happiness as well, nor did he ask himself how from the same source could spring both happiness and hate.

"Mustn't forget Suspect F, though," continued Ulyett, "the little restaurant keeper, I mean – Troya's his name, isn't it? He was on the spot like Clarence and Miss Farrar. He admits to being afraid that Macklin was going to give the Judson business to someone else. That might be a motive, led to a quarrel again. Or there's the blackmail idea – aliens in this country are subject to blackmail sometimes. Get told if they don't pay up, information will be given to the police and they'll be deported. I've known that tried on very small grounds – none at all even."

"Yes, sir," said Bobby.

"I suppose you mean there's no direct evidence?"

"Well, sir, there isn't, is there?" asked Bobby. "Troya's an experienced business man, he would know very well what he would be deported for, he wouldn't be bluffed. And I believe they know him at the Etrurian Embassy, some of them there go to his place to dine, even the Ambassador himself once or twice. He would have a pull there if any unauthorized threats were made."

"That's right," agreed Ulyett. "All just vague and confused, like watching a film when you arrive in the middle. Suspicion – lots of it – nothing more – very difficult – an intolerable deal of suspicion to mighty little evidence, as they say at the Old Vic. Shakespeare, you know – or is it Shaw? All the same, anyhow."

A constable made his appearance. He reported that Sergeant Owen's sketch had been shown to the porter who had pronounced it the dead spit of Mr. Phillip Adams.

"That's that," said Ulyett with satisfaction, "and that's Suspect G, and the hottest of the lot, too. What's Mr. Peter Albert doing in a flat taken under a false name in the same building where Macklin lived and then telling you he didn't know him and had never seen him? You've met Albert – what did you think of him? Likely type?" Bobby drew a deep breath. He had to be just before all, for though justice may not be a divine virtue in this world, or else why is one man a six foot Apollo and another a humpbacked dwarf? yet between men it is the first, the most necessary, the foundation of all human good. 'Let justice be done though the heavens fall,' said the old Romans, and so proved they at least had a right to rule.

"Mr. Albert," said Bobby, drawing a deep breath, "is quite young, twenty-seven he told me. Good looking, well dressed, pleasant manner, talked to the waiters as if he knew all the difference was they happened to be doing a different job, outdoor look about him, gave you the idea that if you and he were in a spot together you could trust him to see it through."

Ulyett looked mildly surprised.

"Fallen for him, eh?" he said. "Well, if he's all that, what's he telling lies for, saying he's never seen Macklin?" Bobby had no reply to make.

"Miss Farrar was with him," Ulyett went on. "Anything between them?"

"They said they had known each other since they were children."

"I mean now – engaged or anything like that?"

"I don't know, sir, I didn't ask and they didn't say, but I feel pretty sure they are," said Bobby, his voice carefully indifferent. Lest Ulyett should notice anything if he were allowed time to think, Bobby went on: "We've nothing yet to explain why papers were burnt in the dustbin."

"Is there any reason why we should have?" Ulyett asked. "I don't see why there need by any connection."

"It's just a thing that happened," Bobby answered. "There's one point though, if you notice, that applies to them all."

"I can notice that all right," Ulyett snapped. "Anyone would. What about it?"

"Isn't it a bit suggestive, sir?" Bobby asked.

"Suggestive of what?" growled Ulyett. "If it suggests to you which of the lot's the right one, let me know, will you?"

But to that Bobby had no reply and so held his tongue.

CHAPTER XV
LOW BEECH COTTAGE

The hour had grown late by now and when Bobby reached the little shop in the street behind Piccadilly, it had already closed. But on the threshold, in the act of departing, was that divinity whom Bobby had seen there before. Apparently she did not recognize him for even when he raised his hat and spoke, it was only with evident difficulty that she realized his existence, a little as one realizes the existence of a speck of dust blown down the street.

"I beg your pardon," she said, but very plainly meaning that he ought to beg hers.

"I was asking if I could see Miss Farrar," he explained.

This was such a shock that it brought her to allow her attention to occupy itself with him, as one allows one's attention to be occupied by an unusually troublesome gnat.

"Our establishment has ceased business for the day," she pronounced, and Bobby felt just as the gnat must feel when an unusually decisive hand descends upon it.

"I'm so sorry," he persisted, for though one may be intimidated, duty must be done, "I am afraid I must see Miss Farrar. Is she in? I understand she has living rooms here."

"Miss Farrar is not here at present," was the stern answer. "Miss Farrar is at her country cottage for the week-end. No doubt Miss Farrar will return on Monday morning as usual. Miss Farrar might be able to receive you then."

"Unfortunately I can't wait so long," Bobby answered firmly. "Can you give me the address of her cottage?"

She bestowed on him one slow, haughty glance. Bobby stood his ground quite bravely. She hesitated and then surprisingly revealed that after all she remembered him.

"I suppose you really are police?" she asked. "You aren't the landlord or rates or any of the wholesalers, are you?"

"Certainly not," said Bobby.

"Well, that's something," she admitted, "and it's not traffic lights or leaving the car too long or anything like that?"

"Nothing like that at all," Bobby reassured her.

"Oh, well, then," she sighed, and gave the address, Low Beech Cottage, on the west border of the forest, towards its northern boundary, and so in the same district as The Manor even though three or four miles separated them with a projecting arm of the forest lying between.

Bobby expressed his gratitude to the hat shop divinity for the information and departed in spite of the fact that, her former indifference broken down, she now seemed condescendingly inclined to linger, even to chatter indeed. But he had grown preoccupied, for he was wondering whether this comparative proximity of Low Beech Cottage to The Manor had any significance, and he had been rendered a little uneasy, too, by the apparent revelation that Miss Farrar was pressed for money. He told himself gloomily that when you are pressed for money, most people would be inclined to say that a hundred pounds could be a great temptation.

All the more need then to discover the truth and so clear the innocent from suspicion. For that, after all, is as important a part of a detective's work as is the bringing of the guilty to justice, and to save a good name often means as much as to save a life.

A little cheered by this reflection he went back to the garage where he kept the motor-cycle he had lately purchased – on the hire system – wondered where the next instalment was coming from, wondered whether he would get the petrol he was going to use successfully passed through expenses, and then mounted and rode out Epping way.

It was a pleasant ride once the more crowded streets were left behind. He had picked out his route on a map and near his destination he consulted a constable who had never heard of Low Beech Cottage but was able to indicate the probable direction. Riding on, Bobby found himself presently on a quiet path, running through the forest itself with the tall trees rising up on either hand. It was very still here and very quiet, a contrast indeed to those roaring spates of endless traffic through which his earlier course had lain. Here he rode alone and tranquillity was all about him. It was very dark, too, he had to turn on his headlight and proceed slowly on a route by no means in the best of repair.

Uncertain whether he had not somehow missed his way, he halted, and sat for a moment or two, aware now of the lovely silence that here lay like the peace of God upon the, great still forest.

He thought lazily how tranquil all the earth would seem if it were not for the presence of the quarrelsome and restless race of man. How all this surrounding peace, for instance, would be shattered the moment that he started his engine roaring and clamouring again, how, too, the fumes from his exhaust pipe would poison the sweet evening fragrance of the woodland air. He told himself it would be like an insult to the old forest gods – only that probably they had not yet recovered from the last bank holiday. He became aware that someone was watching him from the midst of a clump of young beeches near by.

In his present mood he would have been willing to believe this must be satyr or faun, but supposing that was hardly probable he switched off his light, said something aloud about having to 'see about it', alighted, fumbled for a moment or two with his satchel of tools, and then made a swift and sudden dash at the cluster of beeches.

"Right-ho, guv'nor, it's only me," said a familiar voice, and Bobby paused and gasped as he recognized Clarence.

"What in thunder are you up to now?" he demanded.

"Same as you," answered Clarence, not without complacence, "keeping an eye on her."

"On?"

"On her," repeated Clarence, a trifle impatiently this time. "She's here all right."

"Where?" asked Bobby.

"Where she hangs out, over there," Clarence explained, jerking a thumb over his shoulder. "Blooming lonely, ain't it? and what's that for? Not natural like, is it? Front gate down the road where it turns. You can get to the back this way."

He led Bobby a few yards through the trees. They reached a footpath and following it for a short distance they came in sight of a small cottage that looked like an old building recently restored. By its side was a substantially built garage, evidently a modern addition.

"She got here half an hour ago," Clarence explained. "But there was a bloke before that. Come along on a bike he did. I saw him coming so I laid low and watched. He nosed around a bit and tried the door and it wouldn't open so he got in through one of the windows."

"Was it open?"

"It was after he worked it a bit with a knife," Clarence answered. "Pushed back the catch with it and got in. Clumsy bloke, but he done it in the end. And he hadn't been in more than ten minutes when the lady come along in her car."

"What happened?" Bobby asked uneasily.

"I heard her squeal once after she went indoors, same as ladies do when took unexpected, and then nothing more."

"You've done nothing, heard nothing else?" Bobby asked.

"I was trying to think what I did ought for the best," Clarence explained, frowning slightly at the memory of the mental effort he had been making, "me not knowing what it was all about, and then I heard your motor-bike. So I says to myself as very likely it'd be another of 'em, and I had better wait and see what's next, me being mixed up in it all as much as seems healthy like and not knowing what mightn't happen next. So when I sees it's you," added Clarence virtuously, "I says to myself, here's a busy I'll park along with – you being a gent, Mr. Owen, sir, and not like some as is always down on a bloke."

"You'll find me down on you all right if you try any monkey tricks," Bobby warned him grimly. "Come along. We'll see what's happened." He began to move towards the cottage, and Clarence followed. "You didn't recognize him, the man you saw get here, I mean?"

"Bloke of the name of Yates," answered Clarence. "One of 'em from Mr. Judson's office, I've seen him there once or twice, it's him as had it in for Mr. Macklin along of him getting the job what he thought did ought to have been his."

Bobby's uneasiness increased. What was Yates doing here? Was it possible there could be any connection between Yates and Olive Farrar? He began to run. In the increasing darkness, as the night drew on, he blundered against the wire fence that bordered the cottage garden, put there to keep out the ubiquitous rabbit. Almost at the same moment there broke out from the cottage a sudden clamour, a sound of shouting, of conflict as of men fighting together, and a thin voice screaming shrilly.

Bobby half leapt, half scrambled over the wire fencing, lost his footing, fell headlong into a bed of lettuces all run to seed. He picked himself up. There rang out two or three pistol shots in close succession. At his utmost speed Bobby dashed towards the cottage, ran right into a rose bush, tore himself free with the blood trickling from a long scratch on his left cheek, and ran on, as once more, as the sounds from the cottage ceased, there prevailed the deep silence of the forest, indifferent and serene above all these noises that so soon passed and were gone.

Bobby was at the back door now. It was locked and though he flung his full weight against it, it resisted. He raced round to the front. All the windows were closed and curtained but here and there, where the curtains did not quite meet, rays of light reached out into the night. He rounded the corner of the cottage and as he did so he heard the front door bang and was just in time to see a figure fleeing down the garden path towards the shelter of the darkness beneath the forest trees.

Bobby shouted what he knew was a futile order to stop. The fugitive paid no attention, ran the faster. Bobby took a step or two in pursuit, but the other was running with a speed and lightness that told it would not be easy to over-take him.

Besides, there was in him a dreadful anxiety, a gnawing fear that gripped his heart with such terror as he had never known before, that dried his mouth till he knew what that old writer meant who spoke of the tongue that clove to the roof of the mouth.

"Follow him, a quid if you catch him," Bobby gasped to Clarence and himself dashed back to the cottage.

"O.K. guv.," responded Clarence and made a great show of obeying.

But he had an innate dislike for pistols and though a quid was a quid, even more emphatically was a bullet a bullet. For a few minutes he pounded along, more or less at random, and then gave it up and turned back towards the cottage.

There Bobby was trying to get in. The door, provided with a spring lock, had fastened when the fugitive banged it behind him. Driven by the unexpressed fear that urged him on, Bobby leaped on the sill of the nearest window. A vigorous blow with his elbow shattered the glass. He put his hand through, undid the clasp, lifted the sash, tore aside the curtain, scrambled inside.

He was in a small hall. No sound came to tell anyone was aware of his entrance. There was a door opposite. He pushed it open. Within was a fair sized room, a 'lounge' is now the fashionable name. At one end was a deep recess with a small table, a dining recess a house agent would probably have called it. Between Bobby and this was a settee, and by the light of a lamp hanging from the ceiling Bobby saw a hand, a helpless hand reaching out from behind the settee as though vainly asking for help.

Bobby stepped forward. He saw plainly who it was lying there. With almost a sob of relief he said aloud:

"Thank God."

From behind Clarence who had followed him – Clarence hated to lead but he was always ready to follow – said slowly:

"That's Yates, that is. Who outed him?"

Bobby knelt down by the side of the prostrate man and saw to his relief that he was alive, probably not even very seriously injured. Apparently he had been knocked out by a heavy blow on the forehead. He did not appear to have been hit by any of the shots Bobby and Clarence had heard and a neat little hole in the ceiling suggested that one at least had been fired in the air, whether intentionally or not. Overturned furniture and a breakage or two suggested however that the struggle had been vigorous while it lasted.

"If she done it, and there weren't no one else here," observed Clarence with a touch of admiration in his voice, "she can hit same as she can run."

"It was a man I saw," Bobby said shortly.

"Ah, nowadays you can't hardly tell one from which," argued Clarence. "Trousers and short 'air and all," he said and added severely: "I don't 'old with it, spank 'em, I says. Did you see the bloke clear what was running, Mr. Owen?"

"Clear enough to be sure it was a man," Bobby answered, though this was an exaggeration, for indeed he had had but the merest glimpse of that fleeing form before it merged into the dark night.

"Well, if it wasn't her what runned, where is she?" Clarence asked.

It was a question Bobby had already asked himself, that already had brought back upon him that gripping, devastating fear he had known before. Leaving Yates lying, since it seemed he was in no immediate need, they began a brief search of the cottage. They soon assured themselves there was no one else there. Besides the lounge on the ground floor there was a small kitchen – or kitchenette to adopt house agent's language – and a tiny entrance hall. Above was a landing, two fair sized bedrooms, and a bathroom. Heat, lighting and cooking, were all evidently done by oil. There was no attic, no place where anyone could be concealed. Bobby looked even in the cupboards and Clarence lowered himself ponderously on hands and knees to peer under the beds.

"She ain't here and she was here," he said with that direct simplicity which sometimes made his remarks memorable, "so it must have been her done a bunk, or who was it and where is she?"

"I tell you it was a man I saw," Bobby retorted angrily. "Are you sure it was Miss Farrar you saw?"

"Got eyes, ain't I?" asked Clarence in an injured tone. "It was 'er as squealed, too."

They were downstairs again. Clarence said:

"If it was a man as bunked, then 'im or this one –" he stirred the unconscious Yates with his foot, "must have gone and been and done something with 'er. Only what?"

"Oh, shut up," almost shouted Bobby. "She must have gone again," he said more quietly.

"Her car what she came in is there still," Clarence said. I ran into it when I was after the bloke what runned, that's why I didn't cop him. If she's gone, she's left her car – and where is she? It's dark and it's late and them trees all round."

Bobby made a great effort to collect his thoughts, to fight down the panic he felt besieging him. His great quality had always been the coolness of mind that never hitherto had deserted him, even in the most critical moments. But now he felt it going. He supposed it was nerves. For the first time in his life he began to under-stand what that word means, a word of which hitherto he had always been more than a little contemptuous. He must summon help, of course. He ought to have done that before. By this time the fugitive he had seen would be safely away. He would be blamed for that, he supposed. He was sure himself it was a man he had seen escaping, but would others believe that when he would have to admit under questioning that he had had but the merest glimpse, and that only in the obscurity of the night? Others, too, would be quick to remember, as he had already done, that Macklin also had been knocked out by a heavy blow on the head. On his confused and fearful thoughts, there broke the voice of Clarence.

"Here's her hat and gloves and bag," he said. "They was in the hall like, on the table."

He was holding out a woman's hat, gloves, handbag. Bobby looked at them gloomily.

"Shows she was 'ere," said Clarence, "so where is she?" Bobby had already noticed the 'phone in one corner of the room. He went across to it and rang up Scotland Yard. Assured that assistance was on the way, he rang off and said to Clarence:

"We'll have a look round outside."

But the illusive Clarence had once more disappeared. He had no desire to be there when that help arrived Bobby had summoned, nor to undergo the questioning which would inevitably ensue. Bobby noticed, too, that the handbag, which had been closed before, was now open, and he was not greatly surprised when he looked inside to find in it no money, but only an empty purse.

"Our Clarence saw his chance," Bobby said to himself, "no proof he pinched the money because he'll swear it was done before by whoever knocked out Yates. I shall get it in the neck for having let him go, I suppose."

But the thought of that was almost a relief compared with the deadly fear he was making so great an effort to control, that he knew well might master him at any moment, urge him to seek relief in some madness of folly or hysteria.

"I mustn't lose my head," he said and forced himself to stand perfectly still, not moving, hardly breathing, for a minute or two.

Then he went outside. It was quite dark now, the last trace of daylight long vanished. He called out once or twice but there was no answer. His voice died away and was lost in the great silence that seemed no more intense amidst the stars above than it was beneath the tall trees all around. He began to make a circuit of the house, every sense and nerve alert, for a fear was on him of what he might find lying out here in the darkness. He was able to make out the garage as a low black mass against the sky. He groped his way to it, stumbling once or twice over hidden obstacles till he found the concrete path that connected it with the house. The door was closed, locked he thought, when he tried it a voice from within called –

"You can go away. I've made up the door and you can't get in."

Bobby leaned against the garage wall, for the moment a little faint with the relief as there rolled away that cloud of fear within which he had walked for these long last minutes.

"Thank God," he said aloud once more and still more fervently and then again: "Thank God."

CHAPTER XVI
COFFEE FOR TWO

Leaning there in the dark against the garage wall, Bobby strove hard to recover a self-possession disturbed and shaken in a way he had never known before. He found he was perspiring slightly, his heart beating more rapidly than usual. He had trained his naturally visual memory till he had an unusual power for recalling in every detail faces he had once seen, but that did not explain the intensity with which now he seemed to see Olive Farrar's, yet not so much in detail, in passionless recountable detail, as in a kind of intensity of presence. Angrily he asked himself what was the matter, and then, because he did not wish to know, he knocked again at the garage door.

"Miss Farrar," he called, "will you please open? There is no one here now but police and an unconscious man in the cottage. He has been hit on the head and stunned. I have sent for help from Headquarters. It will be here soon."

There was no answer but Bobby felt Olive was listening. He knocked and called again.

"There is nothing to be afraid of. My name is Owen. You remember I called to see you at your shop the other day? I can push my card under the door if you like."

He did so and then after another pause she called out to him that the door was locked on the outside so she could not open it. There was a spare key, though, and she told him where it was. He found it and opened the door wherefrom now she had removed the obstructions with which it had been barricaded. A hanging lamp lighted the interior and by its illumination they stood for a moment or two watching each other. Bobby said:

"They didn't hurt you?"

She shook her head slightly, and with a faint surprise, for she had recognized an anxiety in his voice that she did not quite understand. He said:

"You are alone? There was no one with you?"

Again she shook her head, watching him curiously by the light of the lamp shining full on his face. She said:

"Your face is bleeding? You're hurt?"

"It is nothing, only a scratch," he answered.

They were silent again, looking at each other, and why they were silent and why they watched each other so, neither knew. Reminding himself that he was a sworn officer of police and that he had a duty to do, Bobby said abruptly: "What happened?"

"I don't know," she replied at once and with relief, as if glad their mutual silence had at last been broken. She said suddenly: "You said there was a man in the cottage?"

Leaving the sentence unfinished she flashed by him, running to the cottage. He followed. He noticed how quickly she ran. A finely built, vigorous girl, he thought, with plenty of physical strength. He followed her into the lounge of the cottage when he found her kneeling by the side of Yates's body.

"Who is it? I don't know him," she said over her shoulder as Bobby came in, and there was relief in her voice, he thought, as though she had feared it would be somebody she did know. "He's not very badly hurt, I think," she added.

"You have never seen him before?" Bobby asked, and when she shook her head again, he repeated: "What happened?"

"I come here for the week-end," she explained slowly. "It's quiet here. To-night I left them at the shop to close and I came out in my car. As soon as I got indoors almost, I had just taken off my hat and gloves, someone threw a cloth or something over my head. They must have been waiting in the lounge. I couldn't do anything. I was rushed out to the garage and pushed inside and the door banged. So I put some things before the door to prevent anyone getting in, if they tried, but they didn't. I thought whoever it was would go away presently, and then perhaps I could break the door open with some of the garage tools and get out. The windows are too small to climb through."

"Do you think this is the man who attacked you?"

"I don't know, I didn't see anyone. The cloth thing prevented me and then I was just pushed along. It was all done very quickly. I hardly knew what was happening. I couldn't scream. I couldn't kick or anything. I hadn't even time to be scared."

Bobby thought to himself that perhaps she was not very easily scared. She did not seem very much upset by what she had gone through.

"Were you expecting anyone to be here?"

She shook her head but again with a quick glance at him as if wondering why he asked, and he thought, too, that the question disturbed her. With a gesture towards the still unconscious Yates, she said:

"He ought to be moved."

"Better wait till the doctor comes," Bobby said. "Probably he's just been knocked out – concussion, I expect, and the less he is moved the better. Quiet, rest, and warmth is all the First Aid wanted. It's a warm night but it might be a good idea to put a rug over him."

She went away for a moment or two and came back with a warm travelling rug she arranged over Yates's body. She said to Bobby:

"Do you know who he is?"

"I think his name is Yates, he's in Mr. Judson's office," Bobby answered. "Can you say why he came here? Has he ever been before?"

She shook her head but said nothing for a moment or two. She was evidently thinking deeply. She said after a time:

"If he is one of Mr. Judson's clerks, he would know Mr. Macklin?"

Bobby wondered if her remark meant that she saw in this connection between the two men an explanation of the presence of one of them in her cottage.

"Does that suggest anything to you?" he asked. "Has Mr. Macklin ever been here?"

"Not that I know of," she answered. "I don't see how he could know I had a cottage here. How could he?"

"Yates did apparently," Bobby observed gloomily, and this time he thought she had denied too much too readily.

"I am going to make some coffee," she said. "I'm feeling all in."

She went into the tiny kitchen. He followed and stood in the doorway – there was hardly room for two people in the kitchen itself – watching as she busied herself lighting the oil stove and filling the kettle from a filter into which ran apparently, rain water from a big tank outside. He found himself wondering whether all this bustling activity so suddenly developed, was to avoid his questioning, or perhaps to give her time to think before she answered. Well, she would have more and worse questioning to face soon, he supposed, and from that nothing could save her. She was grinding coffee beans in a small mill now and she said to him:

"By rights they ought to be freshly roasted, but you can't have everything in a week-end cottage."

"No," he agreed, though wondering if her words had a hidden meaning and, if he were right in thinking he detected a touch of mockery in her voice. "You are sure you have no idea what Yates wanted here?"

"None, how could I? I've never seen him before." She went on with her task. When she was brewing the coffee, she said to him: "You will have some, too?"

"No, thank you," he answered.

"I thought," she explained, "from the way you were staring, you were dying for a cup."

To his intense annoyance Bobby found himself blushing. He was furious. He had had no idea he had been watching her like that, but now he realized, that his eyes had been following every action of hers as she moved to and fro in the little kitchen, intent upon her coffee making. He knew that he could reconstruct in memory every single little action of hers, the curve of her throat as she turned to look for something she wanted, the gesture of her lifted arm as she took down from a shelf the crockery she needed, the kind of grave attention with which she arranged the tray she had now ready. In spite of his refusal she was preparing two cups and he had an idea that though she had never once glanced at him, she had really been watching him almost as closely as he had watched her. She said thoughtfully:

"But perhaps you only stared because you were afraid I might run away. Keeping an eye on the suspect, I suppose?"

"Are you suspect?" he asked moodily, well aware now of the mockery in her voice.

"If I am not," she flashed back, "why am I honoured by the presence of a policeman in my house – uninvited?"

"If a policeman wasn't in your house – uninvited," Bobby retorted, "you wouldn't be in it yourself – you would be locked in your garage still."

"Yes," she agreed gravely. "Apologies."

The coffee was ready now and she poured out two cups. Bobby said:

"Is there anything missing?"

She shook her head.

"Nothing in the place worth taking," she declared. "You heard no one else arrive?"

"No, no one."

"Can you make any suggestion who attacked Yates?"

"I haven't the foggiest."

"Could it have been Mr. Peter Albert?"

She had been in the act of lifting her coffee cup but at that she started violently, so that coffee splashed on her frock and on the floor. She put down the cup untasted. She said:

"I don't see why anyone should think so."

"Do you think it's possible?"

"Oh, possible, I suppose, anything's possible." She paused and burst out passionately: "Have you got to ask me all these questions?"

"I am afraid you are going to be asked a great many questions," Bobby told her. "You will certainly be asked a good many more times by a good many different people if you have really no idea what Yates wanted here."

"Well, I haven't," she answered. Her voice was sulky now, a little afraid as well. She drank her coffee and filled her cup once more. It was very strong, almost black. She made no attempt to press Bobby to take his that was still untasted. She said: "I've no idea what you want here, either."

"I was instructed to get a statement from you," Bobby explained. "A man has been murdered. You were on the spot at the time. Anything you can tell us may be a great help, anything at all. You were present sometimes at Mr. Judson's parties at The Manor, I believe. Macklin was there too generally. Anything you can tell us may be important. Even if it's only negative, it helps to clear the ground. Then you are friendly with Mr. Peter Albert. You are very old friends. Our information is that Mr. Albert knew Mr. Macklin, though he denied it. If you can tell us why he –"

She was on her feet now, blazing with indignation.

"Do you think I'm going to spy on my friends," she flamed. "I think it's loathsome to be a policeman." Bobby was used to attacks on police work, from indignant motorists convinced that laws were only for the other fellow, from city gentlemen whose business activities in finding the dearest market for the cheapest shares were being hampered, from club proprietors who could not understand why a willing buyer and a willing seller – of champagne – should have to look at the clock before concluding their bargain, indeed from all those citizens who are convinced that the police are really a great nuisance and far too fond of interfering with other people. As a rule Bobby, like most of his colleagues, made no attempt to answer these reproaches which they all took as part of the day's work. But this time there was an accent in Olive's voice that stung.

"I'm sorry," Bobby said. "I don't think it is loathsome myself to have the job of looking after public order, keeping the King's peace they used to call it years ago. Do you remember at school reading that in the days of one Saxon king the peace was so well kept that a woman with her bosom full of gold could walk in safety from one end of the country to the other? Well, that's the job of the police and I don't feel it's loathsome."

"No. Sorry," she said. "Apologies again. I seem to spend my time apologizing, don't I? But I shan't tell you anything about any of my friends."

"You don't trust them then?"

"What do you mean?"

"If you trusted them, you wouldn't be afraid of the truth, would you?"

"Well," she muttered, "there's such a lot you don't know."

"That's why I'm asking you questions," Bobby pointed out very reasonably. He added slowly: "It's why you'll be asked a lot more."

"I won't answer," she told him and added: "Nobody can make me."

"Oh, no," he agreed. "There's been a murder," he added, looking at her.

"I know that," she retorted. Her voice had grown shrill, she looked pale and excited. "Well, Chinese women and children are blown to bits by the thousand and nobody does anything. Sailors are drowned in the Mediterranean, people are shot wholesale in Russia and Spain. What is one murder, more or less, against all that? Haven't we all been shown what human life's worth?"

Bobby had been standing all this time but now he sat down heavily and he looked very tired.

"You have answered most of my questions now," he said. "I rather wish you hadn't. Of course, I thought it was that before."

"I don't know what you mean," she said uneasily.

He was trying not to look at her. To keep himself from doing so, he began to talk, more or less at random.

"I don't know anything about all that," he said. "It's all over my head. I don't know whether human life is like striking a match at night and you blow it out and it's dark again or whether it's the only thing that really matters in the whole Universe. I don't know whether snuffing out a life is like pouring away waste water or whether it's denying the purposes of God – which is a bit of a responsibility. Our job in the police is just to see the rules are kept, because if they aren't, there's such an awful mess all round."

"I wish you would drink your coffee," she said unexpectedly. "Do you really mean there's something I've told you?"

He nodded.

"Must you she began and paused. "Do you –?" she began again and paused once more. "You needn't tell anyone else, need you?"

she asked in a sudden rush of words that were all jumbled one on top of the other.

He did not answer that. She jerked her chair nearer to his, till they were' sitting almost side by side. She put her hand out towards his. In a very low voice she said:

"I didn't mean to, can't you forget it? won't you?"

It was such a barefaced, almost innocent attempt to beguile, more like the coaxing of a child than anything else, that Bobby almost smiled, even though his mood was far indeed from smiling. At that she lost her temper. She jumped up and stood facing him, her fists clenched, her face furious, contorted with a spasm of rage that should have made it as ugly as anger always is, but somehow failed to do so.

"I don't care," she cried, "I shall say I didn't and I didn't either because I didn't mean. I think you're just Beastly. Go on. Arrest me. Why don't you?"

He made no answer to that. She went on after a pause. "I didn't murder Mr. Macklin and I don't know who did and I'll never say another word to anyone."

She was walking up and down the room now. His eyes followed her, but he still said nothing. She said, still walking up and down so far as the narrow limit of the tiny room permitted:

"I suppose you think you know who it was."

"I think you think you know," he answered then.

"I don't. Who?" she cried, facing him with a kind of controlled fury.

"Peter Albert."

"Oh, oh," she gasped. "I don't. I don't. I don't," she cried, her voice rising hysterically. "How dare you say I do?"

"I suppose because it's the truth and nothing matters but the truth," he answered.

The sound of cars drawing near became audible. They both listened.

"They'll be here in a minute or two," Bobby said.

"Peter's not a murderer," she muttered.

"What I said," Bobby answered gravely, "is that you thought you knew he killed Macklin." He went to the door and opened it. "It's the superintendent," he said. "Superintendent Ulyett."

At the door of the cottage, in the light of the lamp shining behind him, Bobby stood waiting the arrival of the help he had summoned. The big police car drew up outside, a little past the entrance gate where stood Olive's car turned ready to be backed into the garage as she had left it on her arrival. She had followed Bobby to the doorway and was standing close behind him. She said to him in a low, unsteady voice:

"Are you going to tell them what I said?"

He had no answer to make. He felt a little dizzy and he was glad of the cool night air blowing in on them now he had opened the door. He watched the tree tops across the lane bowing right and left as the soft breeze blew. He said bitterly:

"You don't trust him much, do you? If he is innocent, what is there to be afraid of? If he isn't – is he still your – friend?"

"Yes," she answered, though so softly he could hardly hear the word.

"Ah," he said, and then they were both silent.

The police car had now been manoeuvred past the obstruction caused by Olive's car that so nearly blocked the narrow lane wherein her cottage stood. Ulyett came striding up the garden path, followed by two or three others. An Inspector Simmonds was among them, a man Bobby was not glad to see, for Simmonds was one of those who liked to describe Bobby as a favourite, a 'pet', and to declare that such success as Bobby had achieved was due merely to his having been given special opportunities.

"If you want to be in the Cabinet," Simmonds was fond of saying "you've got to start by going to Eton. Then you get the chances. Same here. Mr. Blooming Favourite Bobby Owen gets it handed to him on a plate. All his bleeding lordship has to do is to mind not to let it drop."

There was a chair in the hall. Olive was sitting on it now, or rather, she had collapsed upon it. Her head drooped, her hands hung helplessly, she looked pitifully broken, only half conscious. She did not even raise her eyes, she seemed unaware of it, when

Ulyett came striding in. He looked round quickly and uttered the traditional police inquiry.

"Now then, what's all this about?"

Bobby did not answer. He made a step or two towards Olive, his attention concentrated on her. Ulyett said angrily:

"Well, what's the matter with you, Owen? Gone deaf?"

"Pretty girl," commented Simmonds from behind.

Bobby swung round quickly, recalled abruptly to discipline and duty.

"I beg your pardon, sir," he said. "I thought Miss Farrar was going to faint."

"Where's the doctor?" Ulyett asked, and then as a middle, aged man came up, he said to him: "Oh, doctor, have a look at that girl, will you? Is she drunk or what?"

The doctor went forward. Bobby repressed a wild desire to hit Ulyett, a still stronger desire to kick Simmonds who had giggled audibly. The doctor smelt Olive's breath, looked at her eyes, felt her pulse, spoke to her, shook her slightly. She took no notice, she seemed hardly aware of him. He said:

"Dazed condition. Shock probably. Not drunk, no sign of drugs. What's it all about? Hasn't had a blow or a fall, has she?"

"Well?" Ulyett snapped at Bobby.

"I had your instructions to take a statement from Miss Farrar," answered Bobby. "She was not at her town address. This address was given me. I came on here. I found Clarence apparently watching the cottage. While I was talking to him we heard pistol shots. I saw a man running away."

"Didn't you stop him?" demanded Ulyett.

"I hadn't the chance, sir," Bobby defended himself. "I only had the merest glimpse of him."

Simmonds coughed. It was a cough eloquent, expressing surprise, doubt, dissatisfaction, ironic amusement. It said as plainly as possible that any police officer of intelligence or energy would have pursued and captured the fugitive. It was perhaps the influence of that cough that made Ulyett demand next:

"Didn't you follow him?"

"No, sir, it seemed useless in the dark with the start he had."

"I suppose he would be armed, too," murmured Simmonds in an audible aside.

Bobby flushed at the insinuation but took no other notice of it and continued:

"Also I thought I ought to find out what had happened. The door was locked but I broke a window and got in. In the room there" – he nodded to the door of the lounge – "I found an unconscious man on the floor. Clarence identified him as Yates, one of Mr. Judson's clerks, living in the same block of flats as Macklin. There was no one else in the cottage. I found Miss Farrar locked in the garage. I released her. She was in a very distressed condition. She said as soon as she arrived she had been attacked, put in the garage, and locked in. She did not see her assailant and had no idea who it was."

"Where's Clarence?" demanded Ulyett.

"He's not here now, sir," Bobby answered. "He cleared off."

Ulyett greeted this information with a formidable scowl.

"Didn't you stop him either?" asked Simmonds in a very surprised tone.

"He took an opportunity when my back was turned and I was occupied with Miss Farrar," Bobby explained, flushing again.

Ulyett continued to scowl.

Bobby perceived that the official report was going to be that he had handled the situation badly. Simmonds said:

"Oh, well, of course, if you were busy with the young lady – pretty girl, too."

Sergeants do not answer inspectors, so Bobby said nothing, though not all the discipline and duty in the world could prevent him from going first very red and then very white. The worst of it was that he did not feel quite sure that Simmonds' sneers were altogether groundless. If it had been some other girl or woman – or a man – would not his attention have been more generally alert, less exclusively occupied than it had been?

"Then the young lady wasn't quite so done in all the time as she seems now?" growled Ulyett. "What about Yates? Doctor, will you come in here?"

The doctor, who had prepared a restorative he had been trying, without success, to get Olive to swallow, said crossly:

"It's shock, she's quite dazed, coma."

"You keep an eye on her, Simmonds," Ulyett ordered.

He and the doctor went into the lounge. Bobby stood in the doorway, waiting to be questioned. Inspector Simmonds looked curiously over his shoulder. The doctor knelt down by the still unconscious Yates. Ulyett occupied himself with examining the signs of conflict. He looked at the bullet hole in the ceiling and said:

"Good sized revolver bullet, I should think."

Then he looked into the kitchen and saw the tray with the coffee and two cups on it. He said:

"Who had this?"

"Miss Farrar made it for herself, sir," Bobby answered. "She said she felt she needed it. She poured out the second cup for me."

"I suppose it was while you were having your coffee with her that Clarence slipped off," Simmonds observed from behind.

"The lady was all right then, was she?" asked Ulyett. "Dazed condition came on later, I suppose? Did she say anything before it came on, Owen?"

"She made no actual statement, sir," Bobby answered, thankful he had time to think what to say and to choose his words. "She told me she would refuse to answer any questions. What she did say, though, gave me an idea of what was in her mind. But it is only a guess, not anything she actually said. What I thought was that she was afraid Mr. Peter Albert might be the man who killed Macklin. But there again I didn't gather that she had any real reason or knew any direct evidence. It seemed rather that she was just afraid it might be him."

"Well, that doesn't amount to much," grumbled Ulyett. "We knew before it might be Albert all right – or anyone else almost. Anyhow, we had better see what she has to say for herself now and if she isn't fit to answer questions yet, she'll have to go to hospital with some one to see she stops there. If we have to, we can charge her – suspected assault. She may have knocked Yates out and then been shoved in the garage by pals of his. I suppose this Yates bird had better go to hospital, too, doctor, hadn't he? We can charge him with being a suspected person found on enclosed premises. How long will it be before he can talk?" '

"Oh, he should be all right before long," answered the doctor. "He's concussion. The girl's a shock case – hysteria condition."

"Hysteria – that's kicking and screaming, isn't it?" Ulyett asked doubtfully.

"Sometimes. Sometimes it's passive," the doctor explained. "It might pass off quickly. You called me away before I was quite satisfied. I'll have another look, shall I?"

"Right," said Ulyett, but when they returned to the small entrance hall, there was no sign of Olive.

"Hullo, what's this?" Ulyett demanded, glaring round.

"I had a suspicion the coma wasn't so deep as it appeared," said the doctor with satisfaction. "Up and off," he added to Ulyett.

"Simmonds," roared Ulyett, "didn't I tell you to keep an eye on her?"

"I thought I thought stammered Simmonds, "I thought..."

Discipline and duty are discipline and duty, but Bobby had his full share of normal human nature and though he said nothing he made little effort to conceal a certain complacence that stole into his expression as he watched the unhappy, floundering Simmonds.

Nobody had seen her go. They had all assumed her incapable of movement. Ulyett was a dreadful sight as he stood there, almost literally swelling with indignation. As for Inspector Simmonds, he was almost literally shrinking where he stood. Fortunately for him, Ulyett could not say all he wished, since he felt he himself had shared the general impression and should have issued more explicit instructions. With an unconscious man, badly knocked out, and a girl in a state of apparently complete collapse, further precautions had certainly seemed unnecessary. But Ulyett knew well he would have accepted no such excuse from any subordinate.

"She may be anywhere by now," he muttered, half aloud.

"Funny thing," observed the doctor, "women often seem to know instinctively how to put it on. When a man wants to do a bit of malingering he works it all out beforehand – difference between the reasoning and the intuitive qualities."

But the interesting and instructive discourse thus begun, for the doctor was evidently warming to his theme, was interrupted by a fresh roar from Ulyett and the sound from without of a departing car.

"She's got that car of hers, she's off in it," he cried.

They all rushed in a body out of the cottage and along the garden path to where the cars had been left. Respect for his superiors satisfied Bobby's conscience that his place was in the rear. As he ran he wondered what Olive hoped to effect. An hour or two's respite perhaps, but what good would that be? Or did she not understand how widespread and effective would be the search for her that now of necessity would be begun. He experienced a horror of the prospect, he knew too well what it meant for those who become the object of a nation-wide hunt. He tried to think what he could do, as they all rushed down the path, Ulyett's bulky form leading, for he had been nearest the door and first through it when the sound of the departing car had given the alarm. In the distance they saw Olive's tail-light disappear and heard her sound her horn, as if in a final message of farewell and defiance.

"Get after her, get started, get the car going," shouted Ulyett. "Hurry. Marks, jump to it."

Marks was the police chauffeur. He said:

"Yes, sir. It'll take time, her nose is the other way. Have to turn her, sir, and it's very narrow here."

Olive's car had been left headed towards town in the direction whence both she and the police had come. She had turned it on her arrival with the intention of backing it into the garage. But the police car was still headed as it had been left when they reached the cottage. Evidently by the time the car had been turned round and pursuit was practical, Olive would be far away.

Ulyett expressed himself in fluent but unofficial language. It relieved his feelings but not the situation. Bobby said:

"Beg pardon, sir. I came on my motor-bike. I left it just behind the cottage. I could try to catch up with Miss Farrar."

"Right. Get on with it," said Ulyett promptly.

Bobby raced away. Ulyett wiped his forehead and said to Simmonds:

"He may be a pet and a favourite and all that, but somehow he's always there when he's wanted."

The head-light of his cycle was still on, so Bobby had no trouble in finding it, and a motor-cycle has the advantage over a big car that to swing it round in no matter how narrow a path is perfectly easy. In a moment Bobby had mounted and was flying along a road – a narrow lane, rather – that was however quite straight, so that he could still see a rear-light in the distance.

He supposed it must be hers. He felt he must overtake her at all costs. She must be persuaded it was useless to try to evade the police, much better in every way for her to go to them voluntarily than to await inevitable discovery and arrest.

He supposed that probably her intention was to warn Peter Albert. But that was no good either. Warning him only meant directing fresh suspicion on him. Indeed what could she say except that he was one of several suspects and must be prepared for severe questioning by the authorities? But he must know that already, couldn't help. Anyhow, there was no real evidence against him. His occupancy of a flat in the block also inhabited by Macklin might have a dozen satisfactory explanations. Yates lived there, too, for that matter. Besides, Bobby felt instinctively that Peter Albert was no murderer. He had not the air. That missing hundred pounds seemed to Bobby's mind to prove his innocence. Of course, instinct can deceive, one can never be sure. Human nature is too strange a thing ever to be certain of. The most unexpected people do the strangest things. But then again there was always that missing hundred pounds. Peter Albert had plenty of money and in any case was certainly no thief. The fact of the stolen money seemed definitely to let him out. Also, and even more important, Olive was his friend and plainly trusted him still, in spite of all her fears.

Only, he reminded himself once more, anyone can be deceived and place his trust, her trust, wrongly.

Bobby told himself that all the same it would take quite a lot to make him see Peter Albert in the character of a cold-blooded murderer.

The exhilaration of speed began to possess him. This new cycle of his had a pretty turn of speed and now he was roaring through the night at something like a mile a minute.

But he did not seem to be gaining much.

Luckily it was night and on the road there was no other traffic.

By this time though they ought to have been right in the town again, if Olive was making for her home in London as he had assumed.The road itself, for they had not turned out of it, must have swerved eastward somehow, for now they appeared to be running north-east by east. He could tell that by the position of the north star, shining on his left.

What did that mean, he wondered?

He became aware that another car was following them. It was close behind. It was travelling at the same outrageous, reckless, magnificent speed. It must be in pursuit of them since no other reason could explain such a speed or adherence to the same route.

If it was a police car, pretty quick work.

Only was it?

CHAPTER XVIII
PURSUIT

They had come into a main road now, one of those main roads where modern conditions have abolished the nocturnal pause and decreed that though the night cometh man must still work. Here all through the twenty- four hours, the great lorries rumbled to and fro, all the twenty-four hours the coffee-rooms and the garages were open, ready to give aid and refreshment to man and machine, and all through the hours of darkness, too, here and there by the roadside flickered small furtive fires as signs that by them less legal rest and refreshment could be obtained.

Fortunately tonight most of the traffic seemed headed London-wards, probably in order that delivery might be made in good time in the morning. It was therefore largely confined to one side of the road; so that Olive in her small, fast car, Bobby following behind, behind them both the unknown following car, had a comparatively clear way, since they were travelling in the opposite direction.

Even so, time and again, they all missed disaster by fractions of an inch as they fled on, scraping in narrow places by huge laden lorries with less than the thickness of a hand between them and the utter destruction the merest touch at that speed must have involved.

"She's crazy, crazy, crazy," Bobby thought again and again as he saw the risks she took, risks greater for her who led, less for him who followed, less, too, by the fact that his cycle took up less space than her car; as he heard too the startled lorry drivers shouting their anger as he flashed by after Olive's car had missed them so narrowly.

As for the larger car, leaping in pursuit behind, Bobby had no idea how its driver managed to avoid catastrophe. Perhaps the lorries warned first by Olive's frantic passage, then by his own, scarcely less frantic, drew in further to one side to give more room to the next madman.

Once or twice Bobby fancied that this third car was obliged to slow down. If so, it soon caught up again, for it kept steadily in its place about two hundred yards in the rear.

"They've speed in hand," Bobby thought; "they don't want to overtake us – yet. Why not?"

And then again he thought:

"Who are they?"

But to that question there was no reply.

Nor had he much time to consider it, as they rocketed through the night, this strange, bizarre procession, cheating catastrophe with every mile it traversed, the coffee-houses and the garages tossed behind almost as soon as they became visible, the lorry drivers with hardly time to shout their anger and their fear before light car, motor-cycle, bigger car, had flamed by and were gone.

Many a garage, many a coffee-house, heard the tale that night, in many the tale of that wild race through the night is still told – with additions.

In an earlier age indeed the story would soon have been that those cars and their drivers were of no mortal breed or make, so far indeed did it seem that they passed the limit of the possible, so little did it seem such dangers could be run, such risks taken and evaded, by those of the common race of man.

"The girl's mad," Bobby said to himself once more.

He was extracting from his cycle every ounce of speed, even the rosy optimism of the manufacturer had boasted it could give. But though he held the light car ahead he could not overtake it, and always at the same distance behind, roared the bigger pursuing car.

Bobby was fairly sure it couldn't be a police car. It had speed in hand, too, as was proved by the way in which if it ever dropped behind, it quickly recovered position again.

"There's going to be an almighty smash before long," Bobby said to himself as there came wild shouting from a coffee-stall they rocketed by.

A couple of lorries drawing up, one just starting off again, left here small room for passage. Olive only got past by ripping away fifty feet or so of fencing of which the impact sent her car literally leaping in the air, so that for two and twenty measured yards its wheels were off the ground.

That it did not turn a complete somersault was sheer miracle; that in fact it alighted on four wheels and went speeding on its way, was yet another. The keeper of that coffee-room still tells the tale, still shows the spots he marked and measured, where the wheel tracks showed exactly how the car had left the ground, shot through the air, come down again on the level roadway to continue its wild onward rush – and often indeed does he get called a liar for his pains.

"It's the speed done it," he retorts, "at a speed like that, no one knows what'll happen – smithereens most like, of course, but times it's all too quick even for a smash to catch up."

On his cycle that took up so much less room Bobby ran less risk in getting by. The big following car slowed down by necessity, since even on this night of miracle there had to be a limit to the possible. For a time Bobby thought it had been shaken off. But presently it was there again, keeping as before its old position, two hundred yards or so behind.

"Speed to spare," Bobby thought.

A little to his own surprise he was finding a fierce joy in this madness of speed, this juggling with disaster, this drawing lots with death, this awareness of the night and all things in it flung behind as smoke tossed on the wings of the storm. It was physical life lived at its utmost. It was as though they had exceeded Nature, defied her laws, flung her a challenge, as in triumph they escaped the poor limits she thought she had imposed when she gave to man but one poor pair of legs, and let the greyhound and the deer mock him with their swiftness, and the darting birds scorn his immobility.

But what greyhound or deer had ever fled or pursued like this? what in comparison with this was the swiftness of the swoop of the falling bird?

Speed! The intoxication of it ran through his veins, fired his brain, laughed in exultation with every throbbing pulse all through his being.

Speed! It was speed, the madness, the wonder, the folly of it, that had made him almost forget his errand, forget indeed everything but itself, as it was speed, too, he supposed, that had made Olive mad.

Speed! Well, if it ended in death, as he knew was more than likely but hardly cared, at least they would have lived as none had ever lived till these days, as few indeed knew life even to-day.

Speed! How lovely, how fond, how foolish a thing when the joy of it seemed worth the purchasing even at so great a risk. He wondered a little if the soaring birds, too, thrilled to this beauty of swift motion, or the earth itself as it swung on its path through space at a speed to which his own was as though he stood still and dreamed.

Yet none the less, for he was not quite drunk with speed, he was aware of a considerable relief when he found they had turned into a quieter road, one without lorries, coffee-rooms, bungalows, one where it seemed that they fled on through an uninhabited land, where they had perforce to go less recklessly, compelled at last to some show of caution by the twistings and turnings of the road.

None the less Olive still kept the lead, Bobby still found himself unable to overtake her, the stranger car behind still kept its self-appointed place, some two hundred yards in the rear.

"She can drive all right," Bobby found himself muttering as he watched how Olive swung round bends, cut corners, avoided the traps laid continually by tangled hedge or hidden ditch.

He became aware of a new smell in the air. The land was flat now and he thought:

"We're getting near the sea – well, that'll stop us."

Then he remembered that Peter Albert had spoken of possessing a yacht.

"That's it," he thought to himself. "Silly," he mused. "She means to warn him and she thinks they'll be safe if they can get to sea."

He glanced over his shoulder. The big following car was still there. Olive was making straight for the sea, as if she meant to drive into it. But the road was curving now and soon they were rushing along by the shore, between the sea and the land. They came to a bridge, crossing a small creek. Over it, Olive slackened to a more reasonable speed. She went slower still. She brought her car to a standstill. The road was narrow here, sand on one side, an expanse of rough, coarse tangled grass on the other. She sounded her horn, a long blast and a short, a short and a long again. A signal evidently. She switched off her lights. When Bobby, jumping down from his cycle, ran to her car, he found it empty and of her there was no sign.

"Miss Farrar," he called and then: "Olive! Olive!"

There was no answer. The big car that had followed them so far and so faithfully drew up at a little distance.

Its powerful headlamps shone full on Bobby standing by Olive's empty car.

He shouted again.

"Olive! Miss Farrar! Olive, where are you?"

Darkness and silence. No other answer. Man might be able to laugh to scorn Nature's will to forbid him those ecstasies of speed she allowed other of her creatures, but the night has still its power, not yet is it wholly conquered. In the towns indeed no longer is it permitted full sway, but out here, between the land and the ocean, man was as powerless against the deep and hidden night as ever were his primeval ancestors.

Even the headlamps from the big following car had been switched off. He had an impression that its inmates had alighted, were approaching. The air, freed from the clamour of three engines, was full now of the gentler murmur of the breeze, of the sound of little waves lazily advancing, indolently retreating on the level sands of the shore.

Bobby crouched down, putting his ear to the ground. He could hear cautious steps coming slowly along the road. He could make out, too, a group of three or four men vaguely outlined against the sky. They were coming silently, slowly, yet somehow with an air of purpose, too. Nor indeed was it likely they had come so far and so fast without a settled purpose and resolution clear in their minds. There was a threat, Bobby felt, in that slow and cautious approach of theirs, though nothing to show whether that threat was against him or against Olive – probably it would of necessity include them both.

"Oh, all right, that's O.K.," he shouted. "Hurry along then. I'll follow. Tell them to carry on and be quick back."

He could see that the approaching figures, barely visible against the skyline when he stooped, lost in the darkness when he stood up, paused to listen. He hoped they would wonder what his cry meant and for a moment hesitate and be confused. He began to run, as silently as he could, stooping low. At a little distance he stopped and lay down flat on the ground, to watch and listen. He supposed that if when Olive sounded her horn, as she had done when she stopped her car, she had really intended a signal, then soon there would be an answer of some sort.

He had an idea, too, that the answer was one of which there would soon be desperate need – both for her and for him, he thought.

Unless indeed her signal had not been one for help but merely to convey a warning. In that case all might be well in the sense that she might be making her escape in a darkness that would render pursuit almost impossible. Besides, she might know of some place of refuge near enough for her to reach it on foot.

Anyhow, there was nothing he could do but lie still, wait, watch. Olive evidently did not mean to reply to his call, and in this darkness, in a neighbourhood probably more or less familiar to her but unknown to him, it was hopeless to attempt to find her, even had there not been the menace of these unknown pursuers who had followed them both and who must have some aim and intention of their own.

"If I'm right no doubt of that," Bobby thought, and supposed that if he was, there was little at which they were likely to hesitate.

A body buried here in the sand, in this lonely spot, might not be found for years, perhaps never.

Suddenly a Verey light sailed up into the air. It hung for a little, throwing a white radiance all around. Bobby, flat on his face, lay flatter still. He saw the sea in front. Behind were a few stunted trees and bushes and what seemed a stretch of open field. There was no sign of human habitation. By Olive's deserted car stood a group of four men, clustered there and now all looking upward, as though taken by surprise at this sudden light that shone on them from the upper air. Bobby thought one or two of them had weapons in their hands but he was not sure.

Of Olive, he could see nothing.

At a little distance he saw another group of two or three men. They were standing together and one of them was extending a hand in the direction of the first group as if pointing them out.

For a moment all this was visible. Then the light went out. Darkness came again. Bobby, listening, thought he heard quick footsteps, as of men hurrying along.

But he could see nothing and then the sound of steps died away and all was quiet.

Heavy clouds drifting up from the west had gradually covered the whole sky, so that by now not a star showed and the darkness had become intense, oppressive, as by its own weight and the pressure of a coming storm. The headlamps of the big pursuing car had been turned off, too; nowhere was visible even a glimmer of light. If, as Bobby thought probable, a yacht was anchored near, she must be defying all the rules of the sea by showing no riding lamp.

It was very quiet, too, for the breeze had died away, no longer stirring the grasses or the few scant trees by the faint murmur of its passage. Only the monotonous soft lapping of the small waves on the shore remained. Even all that multitude of tiny whisperings that make up the tremendous silence of the night had died away as beneath the menace of the approaching storm.

Yet to Bobby this silence seemed a suspended thing. He was aware of an impression that at any moment it might break into clamour, shouting, uproar. To him the solemn, silent night seemed full of hidden movement, of invisible forms slipping to and fro upon evil errands. He felt as though he were sitting before a dark, impenetrable curtain that at any moment might roll aside to show strange happenings, happenings in which he ought to share and yet how could he when this wall of darkness and of silence cut him off? And behind all this lay what may best be described in contradictory terms as a heat of cold terror in his constant awareness that Olive Farrar was not far away – a warmth, for somehow there was a kind of glow in the mere consciousness of her proximity and simultaneously an ever-present chill of fear in his knowledge of the implications of her presence.

There was nothing he could do but wait, listening, watching, alert for any hint of what might be going on around. Once he was aware of footsteps, light and hurrying, but they ceased and all again was still before he could be sure of their exact direction. Once, too, he heard someone sneeze. The explosion of a bomb could hardly have been more startling, and then again he thought there was a sound of cautious whispering on his right, only that now this seemed to come from his left. But then perhaps that might be someone else. He had experienced a strong desire to stand up and shout, to exhort those he knew were somewhere close by to show themselves, to explain what it was all about, to submit to the impartial ruling of the law.

But to do that would be only foolishness, for here he knew were those who challenged and defied the laws that stood between them and their desire. Nor had he now at his command that force on which law must rely against the will of violent men.

What he wondered most was whether these two groups he knew of, those who had followed himself and Olive in their big pursuing car and those of whom he had caught a momentary glimpse before they sent up the Verey light, were searching for each other – or it might be endeavouring to avoid each other – and in what relation Olive stood to the one and to the other.

Then, too, what had become of Olive?

Hard to lie still and wonder like this tormented by so many doubts, and yet what else was there to be done?

If, as he supposed, those of the Verey light group were Olive's friends, then perhaps by now they had found her, or she them, and it might be that even at this moment a boat was conveying her out to some waiting yacht.

He did not know whether he hoped this was so or not.

It was of course possible that even in such bewildering darkness he might by persistent groping be able to find the road, rough as it was, that must run somewhere between him and the sea. Then, if he followed it by the way he had come, he would reach presently that stretch of it where Olive's car, his cycle, the big pursuing car had all been left. But that would involve considerable risk of an encounter that would probably end all chance of securing any information as to the significance of these events – or at any rate any chance of being able to communicate that information to anyone else. Also, though this consideration he did not admit into his conscious mind, it would end any hope of being able to give any aid to Olive whom he must believe was mixed up somehow in very dangerous and unlawful happenings.

Somehow, too, it seemed a small and even unimportant thing, here on this remote and solitary shore before the vast indifference of the sea, that he represented all the power and the majesty of the law man has made for his own protection and that counts for so little against the august lonely splendour of sea and land and sky.

A soft, low voice from close behind, though he had heard no faintest sound to tell that anyone approached, murmured:

"I can see you. Don't move. If you do, I shall shoot you. I've got a pistol."

Bobby turned his head. He could see nothing but while he had been engrossed in his thoughts he had raised himself to a sitting position and so perhaps had become visible against the sky.

"Is that you, Miss Farrar?" he said, and in spite of himself there was in his voice a kind of eager joy born of his knowledge that she had not yet joined her friends, vanishing with them beyond his reach and knowledge and yet leaving to him the duty of launching after her an inevitable, an unavoidable, an inexorable pursuit.

She heard that strange tremor in his voice but she did not understand it, though vaguely it troubled her. She said:

"I've got a pistol. I know how to shoot. I've learned. It's quite easy."

"Oh, yes, quite," agreed Bobby and oddly there flashed into his mind a familiar quotation:

"Methinks the lady doth protest too much."

All the same a loaded pistol is apt to go off, anyone can pull a trigger, at point-blank range a hit is more likely than a miss.

"You must promise," she went on, "you'll never say a word to anyone about what I told you. Or – or –"

"Yes. Well?" he said.

"I shall shoot," she declared.

He did not answer for a moment or two and he listened intently to her quick and uneven breathing.

"Oh, well," he said at last, "I suppose you mean about Mr. Albert?"

"You'll promise?" she asked.

"Of course I won't," he snapped, "and mind what you're doing with that gun. If it goes off – well, neither of us will ever get over it."

"What do you mean? I don't care," she said quickly. There was a touch of hysteria in her voice, he guessed she was at breaking point. Anything might happen. It was all very funny, he thought. But then life was a funny business at the best. At least, not life. It wasn't life that was funny. Human beings. They got themselves into such odd fixes. This, for example. Here was the kind of girl whose normal, healthy, happy interests should be tennis, frocks, cream buns, the next dance, threatening to commit murder by a lonely shore in the darkness of the night. Incredible, of course. But there it was. Funny, too, that the girl was one who, from the first moment he had seen her, had roused in him an odd complication of feelings he had not yet had time even to attempt to understand or to analyse. Only into those feelings had never come a suspicion that some day she would be threatening to shoot him.

"Why don't you answer?" she said when still he did not speak. "You think I don't mean it, I wouldn't dare. I would, I will, I must, I've got to. You can spoil everything, ruin everything."

"I suppose everything means just him? muttered Bobby.

"It means everything – oh, everything," she answered. "Oh, more than you understand. Oh, why don't you promise? If you... don't..."

Again that note of hysteria had come back into her voice. It had all been too much for her, he supposed. He realized that they were both in deadly danger – he, because very plainly she was in a mood in which she hardly knew what she was doing, she, because, if she did it, there would come a time when she would understand.

"I suppose you care for him an awful lot?" he muttered gloomily.

"Promise," she repeated as if she knew no other word. "Promise."

"Miss Farrar," Bobby answered then, "I don't know exactly what all this is about, though from what we do know, I can make a pretty good guess. But that isn't because of anything you said. Mr. Albert has a flat in the same building where Macklin lived. You were close by when Macklin was murdered."

"He wasn't," she said, "it wasn't – like that. Not murdered."

Without heeding this, Bobby continued:

"It's not difficult to put things together. You were both in that restaurant, too – the 'Twin Wolves', I mean. It'll have to go in my report. It wouldn't make any difference if it didn't. It's all plain."

Olive's voice had been rising as she forgot the necessity for caution. It had grown quite loud, a little shrill even, as she said:

"You mustn't – I mean any report. You think I'm just a girl. I don't care, I've got to, I must. Nothing matters, nothing else. I mean you must promise."

"No," he said, as she paused.

"But you must, you've got to," she insisted. "Oh, why won't you understand? why won't you believe –?"

He did not answer this. A kind of bitter clarity of insight had come upon him so that he realized it was quite likely she might pull the trigger of her weapon at almost any minute. Women worked themselves up like that at times under the strain of strong emotion. They got one idea into their heads and it possessed them and they could think of nothing else. In a way it was a kind of perversion of the mother instinct. A mother with her baby was not meant to think of anything else, just as this girl now could think of nothing but the fear that filled her mind and her notion that it was for her to put right what she evidently still believed her words had been responsible for. And as he thought all this he fancied, too, that he heard again faint approaching steps and once or twice even a murmur of soft whispering. But whether it came from the right or the left he was still not sure, for first he thought it came from one side and then it seemed to be from the other direction – and yet was not that a new scraping sound, as of a cautious foot against a stone, from almost directly behind?

He did not answer Olive. He was listening intently. He was certain someone was near – either by chance or in knowledge of their own proximity. He wondered who it was – the Verey light group of, presumably, Olive's friends, or the group of those unknown pursuers of whose identity and purpose he had been able to form no idea? Whoever it might be, probably the sound of their voices as he and Olive talked, had betrayed their whereabouts.

Silence came again, and Bobby thought that perhaps he had been mistaken or that those he had heard had merely been passing by, ignorant of their presence. Olive said:

"You are making me have to shoot, I shall have to. Our lives don't matter –"

"Well, they do to me," Bobby interrupted and could not help adding:

"Both yours and mine."

"I've got to, I've got to, I must, oh, why won't you understand – ?" she panted, in her voice terror and despair most oddly mingled with a kind of almost childish irritation.

He put out his hand. It fell upon hers. He felt the pistol in her grasp. He took it from her. She did not attempt to resist. She said in a very surprised tone:

"You've got my pistol."

"I don't like the things," he explained gravely and he flung it as far away as his strength permitted. He said: "You pull the trigger and it's done for good. What are you crying for? There's nothing to cry about. I wonder if you would really have fired?"

"Yes, I would," she answered with passion through her sobs. "Why didn't I?"

"Well, I'm jolly glad you didn't," he said. "For both our sakes. You would have hated it afterwards. You must think an awful lot of him. I would stop crying if I were you. I wish you would."

But the violence of her sobbing did not diminish. He put out his hand again and touched her gently. She shuddered away. He said once more:

"Well, crying's no good. I suppose those people who sent up that firework thing are friends of yours?"

"They'll kill you if they find you," she muttered. "Unless you'll promise..."

"Bit fond of killing, aren't they?" he suggested.

"You and your law – you kill, too," she retorted. "That's true," he agreed gravely. "All nature lives by killing, doesn't it? A law of life, I suppose." Then he said: "One man has been killed already – Macklin."

"It had to be," she muttered, and then again with passion she said: "Not one man only – hundreds, thousands, little children, too. Spain, China, Africa, everywhere. What's one more?"

"Well, one more, I suppose," he answered, and added: "They're coming – someone. They've heard us, sure to. Listen. Will it be Mr. Albert and his friends?"

"I don't know – if it is –" she said and left the phrase unfinished.

"They'll kill me?" he suggested. "Their responsibility," he said more lightly than he felt, for he guessed his were words that ran too near the truth. "Suppose it's the other lot?"

"Then most likely they'll kill us both," she answered promptly.

"Jolly," he remarked, "and if it's both lots, perhaps they'll start killing each other. On the whole," he added thoughtfully, "I hope it is both lots."

"You had better go," she whispered. "It's so dark, no one could find you, if you were quick."

"And you?" he asked. "It might be the second lot, you know – those who followed us. Come along."

"No, we mustn't stay together," she told him. "I don't know what'll happen now. If I had shot you it would be a lot easier. I'm glad I didn't. I wish it had been me – shot, I mean. I'm so cowardly, a coward, afraid. It's no good. Peter said so once. I wish I never had – begun, I mean. Oh, it's awful, such a muddle."

All this had come out in a rush, an incoherent rush as of her deepest feelings breaking loose beyond any clearness of expression into a deep cry of bewilderment and fear. Then she was gone on swift, light feet, slipping away into the dark that opened to receive her and at once closed behind her, as it were, an impenetrable door.

He started to follow, running. His foot caught in something and he tripped and fell. As though the sound of his fall had been a signal long awaited, there burst out at once a clamour of shouting, of running steps, of blows given and returned.

In the darkness dim forms blundered to and fro. A sudden unexpected flash of lightning from the clouds that, unknown to them all, had been gathering overhead, lit up the scene for a moment, the sea, the shore, the figures of men frozen, as it were, into immobility by that momentary blinding light, a daunting light as though an unknown power above were not willing that what was being done should be hidden by the darkness. It vanished and all again was hidden in the black night. Someone screamed:

"Look out! Look out!"

Someone else cried:

"There he is."

There were other cries, confused, bewildering, contradictory, and at a distance someone called in agony on the name of the Mother of God.

Bobby stood still bewildered, uncertain what to do, what to make of this sudden rush of conflict. Big, heavy drops of rain began to fall, and out at sea the thunder roared. The storm was about to break. Bobby had no idea what to do, but he supposed he must do something. He wondered what had happened to Olive. He would have called her name, but he felt it would be useless to do so. Amidst the hurrying, rushing steps around he tried to distinguish one, light and quick, that might be hers, but he could not. He shouted:

"Police. I am police. Police are here. What –"

But he got no further. Someone hit him from behind and he collapsed forward on his face, unconscious, just as the rain began to fall like a sheet of water suddenly let down.

CHAPTER XX
AT SEA

When Bobby recovered consciousness, he lay for a long time watching a swaying, swinging ceiling just above him, wondering vaguely why it seemed to be so continually shifting its position, conscious of a very bad headache, occasionally asking himself where he could be and what had happened, but far too languid to worry overmuch about such questions.

Then gradually memory returned as the picture of last night's events began to form itself in his mind, the madness of that nightmare race through the darkness, the silence and the stillness of the long wait by the sea, the voice of Olive Farrar by his side, fierce, threatening, and bewildered.

He found himself smiling a little. Something deep and fundamental in himself, something he had hardly known was there, something primeval, reckless, individual, though sublimated by discipline and the tradition of civilized life into a strong sense of duty, seemed as it were to laugh an answer to his memory of Olive and that menacing pistol she had held.

"She would have done it all right," he told himself. "She's got guts."

"A man's mate," he thought again.

He wondered what had happened after he had lost consciousness, knocked out, he supposed, from the testimony of that aching head of his, and why he had been brought here. On board ship apparently – Peter Albert's yacht at a guess. A nice fuss there would be when his motor-bicycle was discovered by the shore and no trace of himself. Scotland Yard would be very annoyed. Scotland Yard did not expect its officers to vanish mysteriously. When he got back, if he ever did, he would be at once instructed to submit a written report, justifying his disappearance. It seemed very clear to Bobby that he wasn't going to come out of this affair with much official credit. He frowned uneasily at the thought and then his frown changed to a smile as he thought again of Olive and that pistol of hers which might so easily have gone off. Still smiling at the memory he dropped off into a deep and refreshing sleep.

The sound of voices woke him. A man was standing in the doorway of the tiny cabin. Bobby recognized him as Peter Albert. Peter was speaking to someone standing behind him. He said:

"They're still there, close on our starboard beam." Then he said: "Chap looks all right to me – pleasant dreams from the grin he's got. I say, Olive, isn't it about time you got a sleep yourself?"

"I'm all right," answered a voice Bobby knew was Olive's.

"You've been sitting up all night though there's nothing really to worry about – a crack on the head isn't all that serious. He'll be all right when he wakes most likely. You'll be breaking down yourself if you don't look out. No good playing the fool the way you are."

There was no answer to this. Peter Albert went on irritably: "You're only making an ass of yourself."

"I'm going to stay till he wakes," Olive answered.

Bobby was careful to keep his eyes closed and to assume as regular and deep a breathing as he could.

"You always were as pig-headed as they make 'em," grumbled Peter Albert.

Bobby found himself torn between the necessity of continuing to be asleep in case Olive went when she knew he was awake, and his desire to resent with instant physical violence these blasphemies that Peter Albert was permitting himself to utter.

The dilemma was resolved by Peter Albert's departure, still muttering to himself rude and inconceivable things anent Olive's general intelligence and extreme fondness for having her own way. Bobby heard Olive, who had apparently been standing behind Peter, come into the little cabin. She stood by the bunk where he was lying and he thought that she was bending over him. He continued to keep his eyes carefully closed, to breathe slowly and regularly. He would have liked to risk just one peep, to see what her expression was as she watched him, but he knew well that that expression, whatever it might be, would change the very instant she knew he was awake.

He heard her move away. Presently he ventured a peep. She was sitting at the open porthole, looking out over the sea of which now and again Bobby got a glimpse as the yacht heeled over. They were travelling, he thought, at a fair rate of speed, and one that was increasing, for the throb of the engines was growing much more perceptible. A motor yacht, he supposed, the one Peter Albert had spoken of at the Twin Wolves Bobby fancied, too, that the wind was freshening, that they were running into rough weather. It seemed pleasant to him to lie there idly, without thought of either past or future, and watch Olive sitting so close by his side. Without turning her head she said:

"Have you been awake long?"

"Oh, well," said Bobby, slightly disconcerted.

"How do you feel?" she asked.

Bobby considered.

"A bit empty," he decided, naming what had now become his most prominent symptom.

His head had ceased aching, his mind had cleared, only a certain lassitude remained, a feeling that it was more agreeable to lie still than to move. Olive said:

"I'll get you something to eat, but let me look at your head first."

As she spoke, she undid bandages that had been placed round it and felt with care an exceedingly large lump.

"Does it hurt much?" she asked.

"Well, it does rather awfully," Bobby answered in a deliberate bid for sympathy and was well rewarded by the grave expression her countenance now assumed.

"The skin doesn't seem broken. I'll put some more boric ointment on," she said.

She became busy and very soon had the bandage in position. Bobby said:

"This is Mr. Albert's yacht, I suppose. What happened?"

"We had to bring you on board, we couldn't leave you there," she explained. "You had had a blow on the head, you might have been killed."

"Take more than that to kill me," Bobby boasted, and she gave him a look he did not for the moment understand.

"You mean if I had fired off that pistol," she muttered.

"I didn't," he protested eagerly, for indeed he had only wished to show off a bit and to pretend that he thought nothing of being knocked unconscious. "I say, Miss Farrar."

He paused and they remained for a moment or two looking at each other. She had always been pale, but now Bobby thought that her pallor was- ghastly. There were dark lines under her eyes, she gave an impression of being at the very end of her endurance and yet, contradictorily, of having still reserves to draw on – perhaps it was that her bodily powers were exhausted but that a spiritual energy still remained. She said abruptly:

"I'll get you something to eat – I expect it's food you want."

She went away, leaving him with his mind full of many thoughts. Before long she was back with some hot chicken broth. She gave it him and found a dressing-gown for him to put on when he sat up. She said:

"Peter says I'm to tell you he's sorry about having had to bring you on board. It was raining in torrents and we didn't know how bad you were. It seemed the only thing to do, it's lonely there, miles from any house."

Bobby was too busy with the chicken broth to have any time to answer this. She took away the empty bowl and came back presently with an omelette.

"Did you make it?" Bobby asked after a time, surprised to discover that it contained ham, still more surprised to find how different it tasted from all the other omelettes he had ever known.

She nodded abstractedly, and then with a faint smile she said:

"Peter only cooks with a tin opener."

Bobby continued to devote himself to the omelette. Astonishing how hungry a clip on the head could make a chap. He said presently:

"What happened after I was knocked out? Who were those other chaps? Was it they knocked me out?"

"I'm afraid it was one of the men on board," she answered. "It was dark, he didn't know, he thought you were one of – of the others."

"Who were they? What became of them?"

"I don't know," she answered, though whether this applied to the first question, or the second, or to both, did not seem clear. She went on: "It was so dark, no one could see anything. Peter had his boat and we got in and rowed away and that was all. Of course, we knew you weren't one of them, and we knew if they found you they would most likely just leave you there."

"All the same," he said presently, "I wonder why you didn't – I mean, just leave me there?"

"You might have died, there wasn't any chance of any help coming," she answered moodily. "I know what you are thinking. It seemed the only way, the pistol. I thought everything would be ruined unless you promised not to tell anyone."

"Oh, well," said Bobby, a little regretful that an omelette was so small, so transitory a thing.

"I think I was I can't explain," she continued. "I think it was partly driving so fast – the speed."

"Like being a bit drunk," observed Bobby sympathetically. "I know – you don't care about anything, just speeding is all that counts, goes to the head all right."

"I think I was like someone else," she said.

"Like Joan of Arc or Joan of the Hatchet?" Bobby asked.

At that her pale face went crimson.

"You're laughing at me," she said, and then with a little gulp: "I suppose you're right."

"I'm not laughing at you a bit," Bobby protested. "I know just how you felt. You believed you had told us things we didn't know. You thought you had betrayed things, that you were a traitor and you must do something to put it right, anything. You felt you must get me to promise to hold my tongue and you didn't know how else to try. Well, of course that was all wrong. You hadn't said a thing we didn't know all about long before."

"You said –"

"Oh, yes, what you told me made me sure we were on the right track. But then we knew that, and even if we hadn't we should have followed it up all the same. We always do. That's our strong point, I suppose. Once we start we never let up. Can't. No way of stopping the machine once it gets going. You see, it was plain enough. I got told off when I said to our Super. – Ulyett his name is, the big man who turned up at your cottage – when I told him there was one thing quite plain. He said any fool could see that."

"What –?" she asked.

"That it's all an Etrurian show. Everyone knows a good many Etrurians don't like either the Redeemer of their country or the way he redeemed it, just as a good many Italians don't like their Duce and a good many Germans don't like their Hitler. Well, everyone concerned in Macklin's death had something to do with Etruria. Mr. Albert's half Etrurian by birth, even if he did opt for British nationality, and I rather wonder why. Judson does a big trade with the Etrurian Government and they owe him a lot of money. That means he has to do what they tell him or he won't get a penny. Wonderful the hold a debtor has on his creditor. That's why the City backs up all the dictators, Hitler and Mussolini and the rest. They owe the City pots of money so they put the screw on and say if you don't do as you're told, if you don't switch us all the trade you can, if you don't, for instance, give us your shipbuilding orders instead of letting the Tyne have them or the Clyde or Belfast, we'll see you don't get paid a penny of what you're owed. Well, of course, that jolly soon brings the City to heel. Money has no smell and money knows no loyalty either. Then again the 'Twin Wolves' is an Etrurian restaurant and restaurants are very handy for secret service purposes. Our Special Branch at the Yard knows all the dictators keep a secret service in England. It's jolly difficult to deal with, too. They don't do much over here, all this business – Macklin getting done in I mean – is exceptional and the Dictators don't like it any more than we do at the Yard. Upsets them as much as it does us. Their idea is to get to know what's going on among their nationals, and if any of their nationals don't behave, then to make their relatives at home suffer for it. There's a meeting of the Etrurian or the German or the Italian colony. We can't object. The Americans in London meet to celebrate the Fourth of July, for example. Why not? Quite right and natural. The difference is that if an American stops away – well, he misses meeting other Americans in a pleasant social afternoon. If one of the dictator country nationals stops away from their meetings, he's soon asked why. If he can't explain – well, his sister or his cousin or his aunt at home hears about it. Another point about the Macklin affair is that papers had been burnt outside the house – very carefully burnt. Attempts, too, had been made to hire a man called Clarence to do some dirty work. Easy enough to put all that together and see Etrurian politics were behind it all, and that Macklin was pretty certainly one of the Etrurian Government's agents – one of the Redeemer's destroying angels as they call his secret service people. But there wasn't much to give us any reason for suspecting one person more than another till we found Mr. Albert had a flat in the same block as Macklin. I don't know whether that will be considered strong enough evidence to act on, or if there's anything more, and my opinion won't be asked. There it is, you see, everything's known on both sides – Mr. Albert must have known his having that flat under an assumed name would make our people want to ask him a few questions. I'm jolly sure if Mr. Albert were an Etrurian subject he would be asked to leave the country. As he is a Britisher, I don't see what they can do – unless they've more evidence than I know of. An alien can be expelled on suspicion. For a Britisher there has to be proof to satisfy a jury."

"They'll try, I suppose," Olive said, "to get more evidence I mean?"

"They will," said Bobby grimly. "And remember, the police have nothing to do with motives, nothing to do with punishments. Our job is keeping order – to see that the simple people are kept in their right as the Psalm says."

"Macklin had nothing to do with simple people, he was a spy," Olive said.

"That's not for the police to judge," Bobby answered gravely. "All we have to do with is the truth of what happened. There's nothing more important than the truth. If we only all stuck to the truth, we should jolly soon all be back in the Garden of Eden again. Look here. What's going to happen next? You don't know what an awful fuss there'll be when I don't report."

"I suppose so," she agreed. "Peter was saying that. I'll tell him to talk to you. We're out in the North Sea now. We have to make for a certain spot there. It's about his wireless – directional short waves. He sends out news – everything the Etrurian papers aren't allowed to publish, all about what the Etrurian People's Party is doing."

"Oh, I say," exclaimed Bobby interested. "I've heard about that. The Etrurian Government's rather worried – they were bothering our Foreign Office, said it was being sent from British territory and would we stop it, and we said, certainly, if it was, but it wasn't."

"It isn't," Olive said. "Peter sends it from out at sea – different every time. Sometimes from the Atlantic coast of Ireland, sometimes far out, sometimes from the Channel, to-night from the North Sea."

Peter Albert came to the door of the cabin.

"Talking about Macklin?" he asked, "who killed him? does that matter?" He turned to Olive: "That motor yacht is closing us," he said. "She's twice our size – more. She's just astern now. I don't like it. Looks to me as though she were waiting – waiting till it's dark."

CHAPTER XXI
PETER NODS

Quietly as this was said, the words seemed to convey a sense of closely threatening danger, of some obscure yet imminent threat. Olive could hardly have become more pale, but her gaze wandered again out through the open porthole as though she sought a refuge far away, since near at hand she knew that there was none. Peter Albert was silent, too. Difficult to say what there was about him conveyed the impression, but none the less he gave Bobby the idea of a man who knew the end had come but who none the less would throw into the conflict every ounce of energy and power he possessed. He looked like a man with his back to the wall and it may be that never than then do those of British stock fight better – as Haig well knew in the dark days of 1918. Peter said to Olive:

"You might go and have a squint – see if you think it's her again."

Olive got to her feet and left the cabin without a word. Bobby said:

"Well, I'll dress." He got up and began to put on his clothes which had been lying on a chair near, neatly folded. After a pause he said: "What's it all about?" When there was no answer to this, he said: "I'm still wondering why you brought me on board."

"Eh?" said Peter, as if wakening from his own thoughts. "Oh, that? Oh, that was Olive. She said she wouldn't budge unless we fetched you along." He scowled. "You might as well talk to a lamp-post as that girl," he complained, "once she gets any fat-headed idea in her head. Said it would be murder – leaving you."

"Murder?" repeated Bobby, and to him the word had a heavy sound in that small confined space, a sound he did not like to hear, for it reminded him of many things.

But Peter did not seem to notice.

"Lonely sort of spot," he admitted. "Not much chance of help. Raining, too – regular downpour, thunder and lightning and all. Of course, we didn't know how bad you were. One of our chaps knocked you out. Lost his head a bit – I copped one of his, too." He pointed to his coat where a stain of ink showed. "Luckily all the damage it did was to crack my fountain pen and make it leak. I'll have to get a new one."

Bobby was dressed now. He looked at himself doubtfully in a small mirror hanging on the cabin wall.

"I'd like a wash and a shave," he said.

Olive came back to the door of the cabin.

"I'm sure it's the same boat," she said and went away.

Peter said:

"There's a razor in that drawer. I'll tell Olive to keep out of the way till you've finished. May as well drown clean as dirty, I suppose."

"Thanks," said Bobby, getting out the razor. "Are we going to drown? What's it all about? There's a boat following you? Is it the same lot who were in that car that followed us last night?"

"Not actually the same people – pals of theirs on the same lay, though."

"Etrurian politics?" Bobby asked, diligently soaping his face.

Peter nodded and there came a light into his eyes.

"We want to give our country back her freedom," he said.

"But you're a Britisher," Bobby said. "You told me you opted for British nationality."

"Yes, but only so I couldn't be chucked out," Peter explained calmly. "I'm Etrurian – half English perhaps, but wholly Etrurian all the same. I like and admire England and the English. I think the whole future of civilization depends on the backing you in England give the small free countries – not that there's been much backing lately. But I would sink England, the English, your colonies and dominions, America, too, the whole Anglo- Saxon tradition for ever, if I had the power and if I thought it would help my country one jot, one tittle."

As he spoke there came upon him an ecstasy, as it were, a glow, a fire, a leaping flame of purpose that seemed somehow to lift him high above the level of ordinary life. For the moment it was as though he soared, posed in the heights, transformed from man into a force of nature against which nothing could prevail – not even the finality of death, for there is that which death ends not but makes the stronger. Then as Bobby watched him, wondering a little, he changed and laughed gently and said:

"No need to bore you with Etrurian politics. And luckily I couldn't destroy the Anglo-Saxon tradition if I wanted to and I don't, because that same Anglo-Saxon tradition is our help and our example in Etruria. Since the English are free, why should we remain slaves? I mean of course us of the Etrurian People's Party – not the Redeemer of Etruria and his destroying angels. What I mean is I only opted for British nationality so as to be safe from your Special Branch – they have a nasty trick of cancelling your permit to stop in the country. You aren't Special Branch, are you?"

"No," answered Bobby, "just ordinary crime investigation. Murder, for instance. When there's a murder, I may be put on the job."

"I thought so," Peter agreed. "Murder? That's your word, I suppose. Natural enough. I mean from your point of view. Well, when the house burns you can't be too particular what you do."

"I think perhaps you have not been," Bobby said.

"Blade all right?" Peter asked. "I might have given you a new one – there are some about somewhere, I think. I daresay you can't see it but I've got one aim – the freedom of Etruria, to make it again a country where men can speak their thoughts, where justice is once again justice and not merely the will of the man they call the Redeemer. Nothing else counts. I had an elder brother once. Perhaps you've heard of him. I don't expect you remember. It was in the papers at the time. Seven years ago. Two years before I opted. He was an airman. He flew across Etruria, town and country, dropping leaflets, telling the people the truth, telling them what we were doing, telling them all the things the Etrurian papers aren't allowed to publish, urging them to join us- – the People's Party. For fifteen hours, from dawn till nearly night, he flew the length and breadth of the country, dropping leaflets. Twice he came down at prepared spots for fresh supplies of leaflets and of petrol. He could easily have flown away across the frontier when he had done enough. But he went on. It was towards evening when they got him. Of course, they were bound to in the end. He had nothing to defend himself with even if he had wanted to. The whole air force of Etruria was after him. He knew they would be. Before he went up he said: 'They've got five hundred 'planes and all of them will be sent up to get me.' It was nearly sunset when they did. He crashed in flames. Well, they got him. I go on. They'll get me. But there are others who will still go on."

"Olive – Miss Farrar?" Bobby asked. He was dressed now, he was being very careful to get his tie right. He said: "She is in it, too?"

"Oh, yes, rather," Peter agreed. He added carelessly: "That's why we are going to get spliced."

"You are engaged?" Bobby muttered, undoing his tie and fastening it again. "I thought so," he said.

"Her idea," observed Peter.

"What?" said Bobby.

"If you ask me," declared Peter, "I don't think it's any job for a woman – not getting married, I don't mean, I mean the sort of thing we're trying to pull off. When she asked me about marrying I was a bit bowled over at first – unexpected. I said I must think it over and I had to agree the idea had its points. I made her swear though that when I'm wiped out and she's a widow she'll chuck it. Made her swear on the Bible and kiss the Book as well – she's Protestant, you know. Most of our people aren't, of course."

"There's no question of – of love between you, then?" Bobby asked hesitatingly.

"No, what for? why should there be?" Peter asked in a surprised voice. "Hang it all, she's a jolly sight too fond of her own way for me. I daren't so much as drink a cocktail if she's in sight – if I do I get a lecture a mile long about keeping in form and do I think chaps going to row in the Oxford and Cambridge boat-race drink cocktails? Blowed if I know, and I don't suppose she does either, but that doesn't stop her jawing. You ought to have heard her letting loose when we wanted to leave you on shore last night. We might have been a gang of murderers from the way she talked and a lot of school-children from the way she bossed us around. Of course, she was a bit above herself last night. She had been wanting to do you in, hadn't she?"

"Well, not exactly," Bobby protested. "I don't suppose she meant it."

"She jolly well did," retorted Peter. "She generally does and so she did last night all right. I daresay she was all worked up, though. Driving the way she had been and being followed, and the darkness, and she had got it into her head she had given the whole show away and that if our plans failed and a few hundred people got shot and bombed and so on – then that was her fault, her responsibility and she mustn't let it happen even if she had to put in a spot of shooting on her own. You see all of us, we have the lives of a good many people in our hands – a slip of the tongue and they, not we, face the firing squad; they, or, what's worse, their uncles, brothers, sisters, wives, children, go to the concentration camps. It gets so you feel it going round in your head till you're hardly sane any longer. I've known a man blow his brains out himself rather than stand the strain any longer of knowing what one careless word might mean to others. Olive was a bit like that last night – all wrong, of course. What she told you wasn't any more than your people knew before. But she didn't realize that. You have to know the feeling before you know what it can work you up to. Now she's a bit deflated, poor kid – feels she was rather a fool. I expect I rubbed it in a bit too much, telling her what an ass she had made of herself. I enjoyed it, though. Generally it's the other way, her telling me what an idiot I've made of myself."

Bobby looked at Peter with some disfavour. He disapproved strongly of the general tone of Peter's remarks and yet he did not quite know how to express that disapproval.

"Bossy, that's Olive," said Peter suddenly.

But Olive herself had returned to the cabin door in time to hear this last remark.

"I'm not," she said indignantly, "it's you." She added: "They want to know if they hadn't better change course and increase speed?"

"What's the good?" Peter answered. "They would only do the same. Our chance will be when it's dark – theirs too. I expect they'll have a searchlight. That'll do us if they have."

Olive nodded and went away and Peter explained:

"When it's dark I expect they'll try to ram us – sunk without trace. They may have a gun, but they won't want to use it. Too much noise. Perhaps they haven't one, though. Customs might ask questions. I hope they aren't in touch with one of their submarines. Not likely, though, they wouldn't risk using a submarine so far from their base – sure to be spotted. Their game will be to ram and sink. Quiet. Nothing to attract attention. If there are any questions – unfortunate accident."

"You mean there's a boat following us that means to ram and sink us?" Bobby asked, a touch of incredulity in his voice.

"Got it in one," Peter answered. "She's two or three times our size and much faster, probably. Smash her bow into our side and perhaps a bomb or two to help the good work on."

"Well, I don't want to interfere," observed Bobby, "but why not make for port or get in touch with passing shipping? They would hardly dare do anything openly, would they?"

"Might," said Peter. "They might try the regrettable accident stunt. No one could say anything. Our dear little Redeemer expects results and if he doesn't get them he's apt to turn nasty. He thinks failure is a kind of treachery, and all our dictators do hate treachery so. If we tried to make for port – we couldn't before dark. As for other shipping – well, this is a lonely part of the North Sea. That's why we're here."

"How's that?"

"Wireless. We've got a pretty powerful transmitting set. Propaganda for Etruria, you would call it – information about all the things the Etrurian Government wants kept quiet. There's been talk about it in the British papers. We've four sending stations in all. Two land – Land North and Land South. Two sea – Sea North and Sea South. We are Sea North. To-night it's specially important to get the stuff through. There's one division of the Army ready to move and nearly half the Navy should come over once the Army moves. If that does happen, then the people will rise in mass. There'll be a chance then. They won't merely be machine-gunned and air bombed into surrender. A mob hasn't much chance nowadays against machine- guns and bombs and poison-gas, perhaps. A whiff of grape-shot, Napoleon said, didn't he? The modern dictator can go one better than that. But once any portion of the Army moves, we've a chance. That's why it's so important to get off the messages we have to send to-night. Half an hour should be enough and with any sort of luck we ought to be able to get that in before they can sink us. I say, you know, I'm awfully sorry you've got let in for all this. Much better have left you on shore, only Olive kicked up such a beastly fuss – wrong headed sort of girl, if you ask me."

"Anyhow she cared what happened and that's a jolly sight more than the rest of you did," retorted Bobby with some heat, and then: "What's going to happen to her? Can't you do something –?"

"What?" asked Peter. "She's got to take her chance with the rest of us. Why not? She knows what happened to her mother. After Olive's own father died, her mother married an Etrurian. Olive's English but she was brought up in Etruria. Her step-father was trying to get trade unions going in Etruria. So he was one of the first who was to be arrested, but they couldn't find him so they took his wife – Olive's mother – to headquarters for questioning. She wouldn't tell them anything. She was released after a time but she died within a day or two. She was never conscious so she couldn't say what had happened. Perhaps it was just shock and excitement. She was going to have a baby so probably wasn't up to the sort of questioning the destroying angels go in for. We did hear afterwards that the Redeemer of his country had expressed regrets and issued orders that pregnant women were to be treated gently – when possible."

"I take it," Bobby said, "you realize I shall have to report all this?"

"My dear chap," answered Peter, "that entirely depends on whether you get the chance."

"I suppose there's that," agreed Bobby, aware of a slightly chilly sensation in the pit of his stomach at this intimation of how Peter regarded the position.

"Besides," added Peter quite cheerfully, "I don't flatter myself I've told you anything your Special Branch people don't know already – except perhaps how advanced our preparations really are for the rising in Etruria. And they'll know that soon enough, all the world will know it. There's about me as well. I don't think they knew I was part of the show. We tried our best to keep that quiet – me, I mean. But I'm very much afraid they know it now – couldn't help very well after the Macklin business."

"Did you kill him?" Bobby asked.

Peter nodded.

CHAPTER XXII
DICTATORS' LITTLE WAYS

There was something almost terrifying about that quiet nod, so cool, so unconcerned, so grimly resolute. Bobby had expected prompt denial, perhaps 'avoidance and delay' as the lawyers say, anything indeed but that simple nod of affirmation and agreement. He found himself looking sideways at Peter, as at someone he had never seen before, and Peter looked back at him with his old friendly, frank, sympathetic smile.

"Sorry," he said. "I know just how it is you feel. But there it is."

Olive came back once more to the door of the cabin.

"You're wanted," she said to Peter.

"Right-ho," he answered and went away, but behind him left the cabin full of all that simple nod had meant.

It was some time before either of them spoke and then Olive said:

"Peter's been telling you, hasn't he?"

Bobby tried to answer but somehow the words would not come. Olive continued:

"We both felt we had to get married. It was too difficult as things were." She might almost have been defending herself. "In a way it was settled years ago when we were babies. Everything's fixed up now."

"Yes, he said so, too," Bobby muttered, and once again he seemed to see the simple nod of affirmation which in that one quiet gesture had conveyed so much.

She was still standing by the cabin door, her gaze directed through the open porthole as though she could not bear it should be confined by the strait walls of the cabin. She said presently:

"I'm sorry about last night."

"Oh, that's all right," he mumbled awkwardly.

"It was feeling what I had said might ruin all our plans," she went on. "I expect Peter's told you about the rising there's to be in Etruria – one of the Army divisions is going to move. If anything had got out beforehand it would have meant hundreds of men arrested and shot, and it would have been through me and thinking about it made me go all funny in the head."

"It's all right, nothing happened," Bobby repeated.

"I meant to do it," she said with a sombre intonation in her voice. "I suppose no one ever knows what they mightn't do. It doesn't matter now. I wonder what it's like to drown – they say it's easy but I don't think it can be. Do you?"

"If there's any real danger, can't you send out an S O S?" Bobby demanded. "There must be something –" he said with a gesture almost of despair.

"Peter says we must wait till it's dark and then we ought to have as good a chance of avoiding them as they will have of finding us. If we tried to send out an S O S, they would pick it up first, and ram us at once, and in the daylight we shouldn't stand a chance of getting away. Peter thinks most likely they don't know we know who they are, and they'll expect we shall show lights as soon as it's dark, and then it will be easy."

They heard Peter's step outside. He came back into the cabin and laughed.

"All our chaps want to do something," he said. "I think they would feel better if we all sat in a row and made faces – some sort of action. Our only chance really is just to do nothing – yet. Then our friends will think we don't suspect anything and that when it's dark and we hang our lights out, then we shall be an easy mark – sitters. But we shan't show any lights, and the dark will give us a chance to run, and anyhow we've got to get our messages off at the time arranged or things may get upset. If it doesn't all go like clockwork, the rising may never come off at all, with everyone waiting for the other fellow to begin, and then the Redeemer's destroying angels will be able to get in their shootings and hangings at their leisure. I say, Olive, what about some grub?"

"I'll go and see about it," she said and went away. Peter sat down and lighted a cigarette.

"Tough job, waiting," he said. "Especially for our people – we are a bit of an excitable race, I suppose. Not so much when it comes to action but when it's waiting we do get the fidgets."

"Why did you tell me about Macklin?" Bobby asked. "You know I'm a policeman."

"My dear chap," Peter answered with his friendliest smile, "you've got no proof, have you? You tell your bosses what I said as much as you like, only you can tell 'em at the same time I shan't admit it to them. Besides, I've got a perfect alibi. I can produce a dozen responsible witnesses to swear I was in their company that afternoon."

"But you told me –"

"Not in writing," Peter pointed out. "I don't mind telling you as much as you like, because I think you know it all already. But of course I shall deny it to anyone else. I've arranged for my alibi, or rather a lawyer pal of ours who is in with us, has one arranged for me. Your Special Branch will know better but they won't dare to prosecute, not against my alibi. Besides, we can do a spot of blackmail on our own, if we have to. We've given your Special Branch quite a lot of information about the activities of all the different dictators in England – the whole lot of them. They won't want that to come out. Make an awful stink. Most embarrassing for your Government when it's trying so hard to pretend everything in the garden's lovely."

"It wouldn't be allowed to come out," Bobby said. "You don't know how things can get hushed up."

"You're thinking of the Basilisk affair, and the torpedo that wasn't fired, and the depth charge that wasn't dropped, and the submarine that wasn't there and so it wasn't sunk?" Peter asked smiling. "Oh, yes, I know you English have a genius for saying nothing – most annoying, too."

"It's not only that," Bobby said. "Murder is murder. I know you can pull a lot of strings in England, but not, I think, about murder. What made you kill Macklin?"

"He was in the pay of the Etrurian Government. He had a list of all the Etrurians in England in touch with the People's Party. If he had got that into the hands of the Etrurian Government, it would have meant utter ruin, prison, death perhaps, for all the friends and relatives in Etruria of the people whose names were on it. You don't understand, you can't in your safe, secure England, you can't imagine quiet, harmless people, business people, a lawyer perhaps in ordinary practise, or a doctor, or a University professor thinking of nothing but their own private affairs – their next course of lectures or how such and such of their patients are going on – and then in the middle of the night, because it's generally at night, there are armed police knocking at the door. Next day the neighbours ask no questions, and the tradespeople don't call, and the doctor or professor or whoever it is doesn't come back till the friend or relative abroad has come to heel. And if he doesn't – well, they don't. The little ways dictators have, you know."

"And it was because of that –"

"It was because of that I killed him," Peter Albert said slowly.

For a long time they were both silent. Bobby thought to himself that it was a duty and a right to track down those who themselves had declared war on society, a secret war that had to be combatted and repressed if society was to endure and decent people sleep secure in their beds. But this was different and yet it was the same – entirely different and yet so precisely the same.

Indeed to the complications that life may offer, there can be no end.

Yet none the less, must they be met and faced and straightened out.

"You're thinking you've your duty to do and you've got to do it," Peter said presently. "That's all right – it's one of the reasons why you English are a great people, because so often you put duty first. Only don't call it murder what I did. It was no more murder than it was murder in the war when your officers, as I have read in a book written by one of themselves, shot down any of their men who showed signs of breaking under an unbearable strain. Their duty, I suppose, and it may be your duty to get me hanged – though you won't find that so easy – and in the same way my duty to do what I did."

"You ought to have come to us," Bobby said, but only weakly. "Anyone in the country has a right to police protection."

Peter shook his head, smiling a little.

"What could you have done?" he asked. "The list of names Macklin had was what was important – and for you what was it but a list of names? What harm is there in a list of names? – especially one headed as this was: 'to be asked to subscribe to the Etrurian Hospital Rebuilding Fund.' But we knew what would happen if that list got to its destination. There was an old Professor of the Etrurian National University – a member of half the learned societies in Europe. He was connected with both Olive's step-father's family and mine – her step-father and my mother were some sort of cousin. He was busy with a work on Moral Philosophy – been writing it all his life, more or less. His nephew got mixed up with what in Etruria is called Communistic propaganda – really just about what the Chartists in England were agitating for a hundred years ago. But in Etruria they label it Communism because they know you only have to whisper the word 'Communism' in English middle-class circles and all argument ceases automatically. Look at your Foreign Office. Someone murmurs 'Bolshevism' and at once all there run round in circles screaming in terror. Nervous wrecks, in fact. When they've recovered a bit they wipe their perspiring brows and say: 'Thank God for Mussolini, he may be trying to chuck us out of the Mediterranean but at least he's fighting Bolshevism. Thank God for Hitler, he may want our colonies but at least he's fighting Bolshevism.' I don't know if they thank God for Oswald Mosley, too. Perhaps nobody could go quite that far."

"That's all just politics," Bobby said moodily. "A man can't give himself the right to kill."

"Why not? What right for that matter has any man to deny another's right? Are you God to say this is right and that is wrong, to lay down commandments on tablets of stone? Not that I meant to kill. But we knew Macklin had the list and we knew he was going to hand it over to a go-between for the Etrurian Ambassador. But we didn't know where the meeting was to take place and we didn't know who the go-between was. We watched Macklin and we had observers posted at what we thought likely meeting-places. I was assigned The Manor, Judson's place – and that was where Macklin turned up. I was waiting and I followed him into one of the rooms and asked him for the list. He drew a revolver. I was ready for that because we knew he had bought one from Troya, the little man who keeps 'the Twin Wolves'. Troya had a police permit for a pistol. It's been stolen twice – if you ask me, it wasn't stolen at all but sold. Troya got away with it, though, and we knew about the pistol, and I knocked it out of Macklin's hand before he had time to get to using it. He whipped out a knife then and went for me so I knocked him out. He was pretty badly hurt.

I caught him with the knobby end of my walking-stick and it's a nice bit of ash. I wasn't going to touch him again.

I didn't think there was any need after I got the list of names. I was pretty sure there was no copy and without the list, and the notes of evidence Macklin had got together even the Etrurian Government couldn't pay much attention to his report. I said something like that to him and he began to laugh. He was bleeding where I had hit him and the blood ran down his face while he was laughing. He said he had half a dozen copies but I didn't believe him. He was crawling along the floor, trying to get to the 'phone. I watched him. I thought he was going to call up the police and I didn't care. I had my answer. We had it all fixed up what to say. I should have told the police it was a confidential list of business clients Macklin had stolen to sell to a trade rival and he could prosecute if he liked.

We knew he wouldn't dare. Too much would have come out. It was awfully quiet up in that room. I had never even seen a dead man. What was I saying? Oh, yes, he was crawling to the 'phone and I watched him. He got hold of the receiver. He said over his shoulder: 'I know all the names by heart. I know every one. I know it all off pat. I'll ring them at the Embassy and tell them they shall have it written out fresh first thing tomorrow.' You know, that was a silly thing to say. He shouldn't have said that, should he? After that it all happened very quickly. I got hold of him by the collar and pulled him away. I knew I had to kill him, but I didn't know how. Funny how difficult it is to kill a man. We were rolling on the floor. There was the pistol I had knocked out of his hand but it had gone under a book-case somewhere. He had his knife and he was jabbing at me with it. He cut my hand a little through the glove I was wearing. I had put on gloves because of finger-prints, you know. There was a cushion on one of the chairs and I took it and held it over his face. I pressed it down. Funny how easy it is to kill a man."

He paused. Bobby said nothing. There was a horror in that quiet recital which possessed him utterly. There was sweat on his forehead and he wiped it away. Peter seemed quite unaffected. He might have been talking about a good hole at golf. Bobby found himself mumbling:

"Does Olive know?"

"I daresay she suspects," Peter answered. "She doesn't know. No one does. Except you. I feel better now I've told someone. I suppose you always want to tell someone. I suppose that's why it's always so easy for police to get a confession. There's a kind of wish to tell. I had to do what I did and I would again. It was his life – or that of others and ruin for many more. Well, I've got that off my chest. Of course, I shall deny every word, and I've got my alibi. That's been seen to. Only I think somehow I wanted you to know."

"Why?"

"I don't know," Peter said. "I think we might have been friends – if things had happened differently. I had to tell someone anyhow, and I didn't want it to be Olive. I knew you suspected. I suppose you call it murder?"

"Yes," Bobby answered.

"I thought you would, I thought you would feel like that. Just as well I've got my alibi fixed up."

"I shouldn't trust too much to that," Bobby said slowly. "A sham alibi is – well, it's sham, and shams don't hold. When they know it's you they go on digging up evidence, bit by bit, more and more, slowly very slowly, till in the end they've got enough. I know, for so often I have helped to do it."

"I know," said Peter again. "British. You just go on, don't you? I suppose that's why you always get there. All the same, I had to do it. I could do no other. Luther said that, didn't he? or was it someone else? Anyhow, I say it, too, hang or not."

"You burnt the list of names?" Bobby asked. "That was the ashes in the dustbin?"

"Safer burnt," Peter answered.

"I was thinking it would have been evidence," Bobby explained. "Might have brought it down to manslaughter. I don't know. Now there's nothing to show. No proof. Did you take the hundred pounds that Macklin had?"

"Secret service money," Peter said. "It was to pay the go-between, whoever he may have been. I think Judson myself, but I'm not sure. Perhaps it was a man named Yates."

"Yates? Do you know that was the man who attacked Miss Farrar? At least, he may have been. She told you about that?"

"She said something about it. Looks as if the Etrurian Secret Service had got on to her, too. Luckily there was nothing in the cottage, nothing at all. We used to meet there sometimes and it was a kind of clearing post, registration office in a way. There were two men, weren't there?"

"Yes. I've been thinking since, it's come to me now. I half believe the man I saw bolting was Waveny. Do you know him?"

Peter nodded.

"Olive knows him," he said. "She introduced me once. He and Macklin had a row. He thought Macklin was annoying her. Really Macklin was trying to pump her – they suspected her, they suspected everyone. Dictators always do."

"What made you leave those one-pound notes outside the back door?" Bobby asked.

"Bit feeble, wasn't it?" admitted Peter. "I think the idea was to make it look like an ordinary robbery. I took his watch as well. I threw it in the lake, the revolver and the knife, too. I expect they are there still. I kept the rest of the money. I liked the idea of using our pet Redeemer's own coin against him."

"It'll be traced to you," Bobby said. "Then there'll be evidence."

Peter shook his head.

"All precautions taken," he said. "Another thing, now you know the truth, don't go after anyone else. I may be a bloody-minded murderer, as I expect you're thinking, but I don't happen to care about seeing anyone else let in for what I did. That's another reason why I wanted you to know the truth."

But Bobby found himself wondering if it was the truth. In what he believed to be his country's cause, Peter said that he had killed. It followed then he would be willing to lie, too, if he thought the lie serviceable and if he wished for any reason to prevent the facts being known. Difficult, Bobby felt, to see a clear way through such tangled motives, where right, it seemed, became wrong, and men of good will and honesty of purpose could think secret killings and dark intrigues were justified. And Olive – where did Olive stand in this scheme of things so remote from all ordinary standards? He thrust away the awful thought that would keep trying to force a way into his mind, and yet he knew if it were so, it would make no difference. Whatever the truth might be, the truth remained a part of her. He said suddenly and loudly:

"Precautions my hat. They'll trace the money to you and then they'll have you."

"Changed the same evening at a greyhound racing-track – and not by me," Peter answered. "No questions asked at greyhound racing-tracks."

Bobby made no comment. But he thought that Peter had really a very small idea of the persistence, the methods, the resources, of the C.I.D.

Peter guessed his thoughts and laughed.

"You're thinking you'll get me hanged all the same," he said. "My dear fellow, not you. Though I'm not altogether sure you'll ever get a chance to try."

Olive came again to the door of the cabin. She was wearing an apron now. She said:

"Supper's ready, but the men want you first. They want to know what to do. The other boat's getting up speed. It looks as if they are getting ready."

"It's not dark yet, is it?" Peter asked. "I thought they would wait till then. All right. I'll have a look." To Bobby he said: "Like to come along?" He led the way out of the cabin. Over his shoulder, he said: "I wish I knew if they had a searchlight."

CHAPTER XXIII
IN PERIL ON THE SEA

The question was soon answered. The darkness was rapidly increasing, for always heavier clouds were gathering in the west where the sun, though not yet set, was hidden beneath their lowering mass, so that already the gloom of night was heavy on that lonely sea.

"We had better show no lights," Peter said, and almost at the same instant a beam shot from the other yacht and searched and found them, picking them out in its steady unwinking glare.

"To tell us we are for it," said Peter.

The wind was increasing with every passing moment, blowing in sharp gusts that each time they came seemed to be more violent, to last longer, to lash the sea into a greater turmoil.

A spurt of water splashed over the deck. Two or three of the crew became busy, making all taut and ready for the coming gale. Peter said:

"Thank God for bad weather."

The other yacht had drawn nearer. It was quite close now, running on a parallel course. A man on it was shouting something through a megaphone. It was impossible to catch more than a word or two of what he was saying and to Bobby even what little he did hear conveyed no meaning since it was Etrurian the other was speaking. To Peter, Bobby said:

"What is it? Can you hear?"

"I can guess," Peter answered. "It's 'Dilly, dilly, duck, come and be killed.'"

"They want you to surrender?"

"They want it very badly. They think that if we did they might be able to find out things – with the help of a rubber truncheon. Not for us, thank you. We won't sink the ship or split her in twain, for there's still a chance. But better fall into the hands of God than into the hands of – into their hands."

The man with the megaphone had given up shouting now. Instead they were signalling with an electric light. Morse.

"Same thing," said Peter. "Promises. Pardons. Rewards. Appeals. Invitations to the crew to hand me over. Invitations to me to hand the crew over. Invitations to us all to hand each other over. Why not help the Redeemer go on redeeming? I gather I myself would shortly be made Commander-in-Chief of the Etrurian Navy. Oh, well, it all takes time, thank God, and while there's time, there's hope."

"Can you trust your men?" Bobby asked in a low voice.

"They can't trust the Redeemer, anyhow," retorted Peter and then added: "That's a mean way to put it. Yes, I can trust them and they me, for there is not one of us counts his life the value of a match stalk against our cause."

He lapsed into silence. The winking light ceased suddenly.

"Giving us half an hour to think it over," said Peter. "Good. Half an hour saved is half an hour gained."

Beneath the increasing force of wind and wave the tiny boat was tossing so violently that Bobby had to crouch down in what shelter he could obtain – and that was little – and, by Peter's advice, made himself fast with rope against the risk of being thrown overboard by some specially violent jerk or being swept away by one of the waves that now and again cascaded across the deck. Olive had been on deck for some time, moving to and fro by the help of the life-lines that had been rigged up. She had brought food with her and hot coffee in vacuum flasks, whisky as well, and had been busy distributing it, and urging them to eat, though indeed few of them had much appetite for food. The hot coffee was welcome, though, and so was the whisky. Her task done, Peter brought Olive back to where Bobby crouched, since that was the most sheltered spot there was, or rather the least exposed.

"May as well stay on deck," he said, "better stop up here than risk being trapped down below."

He made fast a rope to secure her by and then brought them two life-belts.

"Put 'em on if you like," he shouted, for the roar of the wind and the splash of the waves was beginning to make hearing difficult, "but I can't say I advise 'em. Drowning's easier quick than slow."

He went away again then and they were left alone, crouching side by side in the darkness and the storm. No lights were showing and all around reigned the black night, save for the beam of the searchlight that crossed it between the two boats, a gleaming bridge as it were. Now and again they could see members of the crew moving silently to and fro, crouching, bending low, swaying to the storm and guiding and supporting themselves by the lifelines. The air was full of spray, now and again a heavy splash, a rush of water along the deck showed that a wave had broken on board. Then the little yacht would reel and stagger beneath the blow and shake herself free and rise again, buoyant and light as before, to meet the menace of the next oncoming wave. The searchlight still followed them. Sometimes it lost them for a moment or two and then it swept to and fro, like a probing finger till again it picked them out, showing them clearly in a tiny pool of light against that enormous background of the tossing seas, the racing clouds above.

Olive had brought the rest of the sandwiches and coffee with her. She gave them to Bobby and offered him whisky from a flask, but that he refused. This was not the time, he felt, for soporifics – a drink of whisky and soda might be all very well as a night-cap, to help sleep to come, but not now. The coffee, however, had been a welcome stimulant, welcome and warming. Though where they crouched together was the most sheltered position on deck, they were both by now drenched to the skin, drenched indeed as thoroughly as though they had been bodily immersed. It was fortunate the season was summer and the wind comparatively warm. In winter they would probably both have frozen to death. Once, owing to some change in the relative position of the boats, the searchlight picked them out as the lime-light picks out the leading actor in a play. Then it moved further back and Olive said:

"Peter's taken the wheel."

They could see him in the tiny wheel-house. But as they were watching he beckoned to a companion to take over the steering and came along the deck. As he passed them, bending to the wind, holding to a life-line, he shouted:

"Half-hour's up."

One of the crew joined him. They talked to each other, shouting to make themselves heard, but speaking Etrurian so that Bobby could not understand. But Olive said:

"It's about trying to shoot. It's Louis Peter's talking to and Louis understands guns."

"Is there a gun?" Bobby asked, and Peter heard and answered:

"No, only a rifle and only about a dozen rounds of ammunition. Louis wants to take a few pot shots and try to smash the searchlight. What a hope, when we're pitching and rolling the way we are."

The searchlight switched off suddenly and the signalling began again.

"The final summons," Peter said. "We'll answer this time. There's an old Etrurian song every child in the country knows – almost like your British 'Rule Britannia'. The first line is 'Etrurians were not born to be serfs'. We'll signal that back. It always," explained Peter, "makes the Redeemer and his pals so beastly cross. They can't very well forbid it because it celebrates the great national uprising nearly a hundred and fifty years ago, but they do hate it so."

He went back to the wheel. Bobby put out his hand and took Olive's. It was very cold. She let it lie in his. They pressed closely against each other. It gave them a little more warmth, a sense of comradeship. Bobby said:

"That coffee was jolly good. Is there any left?"

Olive gave him what remained. She said:

"Peter's very clever. I've heard them say he can do anything with a boat except make it talk."

Bobby was conscious of an absurd thrill of jealousy. He wished he could hear her speak of him in that tone of confidence and trust. But of course she never would, why should she? He was no sailor, knew nothing of handling boats. It surprised him indeed

174 | DICTATOR'S WAY

that he was not prostrate with sea-sickness, but he supposed that the tension and excitement were too great for that. Presumably an imminent risk of death is enough to cast out even sea-sickness. "You're cold," he said, feeling her shiver.

"No, only afraid," she answered.

A great glow of tenderness and pity filled him. He did not know what to say. There was nothing to say. He heard himself mutter:

"I suppose there's not much hope."

Then he was sorry he had said that and after a pause he heard Olive reply:

"In God alone."

The signalling ceased. The searchlight flashed out again, a long finger of light, searching to and fro till it found them, as a child's finger pokes to and fro till it has found the scurrying ant trying to escape. At the same moment Louis, lying in the stern behind the wheel-house, began to fire. The searchlight gave a sudden jerk, as if startled, and then came back and rested on the stern and the man lying there. Little spurts of flame, too, began to come from the other yacht. The rifle fire was being returned. It was all about as useful and as sensible as throwing stones would have been. Not one chance in a million existed of bringing off the direct hit that alone mattered.

"They're getting ready now," Olive whispered.

"They're dropping behind," Bobby said, surprised.

"That's to get up more speed, more room to work up full speed to ram," Olive explained. She said again: "I'm afraid."

Her voice was steady enough but all at once Bobby saw that she was crying silently. Tears were running down her cheeks, all wet and cold already with the driving spray. She was in his arms. He held her closely, pressing her hard to him. He whispered:

"Oh, my dear, my own dear."

She yielded to his embrace. She seemed to find a comfort in the strength of his arms that held her fiercely to him. She said:

"We shall be drowned soon."

"Not yet," he answered passionately, and at that moment life surged so strongly in him that for them both death seemed impossible. It was almost as though he felt within him the power to snatch her from that scene of black desolation, the sea around, the sky above, from the ominous dark thing that was rushing upon them out of the wind and the storm, taking to itself shape in the night, looming up huge and terrible as now it was near and nearer still.

One moment it towered above them, lifted on the crest of a wave. Olive's face was hidden against Bobby's coat, for she dared not look. With despair he watched. The deck heaved beneath them, grew suddenly alive. It was as though a giant hand wrenched the little yacht aside. But for the ropes by which they were secured, both he and Olive would have been jerked overboard. Bobby found himself flat on his face but he was still holding Olive closely to him. Vaguely he was aware of, rather than saw with his eyes, a shape, a form, a something that plunged by in that wild waste of waters so near to them he thought he could have touched it. Vaguely he was aware, too, of shouts, of futile, spitting flames. But one bullet there was that took effect, the only one all through that night that found a billet other than the depths of the sea. It struck the wireless transmitter and put it out of order, so that all hope of sending further messages was ended. Up till now it had been sending out those intended for Etruria, long, apparently harmless somewhat pedantic harangues against dictatorships and abstract praises of democracy that nevertheless contained within themselves, according to a previously arranged code, secret instructions and information for those in Etruria itself in sympathy with those others outside the country who were planning the contemplated rising. The wireless operator came scrambling out of his cabin, crawling on all fours on the tossing deck.

"That's settled that," he shouted in English to Bobby and Olive. "Got most of the stuff through, though." He began to laugh. "Good work, good steering," he said, "pulled her from under at the last moment and now they'll have to come about and find us again."

But that was not difficult, nor did it take too long, for ever that inexorable searchlight swung backwards and forwards till it found them, settled on them, held them. In the stern Louis put his rifle aside, useless now, for there was no more ammunition.

"A pea-shooter would have been as much good in this weather," he grumbled.

"Well, they can't hit us either – if they could, they would be picking off the man at the wheel," someone else told him consolingly.

Indeed, their enemies, too, seemed to have given up firing, for no more little spurts of flame were visible from the other yacht. But it was following, gaining, and once more, borne on the crest of a wave, it came straight at them, fierce and direct on the surface of the sea as any fish in the depth beneath darting on its prey. And once more at the last moment Peter wrenched his boat aside, so that the other plunged harmlessly by.

Bobby said:

"Olive, do you know I love you?"

"Yes, I know," she answered, "but what a time to choose to say so."

"It's why," he explained.

"Yes, I know," she said again, and then: "They're coming again. They won't always miss us."

This time, however, Peter avoided their attacker by a much wider margin, for a fortunate wave swept them apart at the very moment when impact seemed inevitable.

One of the crew came crawling by, clinging to a lifeline, for by now the sea had increased to such a degree that the pitching and rolling of the little yacht made keeping footing almost an impossibility. Coming close to them to make himself heard, he shouted:

"God Almighty couldn't have handled her better." He added, still shouting: "Keep your life-belts handy, the skipper says to tell you. He's working in to run ashore if he can. Our best chance."

With that he crawled away, again to take the same message to others. The searchlight held them still, and, though time had been gained, their pursuer was circling round once more so as to get again into position to ram. But yet once more when she was close upon them Peter wrenched round the wheel to take advantage of a following wave. The little boat leaped aside like a living thing that knew itself its peril, and so another time their pursuer missed them, but by a margin so narrow that the two boats actually scraped against each other and each lost some gear. Then at the moment when impact seemed certain but that the sea flung them apart, as so easily it might have flung them together, a small dark object fell and lay close to where Olive and Bobby crouched. Bobby put out his hand and picked it up and threw it overboard. The sea seemed to split where it fell, the night to divide, a flame roared up and vanished in the waste of water. The yacht trembled, a cataract of water that had been flung into the air came down upon them as from a broken waterspout. Olive said:

"That was only one; they'll throw more next time."

Bobby did not answer. He was thinking ruefully that not much was being left untried. First ramming, and now a bomb, and what next? Olive said to him suddenly:

"Will you kiss me? I should like it if you will. It's because I'm so afraid."

"It is because I love you," he answered and their lips met.

She gave a little sigh of content and he found himself wondering if ever before love had been first spoken of in such circumstances, in such surroundings, in storm and peril, to the accompaniments of bombs and rifle fire, for again there had been an angry spurt of flame running along the side of their enemy, and of these continued attempts to ram and sink.

Peter came by again. For some reason he had given the wheel for the moment to another of the crew and he was walking forward. He was not crouching or creeping as most of the others found themselves forced to do. He walked upright and easily, bending indeed to the plunging of the boat as she rose and dipped to each successive wave, but sure of himself, magnificent against that turmoil of wind and rain and the rush of the blinding spindrift; with one hand only he held the stretched life-line, lightly, more as if from courtesy than of necessity.

"Not so bad so far," he said to them as he returned, a momentary lull in the gale making it easier to stop and speak. "They'll come again, of course, to have another try, but it's not so easy to bring it off in this weather and they've got to hit us the way they want or they might sink themselves as well. That was a bomb they threw?"

"I hope they've got no more," Bobby said.

"Probably a box full," Peter answered. "No expense grudged. What happened, though?"

"He threw it overboard before it went off," Olive explained. "It fell quite close and he picked it up and threw it away.

"Oh, good egg," applauded Peter. "We can't be so far from shore now. Scotland. I've been working in as much as I could. I'll run her slap ashore if I can – fox bolting to earth. Thank heaven, they won't be able to dig us out. If it wasn't for that searchlight, it would be pie to dodge them in weather like this."

The searchlight even as he spoke came again, focused full upon them. He stood in the full glare, balancing lightly on the swaying, leaping, dancing boat, indifferent to rain and wind and flying spray that was about him like a golden cloud in the bright clear searchlight beam. Then he was gone, back to take the wheel once more, and once more their pursuer closed them at full speed, turning herself again into the very missile aimed to strike them down.

CHAPTER XXIV
WRECK

This time again avoidance was not difficult, for the fickle waves, the changing wind, proved once more true allies, and swept the two boats apart before ever the critical moment arrived.

Thus further respite was obtained, for each time the attack failed their assailant had to manoeuvre in the teeth of the gale to get back into position to launch a fresh assault. And of every gain of time thus secured Peter made use to draw in nearer to land, for he knew the Scottish coast must lie somewhere ahead, though indeed by now he had little idea of their exact position.

For they all knew their one hope was to reach the shelter of the land, since they could not hope that there would always continue that mingling of luck and skill by which so far they had escaped so many attempts to sink their boat.

"A race," Bobby thought grimly, "between getting sunk at sea and wrecked on shore."

The hours passed and still this strange and desperate hunt persisted, the bigger pursuing yacht attempting continually to ram, failing now by a wide margin, now by one so narrow that it seemed inches was the measure, a struggle unique perhaps in all the long history of the enmities of men fought out at sea, for though in older days galleys might try to ram each other, never did they engage in chase, avoidance, and escape like this, and though to-day the submarine may be a victim to the ram, that effort, too, is over in a minute, hit or miss.

But this long agony and effort, pursuer and pursued, lasted all through the bitter night; and all through the night Peter stood by the wheel, alert and watchful, ready hand and ready eye, waiting for that instant when by desperate twist and turn he must snatch himself, his ship, his companions from the poised destruction.

By keeping absolute control of his will and nerves, by a patient, still endurance, that leaped at the necessary instant into a passion of activity, by an exact judgment of the one moment when that activity had to spring to such fierce life, again and again Peter succeeded in baffling the efforts of their pursuers, though more than once it was only the fantasy of wind and wave and flowing tide that saved them. Nevertheless, of this, too, of the incalculable vagaries of the weather and the tide, it seemed to his watching crew, as to their enemies, that somehow Peter knew how to draw advantage, like a man inspired, as though the ancient gods of the sea were by his side to advise him and to guide. More than once, too, the moment of danger passed, the gale seemed to take an ironic pleasure in bringing both vessels together again, to run for a time almost side by side, and once Peter only just succeeded in avoiding smashing their own bows into the other's starboard side.

"Smashed her up a bit, but us more," Peter remarked, "and no good dodging being run down in order to let the gale get us."

One piece of luck they enjoyed that was perhaps decisive. Some time after midnight the searchlight began to function erratically. Once it remained pointing straight upwards to the sky for some time before being switched off, not to appear again for five or ten minutes – an interval Peter made good use of by changing course as much as he dared and could in that weather and so for a little throwing off their pursuers. Once or twice again after that had happened the beam failed to keep them in its focus, as though its direction could not be changed quickly. Peter shrugged his shoulders as he noticed this.

"Never bothered to keep the bearings properly oiled, most likely," he remarked. "Our people are fine engineers but rotten mechanics – a sign of the civilised mind. We care for art and intellect, not for machine gadgets."

Towards dawn a whisper ran through the crew that a shore light had been seen and so land must be near. Bobby and Olive were again warned to put on their lifebelts.

"It's nearly high tide," came Peter's message to them, "and we've a shallow draught. I shall run her in as close as we can get and then we must hope that God will be good, and that help will come before she breaks up, or else that when the tide's out, and if the wind drops some more, some of us may be able to get ashore. The other boat probably draws twice as much water as we do and they'll never dare to follow."

Fortune was again their friend, for the wind continued to drop, and presently they found themselves under the shelter of a long rocky promontory which indeed Peter had been able to distinguish in the faint light of a coming dawn and so to avoid by skilful steering, running thus under its lee into the small bay the projecting headlands here formed. A few moments later they grounded on a ridge of rock of which one projection pierced their vessel but at any rate held her upright. For the time, then, they were in comparative safety, unless indeed wind and wave succeeded in breaking up the yacht before they could reach the shore from which at present they were separated by a waste of foaming waters neither boat nor swimmer could live in. But at least they were safe from their pursuer who had turned away and was indeed in sore straits as she struggled to avoid being thrown on the rocks.

Peter had taken the precaution to bring into the wheel-house and keep dry there the yacht's stock of rockets. These he now began to send up, as signals of distress he hoped would be noticed by the watchers of the coast. The lights shone but palely in the pale dawn but they were seen and presently, rescuers began to gather on the shore – only just in time, for fatigue and exposure were beginning to tell on those on the yacht. The framework of the boat was showing signs, too, of breaking up under the assaults of the still heavy seas and the effect of the damage done by the rocks on which she had struck.

Olive was the first to be sent ashore and then the members of the crew, one by one in their turn.

"By all the rules of the sea," Peter explained, as, deserting at last his post, he crawled along the slanting deck to Bobby's side, "passengers ought to go first and the skipper last. But this time I think the passenger that's you must be the last – for once you are on shore I do not know what you will do or say."

Bobby made no answer. The same thought was in his mind, his numbed and frozen mind that yet was now and again shot through by it as by a thrusting flame he dared neither face nor quench. Indeed all that long night of waiting and endurance, broken only by moments of vivid awareness of peril when death hovered and was near at the chance of wind and wave, this question had kept pressing itself upon him. But at any rate he was in no condition physically to react against Peter's decision that he was to be the last to be rescued. Nor indeed did he greatly care. '

"Your bosses can't blame you for not getting ashore earlier," Peter continued, "you're only one against us all and we're armed and you're not. I should hate to think I had got you into a row. But if you tell those chaps ashore I'm an escaping murderer, they might want to make a bother, and I've jolly well got to get in touch with my pals and let them know what's happened. After that, I shan't care what you may think you ought to do. Though I daresay the lads on shore wouldn't pay much attention. Probably they would think you were delirious or something from strain and exposure."

"Perhaps they would," agreed Bobby, who was not altogether sure they would not be right, so much like a nightmare mingling of terror and the glow of strange and deep emotion did the tangled events of the last few hours now seem to him.

"Not much to ask to let me go first," argued Peter, evidently not at all liking the idea. "Look as though I funked it, I suppose. But it's got to be." After a pause he added: "Olive says you and she have fallen for each other."

"She said – that?" gasped Bobby, utterly overwhelmed to hear it, for surely that was an open and intentional admission.

"Quick work, if you ask me," commented Peter. "Rummy night, too, for love making. Not my choice. Making love and waiting to be drowned. You know, I never expected to get through – if I had I mightn't have talked so much. Of course, I shall deny it all now."

Bobby made no comment. He knew well that such a statement as Peter had made would need very strong corroboration before any use could be made of it. It could even be passed off quite easily, as a kind of joke, a pulling of the official leg.

"Olive a bit of a complication, eh?" Peter went on. "I didn't reckon on her. You never can reckon on a girl. A rummy lot. My turn next, there's the last of my chaps gone. You're thinking what you'll have to do. That's easy. Britishers always put duty first, don't they? 'I could not love thee, dear, so well, loved I not duty more.'"

"Shut up," said Bobby angrily.

"Why? It's true, isn't it? And it is a bit of a fix. I didn't reckon on it, you know. Olive never seemed to care a snap of her fingers about anyone before. But there it is. Well, what are you going to do about it?"

With that he laughed, and now that all the others had been safely landed, all except Bobby that is, he went next. After him Bobby was got safe to land, where he was received by a shocked and highly disapproving rescue party, who had been scandalized nearly out of their senses by Peter's airy remark that there was still someone else to come – a passenger.

"I never heard before of crew and skipper being saved before passengers," one of them told him indignantly; "and wouldn't have been either if we had known."

"Ah, but he's a very special kind of passenger," Peter explained.

"Never mind that now," interposed a tall, stout, bustling person, the doctor, who came up at that moment, "they might just as well have drowned if you're going to let 'em all die of pneumonia."

They were indeed all in sorry plight. Olive was already in bed in the nearest farmhouse, protesting feebly that she had no need of hot drinks, hot blankets, hot-water bottles, and having them relentlessly administered by a capable and determined housewife. Bobby distinguished himself by fainting, for the first time in his life, as soon as he got on shore, and only recovered consciousness to find himself in a warm and comfortable bed in a nearby cottage. Perhaps it was a subconscious wish for delay, for time to think and to decide, that at once sent him off again into a heavy sleep. When he wakened it was dark, and night once more, so evidently there was nothing to be done till morning, as his host pointed out when he began to ask about a 'phone. There was one in a farm two miles away, he was told, but he must wait till day, and till the doctor had seen him again, and how about a bite of something to eat?

It was a welcome suggestion, and Bobby made an excellent meal, and then slept again, and when he woke in the morning was once more his own man.

He inquired about his companions and was informed they had all departed in a private 'bus that had been ordered for them from the nearest town. A separate car had come for the young lady and she had departed in it alone. Peter, described as the skipper and profoundly unpopular as having disgraced the tradition of the sea by not being the last man to leave his boat, had spent a good deal of time telephoning, and had left not with the young lady but with the others of the crew. He had also given the name of a firm of lawyers in London who had undertaken, through their Edinburgh agents, to answer all inquiries and make all necessary arrangements.

Evidently the local population thought it all a very queer affair and equally evidently there were a good many rumours in circulation. But those were no concern of Bobby's, and as soon as possible he got across to the farm and secured there the use of the 'phone. He had at first some difficulty in persuading Headquarters it was himself and not his ghost that was speaking. His identity established, however, he was instructed to report at the earliest possible moment and his statement that he had been in the company of Peter Albert was received with evident excitement.

There had been developments in the Macklin case, he was informed. Mr. Albert might have valuable information to give. He must be found as quickly as possible. The department indeed had been busily searching for him all the time all this had been going on at sea. The sooner Bobby got to London and reported in person, the better.

He was even authorized to hire a car to take him to the nearest point where he could catch a southbound express. By that time, it was to be hoped Mr. Albert would have been found.

Bobby hung up and went out to see about a car, wondering to himself if Peter had only escaped perils so many and so manifold at sea in order to stand his trial for murder on land.

Olive, too.

What was her position?

And his own position, and his duty, the duty that he owed and must perform.

The last question Peter had asked him echoed in his mind. What indeed was he going to do about it?

CHAPTER XXV
BACK AGAIN

Not till Bobby was safely seated in the London express did it become fully clear to him that in his confused and troubled mind the real question tormenting him was not what he himself was to do, for his own course of action circumstances clearly marked out for him, but what Olive intended?

Never indeed had he felt more depressed than as he sat gloomily in his corner, staring blankly at the landscape slipping by.

What, he wondered, too, were the developments he had been told of?

What was going to happen to Peter? What would the authorities think of his confession? It had been made deliberately and of purpose aforethought that no risk might exist of suspicion attaching to the innocent, but also Bobby felt as a kind of challenge, perhaps, too, in an effort to soothe a conscience less easy about the taking of life than Peter wished it to appear. Not that the Yard would trouble about questions of conscience. The Yard was a machine for carrying out certain duties and Bobby reflected again that Peter, telling his story, had had small conception of how efficient was that machine.

"I did it," Peter had said, and in effect had added: "What are you going to do about it?"

A good deal probably.

Peter had an alibi, he said. Bobby, remembering that, only felt the gloomier. The fake alibi could almost always be broken down and when broken down often provided the best evidence of guilt.

Bobby thought again of Peter as he remembered him through that long night of terror when the lives of all on the little yacht had hung upon his unfailing hand and nerve and eye. He remembered, too, the passion with which Peter had spoken of his country, of what he held to be a fight for freedom, that freedom of thought and will on which rests man's supreme claim to have been made in the image of God. Once more, too, he remembered that tale Peter had told of his brother flying the length and breadth of his native land, ignoring danger, despising escape, one against five hundred, a dove of peace as it were bearing an olive branch through skies dark with hawk and vulture, till had come the inevitable end – that end which is always also a beginning.

And was the climax of all that to be, Bobby asked himself, the dock in the sordid and shameful surroundings of the Central Criminal Court?

Then again he wondered gloomily where Olive was? what she was doing? why she had gone like that without a word of farewell? what she had meant by what she had said to Peter? Had that acknowledgement, confession, declaration, whatever it was, had that been intended as a farewell, a renunciation – or encouragement?

Little wonder, what with so many doubts and fears making a recurrent sequence in his mind, what with, too, the strain of all he had been through, that it was a very pale-looking, washed-out wreck of himself that Bobby presented when finally he reported at Headquarters.

Superintendent Ulyett was waiting for him he was told, and Bobby was to go at once to his room to repeat his story.

"We thought," Inspector Ferris told Bobby, "you had been done in for good when your bike was picked up and no trace of you. Looked as if you had been dumped in the sea."

"Nearly was," Bobby answered, thinking how often by how few inches the threatening bows of their pursuer had missed crashing upon them. "I hear there have been developments"

Ferris nodded.

"Waveny," he explained. "The Honourable Charles Waveny. Make a splash when he's pulled in – ought to be any moment now. Don't know myself what they are waiting for."

"Waveny – Charley Waveny," Bobby repeated very much surprised. "You mean there's proof, –?"

"That's the development," Ferris told him and then there was no time to say more, since superintendents are not people to be kept waiting.

To Ulyett, Bobby gave a full account of his adventures, and, in view of the suspicions now apparently attaching to Waveny, had the less hesitation not only in repeating Peter's confession but in emphasising that it had impressed him as being entirely truthful.

But Ulyett was by no means convinced.

"How about his having been pulling your leg?" he demanded.

"I can't think that for one moment, sir," Bobby answered gravely. "I don't think any man could have told that story as he did unless it had been what really happened. And I don't see why he should invent it."

"Wants to make fools of us," Ulyett suggested. "Wants the Special Branch to try a fall and get the worst of it and then have to leave him alone. Suppose he's arrested and the charge breaks down, what a chance he would have to cry out about police persecution if we tried to get him over any of this political business. God knows," said Ulyett with a sigh, "we don't want to persecute anyone, all we want is a quiet life and a chance to get home and see the family now and then, but the public will never believe it. The S.B. has had an eye on Mr. Albert for a very much longer time than he let on to you."

"I understand there is new evidence against Waveny," Bobby ventured to remark.

Ulyett nodded.

"Not quite good enough yet, but not far off," he said. "It was what happened at Miss Farrar's cottage put us definitely on to him. Judson has owned up he gave Macklin a job to please the Etrurian Government. They owe him a pile and things will be difficult for him if they don't pay up, which they won't unless he does what he is told. But he swears black and blue he knew nothing about what Macklin did after office hours – or in them sometimes. He tries to argue still that Macklin wasn't in any way connected with Etrurian Secret Service activities here. His idea is that Macklin had a pull with the Etrurians, really believed in their ideas, and on their part they were glad to have someone in City circles to stand up for them. Judson admits he did drive Macklin to The Manor that afternoon. He says Macklin told him he had arranged to meet someone there, but didn't say who, and Judson didn't ask. Judson says Macklin had a perfectly free hand so long as he produced results. He also says he thinks it may have been Waveny Macklin was to meet, because he knows Macklin was bothered about Waveny and wanted to put things right with him. He told Judson about Waveny having threatened him and said it was all a misunderstanding and he would make an appointment with Waveny to clear it up. We've got evidence, too, that Judson's own story of his drive into the country is O.K. He and his car were seen and recognized by two A.A. scouts. So he's out."

"Did he say why he called to see Troya?" Bobby asked.

"No, why should he?" Ulyett asked. "Nothing in it. Business talk, that's all. Troya caters for the parties Judson throws. Waveny's our bird. It seems the bad feeling between him and Macklin was over a girl. That Miss Farrar you went chasing after. She's in it up to the neck."

Nor had Bobby anything to reply to this, but still more gloomily foresaw how Olive, too, would almost inevitably be caught up in the revolving wheels of the great, impersonal machine whereto were due his service and his duty. Ulyett went on:

"There's no doubt about there having been bad blood between Waveny and Macklin on her account. Waveny doesn't deny he was pretty badly hit by Miss Farrar, and he seems to have got it into his head that Macklin was after her, too, and was trying to force her hand by compromising her in some way at Judson's parties. Of course, that may have been all Waveny's imagination – jealousy very likely, and nothing more. Though it's plain enough Judson put on some fairly hot shows. There's proof Waveny had been heard to use threatening language with regard to Macklin. The suggestion is he asked Macklin to meet him at The Manor on the pretext of paying back what he owed him, but really intending to have it out with Macklin in a quiet secluded spot where they wouldn't be likely to be interrupted. Perhaps Waveny just intended to give him the good thrashing he had been heard to threaten. But the thrashing turns to murder, and there you are."

"Is that strong enough to take into court, sir?" Bobby asked. "If we put that to Treasury Counsel, won't they pick a good many holes in it?"

"They'd try," said Ulyett, bitterly, thinking of the many times when what he and his colleagues had thought a water-tight case had gone to the Public Prosecutor's office, only to come back more like a sieve than anything else. "But there's a good deal more than that. Yates has told a story that seems to stand up. He admits he is responsible for the attack on Miss Farrar. He had an idea that Miss Farrar shared the secret that gave Macklin a hold on Judson, and thought he would try to find out what it was – probably thought he would do a spot of blackmail on his own. He broke into the cottage to make a search. Apparently he knew of it from having spent a good deal of time spying on Macklin in the hope of finding out his secret hold on Judson. He never suspected that really it was only that Judson was a big creditor. He was interrupted by Miss Farrar and he admits he threw a cloth over her head and bundled her into the garage. Then Waveny arrived, apparently following Miss Farrar. Probably he wanted a talk with her. When he found Yates there instead he got very excited, according to Yates, and Yates swears Waveny said he would give him a dose of Macklin medicine. It may be that only your arrival and Clarence's on the scene saved Yates's life. That's what he says, anyhow. You saw someone running off. Could it have been Waveny?"

"It could have been, sir. It didn't strike me at the time. It was someone about Waveny's build. I couldn't say more."

"There's more to it, still," Ulyett went on. "Waveny has an ugly-looking walking-stick, formidable looking thing, heavy silver knob. Well, we got hold of that and had it examined. On that handle there are traces of human blood. The group has been established. It's the smallest group known, and it is the one to which Macklin's blood belonged."

Bobby listened in considerable bewilderment. It seemed as though a strong case were being built up against Waveny. He said:

"Yates would hardly show up very well in the witness-box, would he?"

"No, very badly, very badly indeed," agreed Ulyett. "There's more to it. The notes taken from Macklin have been traced. We haven't got them all in, but a number were passed at the West Central greyhound racing-track, and Waveny is known to be interested in greyhound racing. It seems he has a share in a small kennel. We haven't been able to find he's been at the West Central track lately, but he goes there all right, and he would be likely to think a greyhound racing-track a good place for getting rid of the notes. It all fits."

"Yes, sir," said Bobby. "That means taking Mr. Albert's confession for a fake."

"Most confessions turn out duds, don't they?" remarked Ulyett. "I don't think we had better arrest yet, but we'll pull Waveny in and question him as soon as we can find him."

"Isn't he at his address?" Bobby asked.

"No, disappeared," said Ulyett. "Probably with the Farrar girl now she's got back. No trace of her, either, they haven't heard of her at her hat shop, and the cottage still locked up. And why has Waveny bolted unless he's guilty? Why should an innocent man run?"

"Panic," suggested Bobby.

"It's the guilty who panic," retorted Ulyett. "The innocent know they are innocent and so they don't, because why should they? Waveny will have to be brought in, but he seems to have found a good hide-hole for the time. I hope he's not got abroad, though I don't see how he can. We've his passport."

"It's certainly strange he should have vanished," agreed Bobby, vaguely uneasy.

"He'll be brought in soon," said Ulyett, "and when we get him, he'll have a good few questions to answer. Most likely when he sees how much we know, he'll come through with the rest. They generally do."

CHAPTER XXVI
OLIVE'S MESSAGE

It was late before Bobby had completed the full report he had been instructed to write out. He had been told also that though he was to remain in touch with Headquarters in case he was required, yet for a day or two, until he had fully recovered from his recent experiences, he would be excused active duty.

Bobby would much rather have continued to take an active part in the investigation which he felt uneasily might presently lead to very unwelcome and he was still persuaded erroneous conclusions. But to himself he had to acknowledge he had not yet entirely thrown off the effects of all he had been through. He was indeed glad enough to get to bed and once there he slept so soundly it was nearly noon next day before he wakened. A late breakfast or early lunch completed the restoration of his energies, and he was feeling very much himself again when he went out to sit in Regent's Park.

There stretched out in a deck-chair in the sun he went over and over again in his mind the doubts and questionings troubling him.

Had Peter's confession been a fake?

Had the dramatic intensity with which he told his tale been merely an effort of a vivid imagination?

Was there substance in this new case the Yard seemed to be working up against Waveny?

What had become of Waveny?

Were those, the presumed employers of Macklin, who had shown such determination in pursuit upon the high seas, likely to continue their attempts on land?

Above all, where was Olive and why had she also disappeared?

Well did Bobby know as he sat there in the sunshine, gossiping nurses all around and children playing in the sun, that what lay so darkly and so heavily upon his spirits was a deadly fear that presently facts might emerge appearing to implicate Olive.

And what was there he could do but watch and be afraid?

For who could tell into what strange ways Olive might have been led by her friendship for Peter, her devotion to the cause of the Etrurian People's Party? One thing at least that long night at sea had taught Bobby and that was the strength of Peter's character, his capacity for leadership, the burning power he possessed to light others down the path he wished them to follow. Bobby himself could have said, paraphrasing Agrippa:

'Almost thou persuadest me to be a revolutionary.'

Little though would the Yard care for such considerations, little for the motives that might lie behind any breach on British soil of British law. And only too probably would it soon become his duty to aid in the collection of evidence to support any such charge the Yard might have in mind. Yet would not even that be easier than to sit here alone and watch the nurses knit and gossip and the children play, and know nothing of what things were happening elsewhere?

Life hitherto had been simple in a way. He had seen his duty plain. He had done it to the best of his ability, helping to make firm that sense of security on which civilized life must rest. But this was different, this was all dark and tangled, and upon his heavy meditations there broke a familiar voice:

"Morning guv'nor," it said. "You ain't been and gone and got done in then, same as they was saying?"

Bobby looked up, startled and not altogether pleased to recognise Clarence. His first impulse was to tell that worthy to clear off, and then he changed his mind, reflecting that possibly Clarence might have information to give.

"Who was saying that?" he asked.

"It was all over everywhere," Clarence told him.

"Didn't know I was so famous," commented Bobby.

"I wouldn't go so far as that," corrected Clarence gravely as he lowered himself into a deck-chair by Bobby's side, "famous is what's Greta Garbo and Tommy Farr and them sort, ain't it? But all the boys knew about you turning up missing, and some sort of looked pleased like and wished as they had been there to see, and some said that for a busy – well, there was worse."

"Nice of them," said Bobby, quite touched at this tribute.

"Though I did hear," added Clarence, "that up at one of the night-clubs, the Cut and Come Again they call it, there was free drinks going the night they heard."

"Free drinks, eh?" exclaimed Bobby. "Wish I had been there."

Clarence pondered this for some minutes. He was sure there was a catch in it somewhere but was not sure what it was. Finally he saw it and announced triumphantly:

"If you had, there wouldn't have been none."

"Too bad," murmured Bobby.

"I didn't put much stock in it myself," Clarence continued. "When they told me as you was done in, I wouldn't pay for no drinks on the strength of it. I just ups and says: 'Wait and see,' I says. 'Talk of the devil,' I says, 'and up he pops.'"

"True enough," agreed Bobby.

"And I was right," continued Clarence, "for there you is."

"True again," agreed Bobby, once more.

"So as soon as I knowed you was back, I came along."

"What for?" asked Bobby. "Who told you I was back?"

"Same as you blokes knows about us blokes," explained Clarence. "Organization. Brain work. Kept an eye constant, me and my pals, on where you doss, so as to be the first to know if you did pop up again. Which when you did, soon as I knew, I was there watching and followed you when you came out, and here I am. Got a fag, guv'nor," he added abruptly.

Bobby meekly produced one.

"What's it all about?" he asked. "You aren't generally so anxious to interview the police, are you? More often, the other way about."

"Ah, but I'm running straight now," declared Clarence virtuously, "only I'm sort of worried like – upset, if you know what I mean, and not the comfort in a glass of beer there ought to be. I don't want no more nonymous letters, saying as I've put no bloke's light out, especially now the Honourable Charles Waveny has turned up missing same as you was, only with him more like to be permanent like."

"What do you mean? How do you know?" demanded Bobby, sitting upright.

The chair attendant came up before Clarence could reply, but that gentleman waved him carelessly aside, with the remark that his friend would pay. Bobby dutifully provided the required twopence and repeated:

"What do you know about Mr. Waveny? How do you know he is missing?"

"Ain't you blokes been asking about him at every pub he ever used?" demanded Clarence. "But she ain't going to pass nothing on to me this time, not if I know it. If she's done him in, too, that's her biz., but I ain't taking none, not if I know it."

"What do you mean by 'she'?" demanded Bobby.

"That there Miss Farrar."

"If you say things like that, you'll be getting yourself into trouble," Bobby said furiously.

"Sweet on 'er?" asked Clarence, greatly interested. "Lummy, think of a busy being sweet on a skirt what's done in a bloke what –"

"Shut up," ordered Bobby, glaring at him. "What are you talking like that for? What do you think you know? What grounds have you for saying things like that about – about anyone?"

"Missing, ain't he?" retorted Clarence. "And if he ain't been done in, what's he missing for? And ain't she the sort as would do in any bloke soon as look at him? Remember," said Clarence feelingly, "the way she turned that hose right on me and me mouth open, and not expecting nothing like it, so as I ain't hardly got rid of the taste of the water yet, I haven't, it sort of laying heavy on my stommick so I can feel it still."

"I wish," said Bobby, equally feelingly, "it had choked you for good and all, and you listen to me –"

But Clarence didn't intend to, he much preferred that Bobby should listen to him. He swept on unheedingly:

"There's more than that," and Bobby winced a little, so uncomfortably did that phrase remind him of Superintendent Ulyett. "Wasn't it him as was at her cottage that night me and you found her pushed in her garage? After something, wasn't he? and got it, didn't he or why did he bunk?"

"Because he heard someone coming," snapped Bobby. "Don't be a bigger fool than you can help. Waveny's being at Miss Farrar's cottage, even if it was Waveny, proves nothing."

"Ah, you're sweet on her," said Clarence tolerantly, "and if you wasn't, you would see it was only natural like she should want to get her own back after that garage do, and her being what she is, as shown by putting a hose on them as hadn't never done nothing to her – well, there you are. Only there's more than that, which I ain't telling you, for there wouldn't be no sense in putting a man on his own girl, nor it wouldn't be fair neither and against all natural feelings. What I have to say," said Clarence with dignity, getting to his feet as he spoke, "had best be said to others what hasn't got no tender feelings engaged."

By a supreme exercise of self control Bobby resisted various atavistic impulses such as hitting Clarence as hard and as often as he could, forbidding him to dare to say another word, demanding that he should explain himself fully, threatening that if he did he would suffer for it.

But then he told himself that only as big a fool as Clarence himself would pay the least attention to anything that worthy said. Before he could make up his mind what to do, Clarence suddenly turned back and thrust a note-book into his hands.

"If there's any nonymous letter trying to bring me in," he said, "I've got it down in writing just where I was all the time, so as I can prove an alibi and there it is which will show you, Mr. Owen, sir, as I'm innocent of nothing like the babe unborn, and there's the proof as you can read it for yourself."

Very much surprised, Bobby looked from the little notebook so oddly thrust into his hands to Clarence's retreating figure and then back again in continued wonderment. This then was what Clarence had really wanted. He had been badly frightened by the previous accusation made against him and had adopted this method of protecting himself against any future accusation. He had not enough intelligence to realize that what he himself wrote about himself was hardly proof of its accuracy and Bobby smiled at that and then grew grave again as he reflected that at any rate it proved that Clarence was very much afraid of future developments and quite likely had good reasons for his fears.

Turning over the soiled and dog-eared pages of the little book given him, Bobby found to his surprise that Clarence had not been altogether unaware of the need for confirmation. Several of the entries had initials or signatures of witnesses attached, or gave details that could be checked. One, for instance, ran: 'Said how do and was there a hot tip for the three o'clock to Police Constable XX99, who said not to be funny and get out, if not wanting a lick over the head, and did so according.' Another ran: 'Thrown out of the Red Lion, High Street, hitting nose on pavement,' and this was initialled with the note: 'Correct, and warned not to come back.'

"Clarence has got the wind up all right," Bobby reflected, and even though he could not help smiling a little at such careful precautions taken to prove an alibi if one were needed, yet all the same the fear and foreboding dread Clarence so plainly experienced Bobby found communicating itself to him.

He left the park and from the first call-box he saw rang up the Yard and ascertained that his presence was not required. Thence he went on to Olive's hat shop in the side street just behind Piccadilly. From what Ulyett had said he guessed it was being watched, and that therefore his visit would be reported, but then he meant to send in a brief report of his talk with Clarence and he hoped that would be taken as a sound reason for going there. Though he looked round carefully when he got near his destination he saw no sign, however, of any such watch being still.in force. Of course, a newspaper seller or someone like that might have been employed to report any sign of Olive's return. Or the Yard might be contenting itself with ringing up now and again to ask if she were back.

He entered the shop and found there the divinity he had seen before, but this time prepared to be quite human. Also she was evidently a good deal worried. Miss Farrar had not been near the shop since the time when she left for her Epping Forest cottage.

Business matters required attention. Letters were remaining unopened. None of her friends knew anything of her. At the cottage, no sign of her. Altogether it was very worrying and disturbing, said the divinity, now turned into quite a friendly and normal and rather anxious young woman; and Bobby's own troubled thoughts were no easier when he left to report at the Yard and deposit there Clarence's somewhat pathetic little note-book.

Fortunately no one seemed disposed to take Clarence's rambling accusations very seriously or to share the apprehensions aroused in Bobby by his forebodings. It appeared the general impression that for the present at least all Clarence said could be disregarded. He was most likely still suffering from the fright he had experienced when he knew that an anonymous if evidently unsubstantial accusation had been made against him.

"Though I suppose it is just possible," observed thoughtfully the inspector to whom Bobby was talking, "he does know something – for instance he may know Waveny has been murdered now. And if he does, perhaps it's because it was him did the job."

The same thought had been in Bobby's mind, though he had not wished to give it expression.

"If Waveny has been done in and Clarence did the job," the inspector continued, "then it makes it look as if Waveny did in Macklin, and Macklin's pals know it, and they've used Clarence to make it evens. A lot in this case hasn't come out, and the S.B. just look down their noses and won't say anything – probably because they don't know anything. But the Macklin-Waveny- Clarence idea looks right to me, and that makes Peter Albert's confession a fake to help Waveny. He knew his alibi made him safe, he put nothing on paper we could hold him to, and his confession was bound to put us off and muddle things a bit."

It was a plausible idea and Bobby retired to the canteen to think it over and to get a cup of tea before returning home, where he had a second tea since his landlady had it ready and he hated waste. He was balancing the respective merits of going to bed, a quiet read, and a visit to the nearest cinema, when there came a ring at the door and there appeared the servant girl.

"It's a lady in a car," she said. "She says, please come at once because it's urgent and important."

The girl looked quite scared, as though the urgency and importance of the message had communicated itself to her. Bobby got up quickly and went to the front door. A car was there and he was not much surprised to see that it was Olive at the wheel and that she was leaning out and beckoning to him. He crossed the pavement to her. She said:

"Get in. Quick. Quick. Something's happened at The Manor."

"What?" he asked.

"I don't know," she answered, her voice coming in little gasps. "I think it's murder. I don't know. Oh, get in, please, and we'll go and see."

There was a note of terror, of urgency in her voice that made him forbear further questioning. The car door was already open. He got in. Instantly Olive started and they shot away into the darkness.

CHAPTER XXVII
INK-STAINED FINGER

She drove fast, with a swift dexterity and ease, with apparently a complete knowledge of the district, avoiding traffic-lights and crowded thoroughfares by slipping down side-streets, taking more than once chances that showed how desperate she felt the need for haste. Plain, too, was the tension and the strain her pale, drawn features showed, and her eyes, too, no longer aloof and searching as it were things far away, but desperately intent upon the instant. Only once did Bobby speak to her. He said:

"How do you know?"

"The 'phone," she answered in a voice suddenly clear and high as though it might at any moment break into a scream. "The 'phone – a voice – whispering – that's all."

"What did it say?" he asked.

"My name. – that's all," she answered, "that's all – The Manor and my name – that's all." But a moment after she added: "A noise like a book falling – twice."

"Ah," Bobby said below his breath, for it seemed to him that sound of a falling book might well have been a pistol shot.

She gave a look at him over her shoulder, a look full at once of fear, of appeal, of trust, so that his heart gave a sudden leap. Then she turned once more to her driving and he did not speak again.

The Manor gates were open, left probably so by some of the many sightseers recently attracted to the place as people always are to the scene of any sensational crime. They swept through and up to the house and round to the back where Bobby was not surprised to find also open the back door by which once before he had gained admittance to the house. This time just within the door an electric light was burning.

Olive leaped out and ran into the house. Bobby followed quickly and caught her up.

"Let me go first," he said and drew her back and went by.

They reached the great hall. Here, too, lights burned, making pools of clear radiance in the murky darkness that reigned elsewhere. Instinctively they both stood still to listen for any sound that might reveal another's presence, but the silence around seemed absolute. Bobby began to run up the stairs. Olive followed closely behind. On the landing all was dark, save for one thread of light that came from the door, not quite closed, of the room in which, on another day, a dead man had lain. They ran together, side by side, along the wide corridor. Bobby flung open the door, told Olive to wait, and went in. Ignoring what he had said, Olive followed close behind.

Before the 'phone Peter Albert lay supine. His head had been injured and was bleeding slightly. He had been shot three times in the chest. None of the wounds had bled much. Evidently he had been shot down in an attempt to telephone, for the loose receiver dangled just above his head. There were fresh bloodstains on it, just as there had been once before. He tried to lift himself as he heard them enter, but it was a last effort, the last before the spirit went elsewhere. He knew them and called out:

"Hullo, you two," and then in a voice from which the strength was quickly ebbing: – "Same room, same thing, same way, trying to 'phone, too – fair do's all round."

He lay back as he spoke and sighed heavily twice over, and so was it finished. Bobby bent over what once had been the habitation of a human spirit and made sure that now it was void and the spirit gone to another place. He turned back to Olive. Neither of them said anything, but abruptly he found Olive was in his arms, crying and trembling, and that clumsily enough he was trying to soothe her, muttering incoherent endearments, murmuring in her ear the first words that came to him. She freed herself presently and said:

"He always knew it would be this he wanted it, I think he said once what right had he to live when all over the world the dictators were killing, killing, killing..."

Bobby took her by the hand and led her out of the room.

"There is nothing you can do," he said.

She submitted passively. She had become very quiet and still, and she seemed content now to leave everything to him. He found the switch controlling the corridor lights and turned them on. From one of the rooms near he brought a chair and told Olive to sit there and wait while he summoned help. He kissed her and she clung to him and seemed comforted and then he went back into the room where Peter's body lay. He found himself wondering for a moment whether Peter's self was also there, still lingering on the same spot, a little dazed perhaps by so sudden a passing, aware of what was going on and yet unable to manifest or interfere.

For never had it seemed to him more clear and certain that no absurdity could be greater than to suppose that the accident of the impact of a few bits of lead upon its fleshy habitation could obliterate all that splendid vitality he had known under the name of Peter Albert.

Putting aside such thoughts he stood there, looking round intently, with all that concentrated attention upon every visible detail he had taught himself to use. There was a torn paper lying on the floor. It was a torn I.O.U. signed by Waveny. Part of it was missing but enough remained to show what it was. Under one of the chairs was a hat. Bobby picked it up. Inside were the initials: 'C.W.'. In a corner lay a walking-stick, of the kind known as Penang Lawyers. On the silver mount was a stain of fresh blood. Obviously it was not the one Bobby had seen previously in Waveny's possession, for that was in the hands of the police, and also the silver mount of this one was different. But Bobby remembered that Waveny had told him he had two walking-sticks of the same kind.

"Making it plain," he said to himself.

He bent over the dead body and examined the injuries to the head. Serious, he thought, but probably not fatal by themselves. Apparently the blow had been struck from behind. Bobby thought of Peter as he had known him, alert, watchful, active.

"Caught him unawares," Bobby muttered. "I wonder how?"

A chair was overturned, the table pushed aside. On it was some fresh blotting-paper and an unused writing-pad. Apparently Peter had been sitting at it when attacked. As Bobby reconstructed the tragedy in his thoughts, Peter had been struck with the stick from behind and had fallen. His assailant, thinking him either dead or insensible, had left him like that and become occupied with something else. Peter had recovered sufficiently to get to the 'phone, and, probably still half dazed, had called up Olive with the idea of asking her to summon help. His assailant, discovering suddenly what he was doing and probably afraid he was calling up the police, had drawn a pistol and fired, and Peter had fallen with his cry for help only half uttered.

Bending over the body Bobby noticed there was a stain of fresh ink on the forefinger of the right hand.

"Making it quite plain," said Bobby with satisfaction.

He went to the 'phone, and, handling the receiver with great care, rang up the Yard to report what had happened and ask for help. Superintendent Ulyett had gone home but Bobby was told he would be instantly communicated with. Help would be sent at once, and till it arrived Bobby was to stay on guard but take no action. He hung up the receiver accordingly and went back to Olive.

"There is ink on his finger – fresh ink," Bobby said. "Peter was writing when he was attacked. I think that makes it clear. But there is no sign of any pen."

"I saw Mr. Waveny's stick," Olive whispered. "It's the one he threatened to thrash Mr. Macklin with. I don't – understand."

Before Bobby could reply the 'phone bell rang and he had to go back to answer it. It was Ulyett ringing up from his home, apparently for further information, as if he could hardly believe the reports he had just received. Bobby repeated what he knew and while he was still in the middle of his explanations Ulyett interrupted to say the police car had just come for him and he would be at The Manor as soon as it could get him there.

Olive by now was in a very distressed, nervous condition, as if she were beginning to realize more clearly what had happened. He did his best to soothe her and soon help arrived, first the emissaries from the Yard direct, and then Ulyett, so that Bobby was very busy telling his story over and over again and explaining how it was he had been there to make the discovery. Olive, too, had to answer many questions. She had been staying, she said, at a small hotel in Bayswater. She had gone there at the dead man's request, rather, by his insistence. For he had believed they were all in great and imminent danger and that the attempts to dispose of them by ramming and sinking the yacht would be continued with even greater intensity on land.

*"Here, in London?" someone asked incredulously.

Olive did not answer but she looked towards the closed door before which a uniformed constable stood on guard, behind which lay Peter Albert's body.

"He thought they might try to get things out of me they would think I knew," she explained. "Even when I got the 'phone message to-night I wasn't quite sure. I thought it might be a trick. Peter said if I wasn't sure, I must go to Mr. Owen. I wasn't sure to-night, only that it was something terrible. So I told Mr. Owen and he came here with me.

Bobby was conscious of a sudden glow that warmed him through and through, as though all at once he stood in an actual ray of heat. She had spoken as though somehow it were natural for her to turn to him, as though indeed she had a special right to his help, as though, too, in his protection, she felt safe. Ulyett, who was questioning her, asked her what she had actually heard, and almost in the same words she repeated what she had told Bobby. It was told with the dramatic force that is given by utter simplicity and truth, and they were all silent, as if they, too, heard that faint summons whispered over the telephone wire and those distant sounds that had resembled the noise of a book falling on the floor.

Olive had no more to tell and presently she was allowed to go. But Bobby was not permitted to be the one to accompany her back to her hotel. That task was entrusted to someone else and Bobby was told to wait. Then he was told that Ulyett wanted him, and going to the superintendent he found him examining the hat and walking-stick discovered near the dying man in the room where the murder had been committed.

"Waveny again, eh?" Ulyett said. "Looks like it, doesn't it? Same M.O., walking-stick and all. Anyhow, he'll be here in a minute or two, and we can hear what he has to say. We got word he rang up the block of flats where he lives to say he would be back to-day. Did this little job and then bunked off home to put in a spot of alibi, eh? Probably meant to come back here and clear up, or else he panicked after he had done the job. Anyhow, what he's left behind makes it pretty plain."

"Yes, sir," Bobby answered, "only there is ink on his fingers. And no pen."

"Whose fingers? Peter Albert's?" Ulyett asked. "Well, what about it?"

Before Bobby could reply there was the sound of another car arriving and a moment or two later Waveny himself was brought in. He was in a great state of indignation and protested vehemently that he knew nothing about what had taken place. He admitted at once that the hat and stick shown him were his property, but protested he had no idea how they had got there.

"Must have been pinched," he said angrily, "probably you did yourselves, just as you pinched my other stick."

"We didn't pinch it, did we?" Ulyett asked mildly. "I think we asked you for it and you handed it over."

"Same thing," growled Waveny. "Your fellows just said might they have it and didn't give me a chance to say no."

"There was blood on the handle," Ulyett remarked. "The report says it is blood of the same class as Macklin's."

"I know there was blood on the handle," Waveny answered. "I hurt my hand getting out of a taxi and it bled a bit and I daresay some got on the handle. Why shouldn't it? and why shouldn't my blood be the same class or whatever you call it as Macklin's?"

"That can easily be proved by a test," remarked Ulyett, and in fact the test later on proved that, as it chanced, both Macklin's blood and Waveny's belonged to the same, and smallest, class known, one including only about ten per cent of the population.

Waveny went on to deny with still more heat that he had been in hiding. He had simply been away on a motor trip.

"Who with?" demanded Ulyett. "None of your friends knew anything about you, and your car is in your garage and has been all the time."

"I didn't use my own car," Waveny explained sulkily, "and I wasn't with friends exactly. I was feeling a bit down, I wanted to get away from people, and my aunt made a suggestion and offered to pay and so I said all right."

"What were you feeling down about?" demanded Ulyett, and presently it came out, after a good deal of stammering, hesitation and fencing, that Waveny had had a letter from Olive, making it quite plain that, much as she appreciated his attentions, and greatly as she felt honoured by them, she thought it would be better for them both if they saw as little of each other as possible for the future. It was then, on receipt of this letter, that he had gone out to her cottage and found in it, as he believed, a burglar. A struggle had ensued, he had knocked the supposed burglar out, he had been afraid he had killed him, and in a panic, hearing someone approaching, possibly another of the burglars, he had run for it.

He admitted he had had a pistol with him and had fired two or three shots, but only, he insisted, in the hope of frightening his opponent. Under pressure he admitted he had taken the pistol with him with some idea of committing suicide at Olive's feet. But he was rather glad now it hadn't got that far, and perhaps it never would, only perhaps Olive, at the sight of the revolver, since such a threat would have convinced her of his desperate plight, might possibly have relented.

"It was her beastly letter," he complained. "You would have thought she never wanted to see me again."

Ulyett grunted, as if he thought that was no subject for wonder, and wanted to know next what the aunt's suggestion had been.

"She said I ought to study the proletariat," Waveny explained.

"The – how much?" asked Ulyett.

"The proletariat," repeated Waveny simply. "You see, it's this way. Hitler was one of 'em, and see where he is. So was Mussolini, and look at him. Then take that Etrurian fellow – the Redeemer they call him. Been in an asylum for the cure of drug addicts and all that, and see where he is. Then take our own man, Oswald Mosley – always been a rich man and has a rich man's ideas all through – and look at him, or rather, as aunt said, you can't, because he simply isn't there, not visible, except as a bit of chalk on a wall. So aunt said it was a chance for me to catch on where he had got off."

"Good God," said Ulyett.

"Why? asked Waveny, and when Ulyett did not answer he went on: "Besides, she had been hearing gossip about bad company and all that rot and being mixed up with the Macklin murder, though of course I wasn't, and so she said I must take it on, and she said she would cut me off with a shilling unless I did what she told me, and to keep out of the way for a time till the Macklin affair had settled down, and meanwhile I could study the proletariat so as to be ready to go into Parliament."

"Parliament?" repeated Ulyett in a faint voice.

"All our family do," explained Waveny. "It's a bore, but you have to before you join the Cabinet."

"The Cabinet?" murmured Ulyett, whose eyes by this time had nearly started out of his head.

"All our family do," Waveny explained once more, "and aunt said the best way to get in touch with the proletariat and a good start to study their way of thinking and understand them and their ways was to go one of those motor excursion trips – you know 'Visit the Wye in an Arm-Chair' or 'See the Lakes at Sixty m.p.h.' Aunt said it was that sort of proletariat that really counted, because of course what she called the workhouse end don't matter one way or the other."

Ulyett looked round helplessly. Everyone within earshot was listening in awed silence. Ulyett said:

"My God!"

"Why?" asked Waveny. "You said that before," he complained, and added thoughtfully: "People often do when I talk to them."

"Means they think you ought to go into the Church," suggested Ulyett. "Well, Mr. Waveny, I suppose you can give us details of this trip of yours?"

"Oh, yes," agreed Waveny, "it was one aunt chose herself, and of course I had to let her because she was paying. It was 'The Cathedrals of England in Quick Time'. I can't think where they all come from," added Waveny, sighing. "Why, some days we did two, morning and afternoon."

It seemed that Waveny's whereabouts during the last few days was now fully explained. Evidently his aunt had wanted to get him out of the way of any awkward questioning and avoid further possible gossip but not having wished to explain her fears to Waveny had hit on this pretext of a kind of preliminary political training.

But though the details given proved where Waveny had been during the time the police were searching for him, there was nothing to prove an alibi for the moment when Olive had heard the dying man's voice whispering to her over the 'phone and then those sounds she had described as like those made by a book falling to the floor. His own story was that he had had a message over the 'phone to tell him to go to Euston to meet his aunt, unexpectedly arriving in town. But when he arrived there was no sign of her and after waiting for the next train on the chance of her coming by that he had returned home. He had gone to Euston by bus, expecting that his aunt as usual would have a hired Daimler waiting for her, and he had returned home by the same method. He had in fact no proof of his story, and he had no explanation to offer of the presence of his hat and stick at The Manor.

Ulyett looked very glum, for he hated arresting prominent and well-to-do people who could employ K.C.'s of great fame and extraordinarily loud voices. He said glumly to Bobby:

"No alibi. Thin yarn altogether. Hat, stick, on the spot. He may be a Cabinet Minister some day, but meanwhile we've got to pull him in all right."

"Well, sir, if I may say so," Bobby answered, "there's the ink on the finger I mentioned before. If I may explain, sir –"

But Ulyett was staring at him, open-mouthed.

"Good lord, of course," he said. "Ferris told me at the time. I remember now."

CHAPTER XXVIII
FINGER-PRINTS

The 'twin wolves' had never fallen, as Mr. Troya would have said, to providing a cabaret show. To distract attention from a meal of serious and artistic composition by music of the same rank was merely, he said, to prove all concerned unworthy of both. And for such a meal an accompaniment of jazz or even of light dance tunes – imagine consuming 'faisan aux loups jumeaux' to jazz! – was simply further proof of the slow disintegration of civilization and of culture.

It was therefore only the attraction of the food, the cooking, and the wine that made the 'Twin Wolves', despite the fact that it was situated such a long, long way from Piccadilly, almost as popular as a rendezvous for supper as for lunch or dinner. Late as was the hour by now, supper parties were still in progress on the first floor, guests were still lingering over wines of quality at such reasonable prices as no other establishment could rival, and in the side streets adjoining, a recognized parking place, still waited a string of cars of which almost every second one was either a Rolls Royce, a Daimler, or some other in the four-figure group.

Ulyett, as he and Bobby alighted from their own car, looked a little uncomfortably at this display of sumptuous vehicles, uncomfortably, too, at the restaurant itself.

"Suppose we are wrong?" he said, "a bit of an ink-stain isn't much to go on."

Bobby knew that and made no answer. One has to take one's risks.

"Suppose he isn't here?" Ulyett said again.

"Sure to be unless we are wrong," Bobby answered, "and if we are, then it doesn't matter where he is."

Ulyett looked at Bobby with annoyance. All very well to talk in that light way of being wrong. What did a mere detective-sergeant risk? A bit of a telling off and possibly a delayed promotion. But a superintendent! For a superintendent's motto has to be: Never wrong, and those are words that are hard to live up to.

But Bobby, with all the horrible impulsiveness of youth, was already making for the restaurant door, and Ulyett sighed and followed. They entered and a waiter came forward to meet them. It was, he began deprecatingly, a little late, and Ulyett cut him short.

"That's all right," he said. "We aren't here to feed. Police business. Mr. Troya here?"

"He is in his office perhaps?" Bobby suggested. "This way, sir," he added to Ulyett, for he did not want either any delay or a warning given to Troya, and he was fairly certain Troya, if on the premises at all, would be in his office.

On the door of it there hung a notice Engaged but of that they took no notice. Bobby opened the door and they went in. There were two people in the room: Troya himself sitting before a gas fire with a glass of wine in his hand and a half empty bottle by his side and Madame Troya seated at the table. Even at that moment Bobby noticed that the wine was a cheap and rather fiery Chianti, for Mr. Troya's own palate, in spite of the reputation of his restaurant, was one that preferred the more violent emotions. Madame Troya was apparently busy with the accounts and the receipts of the evening. She was a tall, stout, commanding-looking woman with an authoritative air that left little doubt who was the senior partner. It was she who sprang to her feet and came quickly to meet them while Troya himself sat still and frozen, his glass half way to his lips, terror and dismay showing plainly on every feature.

"Police, ma'am," Ulyett said before Madame Troya could speak. He waved her aside. "Mr. Troya, have you any objection to telling me where you have been this evening? "He has been here, all the time he has been here," Madame Troya answered, not allowing Troya himself time to reply.

"Witnesses?" Ulyett asked.

"Without doubt," retorted Madame Troya as though that were a question for which she was well prepared, and she rattled off a number of names till Ulyett stopped her.

"It would be better, I think," he said, "if you would allow Mr. Troya to answer for himself."

It was at this moment that Bobby stepped forward and very neatly and very firmly possessed himself of the fountain-pen protruding from Troya's breast pocket. Troya did not attempt to resist. He looked very surprised but that was all. Madame Troya hardly seemed to notice, though she looked round as Bobby murmured a polite preliminary accompaniment to his unexpected action:

"Oh, excuse me. May I? Thank you so much." Evidently neither of them attached any importance to what he was doing. Madame Troya was busy gathering all her forces to express her anger and her indignation. As for Mr. Troya he was still very pale, and he put down untasted that glass of extremely fiery Chianti he had just poured out.

Madame Troya said impressively:

"I do not understand what reasons, what excuse you may have to offer for this extraordinary intrusion, for this unprecedented outrage on the privacy of Etrurian citizens. But I warn you I shall communicate instantly with our Embassy. Since the advent of the glorious Redeemer of Etruria your Foreign Office has been taught that Etrurians must be treated with respect, with deference. Or your Government will hear about it – your Government of a democracy that knows so well its own futility, its own feebleness before the iron will of the totalitarian states."

"I know all about our Government," retorted Ulyett, making indeed as rash, as heedless, as thoughtless a claim as ever yet man uttered. "What I want to know –"

He went on to question Troya closely. It appeared there was a wealth of evidence to prove his presence during the evening in the restaurant, dining-rooms, service-rooms, the kitchen even, though there while their masterpieces are being produced by the irritable and temperamental race of chefs, the wise proprietor or manager never ventures. None the less it began to be apparent also that there was a gap, an interval of nearly two hours, when Troya had retired to his office, with on the door that 'Engaged' sign the intruders had noticed and ignored, though for any of the staff to disregard it would have meant for the culprit instant dismissal. Naturally, that did not apply to Madame Troya, who volunteered the information that she had been in and out of the office several times during those two hours and had always found Mr. Troya there, busy with his accounts and correspondence.

"Very satisfactory," declared Ulyett. He went across to the window and opened it. It opened as he knew perfectly well, on a narrow, paved alley, used only for the removal of rubbish, that ran between this building and the next. Since Troya's office was on the ground level, to climb through the window into the alley and so proceed unnoticed to the street, would be perfectly easy. Ulyett closed the window and turned to the inmates of the room again. "Wife's evidence, though," he remarked. "Quite all right, of course, but the courts always like a wife's evidence confirmed. Anyone who could do that?"

"Yes, certainly," answered Madame Troya at once. "Major Cathay, the Military Attaché at the Etrurian Embassy. He came in to speak to my husband for a moment. I presume you will accept Major Cathay's word?"

"The word of a Military Attaché is always accepted," answered Ulyett politely. "Can you tell me what time he was here?"

Madame Troya knew to a minute. She knew, she explained, because the Major's watch had stopped and he had asked her what the time was. It happened to be almost exactly, to the hour and minute, the time when Olive had received that whispered 'phone call from the dying Peter Albert at The Manor.

"Very satisfactory," repeated Ulyett, who had anticipated that this interval of two hours covering the time when they knew the murder had been committed would be carefully provided for by a good sound alibi. "Of courses we shall have to ask Major Cathay to confirm."

"Major Cathay will confirm everything we say," Madame Troya told him with a kind of grim assurance in her voice, as much as to say Major Cathay would know better than to do anything else. Her voice changed suddenly, grew shrill. "What's that man doing?" she cried, pointing a finger at Bobby who was busy with a small gadget that looked a little like a scent spray, a camel-hair brush and the fountain-pen he had taken from Troya. He was not a finger-print expert but he knew the technique well enough, and the necessary articles for testing he had brought with him. "What's he doing? what?" she cried again.

"Only testing for finger-prints, ma'am," Ulyett explained mildly.

In a panic she swung round on Troya.

"You wore gloves?" she cried, "gloves?"

"What gloves?" Ulyett asked. "What for?"

But Mrs. Troya had recovered her self-possession that for the moment had been badly shaken.

"It is bluff," she said, "nothing but bluff – impudent bluff. You do not take us in. No." She laughed, though not very steadily. "To-morrow our Etrurian Embassy shall hear of this and then we shall see. The Redeemer of his country does not permit his people to be insulted. To them he is ever as a loving father and you won't find any finger-prints –" She paused again as if something had just occurred to her, something she did not understand. "In any case," she demanded, "why should not a man's own finger-prints be on his own fountain-pen?"

"Why not indeed, madame?" agreed Ulyett, "I'm sure that's what one would expect. Quite natural."

"Then what is the meaning of this comedy?" she asked angrily.

"You see," Ulyett explained, "we are not looking for Mr. Troya's finger-prints, which indeed one would expect to find, as you say, on his own pen, though not of course if he wore gloves for any special reason."

"Never mind the gloves," she snapped.

"A man named Peter Albert has been found murdered at a house called The Manor, belonging to a Mr. Judson," Ulyett continued. "We have reason to believe that Mr. Albert was attacked while he was writing. There is ink on his fingers. As his own fountain-pen had been broken a day or two ago and he had not yet obtained a new one, he may have borrowed another from some other person if he had writing to do. It is therefore the finger-prints of Mr. Peter Albert, not those of Mr. Troya, we are looking for, and whose presence on Mr. Troya's pen may require explanation."

Troya gave a low, strangled cry. Madame Troya swung round upon him.

"You fool," she cried wildly, "did you lend him your pen?"

Troya tried to speak, his mouth opened but no sound came, he shrank back into his chair, it was as though in that one moment he had lessened to one half his previous size.

"You wore gloves," said Ulyett softly, "but you forgot, I think, that Peter Albert wore none."

There was silence for the space of perhaps three-quarters of a minute while no one moved or stirred. It was only broken when from a little distance sounded the voice of a newsboy. He was calling:

"Extra special. Rising in Etruria. Redeemer reported shot. Navy joins rebels."

CHAPTER XXIX
CONCLUSION

Clear and shrill in the quiet street sounded the voice of that Recording Angel of our times – the newsboy. Ulyett went to the door and opened it and called to a waiter.

"Get me a paper," he said briefly. "Quick."

He went back into the room. They all waited silently. Bobby was thinking of Peter Albert, as he had known him first, smiling and debonair; as he had known him on the yacht that had become in his hands almost like a living thing to see danger and avoid it; as he had seen him last, silent and still, life leaving him.

Troya was now sitting forward in his chair, hope and an enormous relief apparent in his expression. Madame Troya kept opening and shutting her mouth. Bobby was reminded of a fish suddenly flung from the water on to dry land. Ulyett was the only one who spoke. He said loudly and firmly:

"These foreigners."

The waiter appeared, bringing in the paper. He eyed the little group curiously, but Ulyett motioned to him to go, and he retired. Ulyett unfolded the paper and ran his glance up and down the columns.

"All there," he said. "He's been put on the spot all right – the Etrurian dictator, I mean. Stood him against a wall and that was that. General rejoicings – so there would have been if he had stood someone else against a wall and that had been that. London Embassy taken over, too, apparently." Ulyett looked from one to the other of the Troyas. "Your pal – Major Cathay. He's gone over to the other side, taken possession of the Embassy, chucked the Redeemer lot outside, and says he is now the representative of the new Etrurian Government – the Government of the People's Party."

"In that case," said Madame Troya thoughtfully, "if he has gone over to the other side – then he will no longer tell lies for us."

"No, he won't, will he?" agreed Ulyett. "How about telling us the truth now yourself?"

"I will," declared Madame Troya with sudden emphasis. "Yes." She pointed at Troya. "Yes," she repeated, "he shot Mr. Albert. He was hired by the tyrant who dared to call himself a redeemer – a redeemer who shed the blood of others, not his own. The Tyrant," she concluded at the top of her voice.

"Meaning the Redeemer?" asked Ulyett mildly.

"I," said Madame Troya with great decision, "I call him the Tyrant as did the millions of my fellow-countrymen who groaned for so long under his abominable rule. He knew, the Tyrant, that Peter Albert was one of the most dangerous of his enemies. Well, he knew it, well he knew that from his yacht, the hero, Peter Albert, wirelessed orders, instructions, messages, organized in short that superb rising of the people of which we have the glorious news to-night. Well knew the Tyrant –"

"The Redeemer?" asked Ulyett as mildly as before.

"The Tyrant," repeated Madame Troya, glaring at him, "hired that man" – an accusing finger designated the restaurant keeper, still sitting upright in his chair, evidently trying to adjust his mind to the news just received – "hired him to liquidate one whom he knew to be his most dangerous enemy and to-night the foul deed was done. Of course, for me," said Madame Troya earnestly, "I knew nothing of it – nothing till he returned, when he at once threatened me with death if I dared say anything, if I did not back up his wicked stories. It was the window, you understand. He put the notice 'Engaged' on the door and then he slipped out by the window and came back the same way. I was to confirm his lie about his having been here all the time, and so was Major Cathay. Oh, but he is clever, Major Cathay, we had no idea he was one of our enemies – I mean, one of our friends."

"Bit confusing" agreed Ulyett, "to remember which side you're on – like our own Liberals, not sure whether they've turned Tory or are really Labour. Go on."

"For months, I have been terrorized, living under the instant threat of death," continued Madame Troya, "but now I will speak out, and to you, to the English police, so loyal, so magnificent, I trust for my protection."

"Terrorized, were you, ma'am?" asked Ulyett, giving a somewhat doubtful glance at Troya, sitting upright, abstracted, and silent in his chair.

"Terrorized," repeated Madame Troya with another glare that very plainly dared him to doubt it. "But do not think that under your British laws, because I am his wife, I cannot give the evidence against him that will enable you to hang him. We are not married. I am not his wife."

"Not even my mistress," sighed Troya. "Never once did she allow me near her – not even the slightest alleviation."

"As if I would, a worm like him, a louse," said the lady to whom now it would be incorrect to refer as Madame Troya. "For that matter, before I came I had to give my husband the most complete assurances. They were unnecessary – look at him and imagine if assurances were called for." As she spoke she jerked a disdainful thumb at Troya. "But my husband insisted. Or he would never have consented."

"Where is he? in England? can you give us his address?" Ulyett asked.

"Head porter at the Embassy," was the prompt answer.

Ulyett nodded to Bobby to make a note of this fact and Bobby said:

"There's something in the newspaper account – oh, yes, here it is: 'Head Porter taken to Hospital, thrown down Embassy steps by former Military Attaché'."

"He did not change sides quickly enough," said the lady with a sigh. "In politics, it is so necessary."

Troya got to his feet and spoke with a certain dignity.

"It is true I shot Mr. Albert," he said. "I did not wish to shoot him. Why should I? They told me he was a traitor. They told me he was working harm to our country, they told me he conspired against our Government, they told me he would bring about a war so that Etruria should be like Spain, butchered to make a German general's holiday. For that I should not have shot him. They reminded me they had made my restaurant famous and if I did not obey, they would unmake it again with tales of bad food and bad cooking till it was once more what it was before they talked up the 'Twin Wolves' into being thought a kind of rival of the Ritz or the Savoy – easy enough when most people only know the difference between a fried-fish shop and a restaurant of class by the prices and the lights. They could have done it as easily as they said, and it was they, too, who sent this woman –here to spy upon the Etrurians in England – on the refugees to find out what they were doing, on the others to see that they did nothing."

"So that's how the lady came here?" observed Ulyett.

"But not for that would I have killed, even though they said that perhaps if I refused, I also, I might find a knife waiting for me one night. But not for that would I have done what they wished. So they tried to hire an Englishman, a boxer, a hired chucker-out at Mr. Judson's parties.

But he would not either, he is what you call a crook but not a murderer. They feared then he would betray them so they sent a letter to accuse him of another crime to frighten him into keeping quiet."

"Silly fool idea," observed Ulyett.

"I do not think they are very intelligent," Troya said slowly. "Such as they never are, for they think it is only stupidity if you are honest, they cannot believe there are some who will not lie, even when it is clever to lie. But when this man, this boxer, refused, they came to me again, though not now to kill, for to that I still said no. They gave me orders. I was to go to The Manor and wait there in the garden for Mr. Macklin who would give me important papers. Mr. Macklin was the agent between the Embassy people and the Etrurian Secret Service agents in England. His flat was the general headquarters. They did not wish the connection between Secret Service and Embassy to be known. I have often been given papers either to pass on to the Embassy from Macklin – I suppose now Major Cathay read them all and kept Mr. Albert informed – or else from the Embassy, instructions I suppose, for Mr. Macklin. Sometimes I would hand them over in place of a bill or with the bill, or sometimes I would put them inside the wine list I took round myself. That day in The Manor garden I knew the paper I was to expect was very important. It had to do with the great rising of which there is this news to-night. I never got it. I waited but I saw no one.

Afterwards I went away. It was the afternoon Mr. Macklin died. I knew nothing about it at the time. I knew everyone suspected everyone else. I knew there was danger. Not that day more than any other, though. Mr. Macklin told me there was a girl he thought knew more than she ought to – a friend of Peter Albert's, a Miss Farrar. He thought she came to Mr. Judson's parties to watch him, and he tried to get friendly with her to find out. That made Mr. Waveny angry, he thought it was a flirtation and he said he would thrash Mr. Macklin. I thought at first it was he who had killed him – Macklin, I mean. Afterwards I thought perhaps it was the girl or Mr. Albert. I was told Mr. Macklin's connection with the Etrurian Secret Service was known, and a flat had been taken in the same building as his so as to watch him and his agents who came there. I suppose now it was Major Cathay who gave Mr. Albert and his friends all their information and that it was because of what he had told them that Mr. Albert went to The Manor to get back this important paper from Macklin. After Macklin was killed, then it was realized more than ever that Peter Albert was dangerous and had to be removed. But they always failed, for Peter Albert, when he was attacked, he knew how to defend himself."

"And all this," broke in Ulyett angrily, "going on under our noses."

He was quite red with indignation and Bobby said soothingly:

"You see, sir, both sides were doing their best to keep it quiet – after all, if no one will tell a detective anything, how is he to know anything?"

Ulyett received this pearl of wisdom with a grunt, and Troya continued:

"It was because they thought I had opportunities that again they came to me. They even spoke of poison – poison in the food or the wine we served. I told them that a restaurant does not so betray its guests."

He paused then. It was odd with what an energy of conviction he uttered this last sentence. Clearly it expressed the deepest conviction of his soul, a loyalty from which nothing would be able to make him swerve, as others might cling to family, to country or to religion.

"They understood that," he went on in a moment or two, "but they tried again, only this time it was different. They showed me a police order sending people to a concentration camp – the one of which all in Etruria know, the one to which those are sent who are meant to die, but not too quickly. Well, the first name on that list, it was my father's. The second name, it was my mother's. One does not permit one's father and one's mother, when they are old, to be sent to a concentration camp, above all, not that concentration camp. For that, then, I agreed to do as they said. But I said to them, his blood, that will be for you to answer at the end of days. They only laughed. What is just a little more blood to add to all the rest? I went therefore this evening as it was planned. I had with me a hat and a stick of Mr. Waveny's. They had got into his flat with false keys to obtain them. That was to make him suspected, and for the same reason they got him out of the way by a sham message, so that for this evening he should have no alibi. They did not care about him, all they wanted was to make a confusion, and if possible prevent it from being known that Etrurian politics were concerned. Also they arranged an alibi for me. Major Cathay was to swear to it. Now, of course, he will not. That is all, and if you hang me, it must be so, but at least my father and my mother will not go to a concentration camp."

Though Troya was duly tried, and even convicted and sentenced, for in England all things must be done in accordance with custom and tradition, everyone concerned knew perfectly well that there was not the least intention of ever carrying out the sentence, knew indeed that in a very short time Troya would probably be a free man again.

For he was able to give a very great deal of very useful information about the proceedings of the Etrurian Secret Service, though that had now become of small importance, since all the refugees had gone home and most of the others were only too glad to be allowed to attend to their own affairs without bothering any more about political ideologies they had never clearly understood. After all, what else does man require here below but leave to work for himself and for his family, to eat and to drink at his need, and for a little to be merry before the time comes for him to depart hence, and what had political ideologies to do with that? So the Etrurian Secret Service vanished, like a bit of putrid meat thrown into the dustbin, leaving only a bad smell behind. But there remained the Secret Services of certain other of the totalitarian states working at full pressure, sending reports home of the secret dispositions of this national or the other, how one was actually a subscriber to the *Daily Herald* and another to the Left Book Club, and how yet another was suspected of having written a letter to the *News Chronicle* and how a fourth had been seen coming away from a Communist meeting! Of all these activities too, and not only of those in England, Troya had much to tell. Certain High Commissioners of certain Dominions were also given interesting facts; and a recently established office in Washington, D.C., United States of America, expressed a desire to be allowed to question Troya in person. So first it was publicly announced that the death sentence on the convicted man in the case known as the Second Manor Murder had been commuted to life imprisonment, and then, not at all publicly, the Prison Commissioners were asked to send Troya to New York, and not to be too exigent about his return.

Olive, too, had to undergo a good deal of questioning, but as Troya pleaded guilty, so that the whole trial was over in about five minutes, she was not called upon to give evidence. At first she had been reluctant to speak, fearing to implicate others. But once she understood that the People's Party Government was firmly established in Etruria, that it was in the hour of triumph Peter had died, that there was no intention, in spite of the solemn trial and sentence on Troya, of carrying out that sentence, she was quite willing to tell what she knew. Some of the details she was able to give confirmed various of Troya's statements.

"I was afraid all the time of what would happen," she told Bobby. "I knew Peter suspected Macklin was a spy. That was why he took a flat in the same building to watch him and his visitors, for Macklin was a kind of general centres I went to The Manor that day to try to stop anything from happening – I was afraid of what the English police might find out. I wanted to tell Peter he mustn't do any more than get the paper from Macklin, the list of names he had got together. Peter did promise, but afterwards he said Macklin knew too much, remembered too much, it had been necessary – what he had done."

Before however she told what she knew – and it was of some value – she again insisted that Troya must not be punished.

"I know Peter would never have wanted – that," she said, "not – hanged. Peter always said he would kill when it was necessary and afterwards sleep as soundly as ever, because there are things that count more than life, things by the side of which life counts no more than the burning of a match. What else is Christianity, why else did Christ die? But those things are rare things and terrible, very few and rare the things that count for more than life. But they exist."

To satisfy her, for experience of a totalitarian government had bred in her a distrust of official statements and promises experience of a British Government during these last few years had somehow or another not entirely dispersed, Bobby was allowed, for he and she were now officially engaged, to take her to a London terminus and see Troya and an American companion comfortably taking their seats in the boat-train.

So, having seen the little restaurant keeper starting off to the New World they themselves turned away to face together the new life waiting for them.

THE END

37082676R00130

Made in the USA
Middletown, DE
18 November 2016